I love you SO WHAT?

TISA MATTHEWS

ISBN: 979-8-9877405-2-1

Cover design by Cindy Ras

This is a work of fiction. Characters, events and incidents in this book are either the product of the author's imagination or used in a fictitious manner. Any resemblance to actual persons, living or dead, or actual events is purely coincidental.

Author's Note

Dear Reader,

Hello! We (Troy & Lexy) are so glad that you've picked up our story! But before you start, there are a few things we need you to know!

1) While our story is the best (duh), it is a companion novel. Book one, *And Then There's You*, *should* be read first! You'll get to meet us over there and achieve insight that will help you love our personal growth and love story even more!

2) If you have read *And Then There's You*–featuring some of our very best friends–then you're ready to dive in! Our story runs parallel to theirs, and we hope you take the time to see why we will be your favorites, instead of cheating and skipping to the end to find out what happens.

3) We hope that you find a new (or renewed) sense of appreciation and respect for bartenders and servers! We work hard so you can enjoy your days and nights out!

Now grab a Mango Cart, and go enjoy our story!
Xo,
Troy & Lexy

To the *ones who got away*
who weren't *the one*—
thank you for letting us go.

CHAPTER ONE
TROY

Senior year at the University of Oregon (September)

Maci's wide, terrified brown eyes are locked on my bike. She must already know it's me with the way fear emanates off her–as if I showed up to this date with a hockey mask and a machete. I pull my helmet off and laugh as I hold my spare helmet out for her. "Have you been on a motorcycle before?"

"Noooope." It's kind of cute how nervous she is and a surprising change from most girls who think my bike is hot in that desperate sort of way–considering none of them actually want to drive it or learn anything about it. Maybe that's too much to ask of a girl, though. It was too much to ask of Emily.

"Guess I get to be your first," I flirt with a sly grin and a wink. Flirting feels dusty rolling off my tongue even though I'm attempting to get back to it, starting with this beautiful brunette from my early morning math class. It's such a natural part of my personality, which might sound douchey, but I'm a quick thinker and great at reading people, and I'm proud of it.

Dinner went well, and conversation was easy. We talked about travel, but I couldn't contribute much. Traveling for me consists solely of summer vacation at my uncle's cabin two hours from here and my weekly ride to the viewpoint where I've brought Maci. Outside of a few trips to California, I haven't been anywhere, but the more I think about it, the more I like the idea of moving there once I graduate. I've lived here my entire life, and I need to get out of this fucking town. I need to get away from anything that reminds me of Emily. It's been two months since our breakup after a four year relationship that apparently didn't mean shit to her. Maci is the first girl I've been attracted to since, so I took that as a sign I was ready for a first date.

I take in the view–my favorite one in Eugene. It's an overlook I come to often. There's a path through the trees that brings you up to the top viewpoint where you can see a good chunk of the town from the University of Oregon to the downtown area and all the houses nearby. It's enclosed by trees, some of them already changing from green to shades of yellow, red and orange now that it's mid-October. I forget Maci is standing next to me for a moment until her voice breaks through the slight rustle of wind through the trees.

"Carley told me you were going to chicken out of asking me to hang out if she didn't talk you into it. Do you think you would have?" Once she's talking, she says the words quickly, as if she regrets asking them and wants to rush to the end.

I noticed she's a little insecure and nervous when she speaks sometimes but in a cute and endearing way. "I guess we will never know," I respond even though I know I would have asked anyway. I've never needed anyone to talk me into doing anything. I only brought it up to Carley because I haven't asked a girl on a date since high school.

Maci's thoughts overlap mine. "This *is* a date, right? I mean it feels date-ish. But just because she's not here, I'm not trying to misread this situation." She's rambling again, and I consider kissing her to get her to stop, but my stomach twists at the thought. My gut tells me what that means. Fuck. I am so not ready for this. I thought I was, but I'm not. I can't see past potential betrayal. Lies. Bullshit. The fact that I can't trust my own judgment or risk falling for someone again.

I push down the rage that's welling inside me thinking about my ex. I wonder how long this shit will affect my life.

Refusing to succumb to my anxiety and somehow make Maci feel bad for no justified reason, I chuckle at her question. Wrapping my arm around her, I squeeze her shoulder lightly as I kiss her hair. I can manage that at least. "Definitely a date, but it's getting late. I should probably get home so I don't sleep through class again tomorrow. Ready to go?"

I pull up to the curb outside Jameson's Bar, flipping out my kickstand aggressively as soon as I've parked. I feel like shit. It's not that I didn't have a great night with Maci. I did. It was good to get out of my house and out of my head for once, but when I dropped her off, I knew I couldn't see her again. Partly because she deserves more than to be a rebound and partly because I don't trust myself to not accidentally hurt her. My head is still so fucked up. I don't know who I can trust anymore, and I can't imagine allowing myself to trust another girl for a while.

Shoving my keys into the front pocket of my jeans, I yank open the glass door hard enough for the bartender, Jess, to look up from where she's pouring a beer under the dim reddish-orange lights above the taps. I take a hard seat on the black leather stool, pinching the bridge of my nose between my thumb and forefinger, closing my eyes and taking a deep breath. I'm fucking frustrated. I know I'm better without Emily. I should be fine.

I'm rattled out of my head when a pint glass hits the dark wooden bar in front of me. I glance up to see Jess already walking away to help two girls at the other end of the bar. My phone buzzes in my pocket, and I pull it out as I reach for my beer.

Maci: *Thanks for tonight! I had a great time.*

Fucking great. Without replying, I toss my phone face down on the wooden bar top, not caring if the screen cracks. I take a sip of my beer in an attempt to wash down my guilt. I'm such an asshole. I should have never asked her to go on a date with me. I don't know what I was thinking.

A rush of cold air hits my neck from the door opening, sending a chill down my spine, despite being dressed in jeans and a hoodie. I turn when I hear her laugh.

You've got to be kidding me.

My eyes lock with Emily's, her laugh stops abruptly, and it feels like all the other sounds from the bar go silent with it. This is the first time I've seen her since she callously broke my heart. Why is she here? Someone else comes into view as Emily steps forward. A hand on her back brings her attention to him as he guides her toward the bar. Oh, perfect. My second favorite person in the world. Am I the only one who wants to punch their favorite people in the faces? As my feet hit the floor, Emily's head spins to face me again, her eyes wide. This time the bastard touching her sees me too, an unreadable expression on his face.

Piece of shit.

I take a step as a hand grabs my forearm. My eyes fall to where her fingers dig into my skin before I meet her gaze.

"Don't even think about it, Troy. I'll call Tony if I have to." Her eyes soften. "She's not worth it."

I stare back and tug my arm, and she releases her hold on me from behind the bar. Jess turns back to the well–her place behind the bar where she keeps ice, glasses and the most popular liquors to make drinks.

She must be convinced I won't start a fight. I've never even punched someone before, but I desperately want to tonight. I take the last sip of my beer and slam the glass down.

It shatters.

"Fuck," I mumble.

"What the hell?" Jess' curse overlaps mine as she spins toward me and takes in the shards of glass scattered over the wooden bar top.

She's about to yell at me, but I cut her off. "I'm sorry, Jess. I'll take care of it."

She sighs, and I feel all the pity she's directing my way. Pathetic.

Luckily the glass broke into a few big chunks, so it's an easy mess to clean. Jess wipes a wet rag over the counter just to be safe and then sets a shot glass in front of me. Reaching for the tequila, she tips the bottle over until the clear liquid is level with the rim of the glass. "I texted Cooper to come get you," she says, not concerned with me or my response.

I scan the room and spot Emily in the corner booth by the billiards room leaned over the table, whispering to my ex best friend. I take a breath as I bring my attention back to Jess. "Thanks," I mumble. I tap the shot to the bar then shoot back the alcohol before pushing the glass forward for another.

Twenty minutes later, my phone buzzes with Cooper's name lighting up the screen. I drop a couple twenties on the bar top for Jess, and when she looks my way, I give her a slight nod as I leave.

The windows of his black 4Runner are rolled down, so I can clearly see Cooper sitting in the driver's seat, his hand draped over the steering wheel. His U of O sweatshirt hood is pulled over his worn-in, black Nike hat, but I can see his face enough to note the familiar look of pity in his eyes.

I open the door and slide into the passenger seat.

Twisting the volume dial left, Cooper turns the country music down to a hardly audible level. "Do you want to talk about it?" he asks before checking his blind spot and pulling into the street.

"Not really." I scrub my hands up my face. He doesn't fight me on it. "It's just... it fucking sucks."

"I know," is all he says, and we drive the ten minutes back to our house. He pulls into the driveway and turns off the car before turning to me. "I think maybe you should consider taking your cousin up on his offer early. You could transfer to a school in California."

"You think it will be this bad for that long?" I groan.

"I don't know, man. Maybe I'm the wrong person to ask, but I think sometimes the only option is to distance yourself." He sighs, gripping my shoulder and squeezing before letting go. I have a feeling he's right.

"I'll get through this year. I'll be fine. Then if I need to leave, I'll go."

"Okay," he says.

CHAPTER TWO
TROY

Three months later (December)

"Are you sure Sophie won't be here?" I ask Cooper as we get out of my car where I just parked on the dark street. I wanted to go to this party tonight specifically because Marcus and Dean throw low-key, no drama parties. Lately we've been to ragers, and I'm over it.

"I don't think so. Dean has a sweet and innocent view of his sister, and she likes it that way, so she won't party around him," he says as he slides his hands into the pocket of his black hoodie.

"Well, that works out for us." Where there is Sophie, there is drama–at least when it comes to Cooper, and me by association. "Maybe you'll actually have a good time tonight without worrying about her. Hell, maybe you'll meet someone new." I know he's still hung up on Sophie, but if she's moving on, so should he. If I can at least _try_ to get back out there after a four year relationship blowing up, he can too. Especially since their relationship was hardly even official.

"Doubt it. It's always the same people." We walk up the gravel driveway then veer around the side of the house, following the sound of crackling flames toward a bonfire so big it lights our path from a few hundred feet away.

Before I have a chance to shift Cooper's attitude, Marcus stops in front of us, a full, red Solo cup in his hand. "Hey, Troy. Coop." Even from this distance, the fire lights him from the side, his well-built frame and man bun casting a shadow on the grass.

"Hey, man," Coop and I say in unison. Marcus lives here with Dean, whose parents have owned the house next to Cooper's parents forever. We aren't super close, but because I've lived with the Montgomerys since I was ten, we've all spent a decent amount of time together. "Big turnout tonight," I say, not recognizing as many people as I expected.

"Yeah, it seems no one left for winter break this year, and I think Dean's girl brought some friends again."

I hit Cooper's arm and get an eye roll in return for insinuating again he could meet someone new tonight. "Oh yeah, I heard he's with someone. Weird as shit. I've never known him to have a girlfriend."

Marcus chuckles. "Yeah, it's strange. But they're great together. We'll see what happens." The energy shift in his last statement seems contradictory to the previous one and piques my interest, but I don't push the subject.

"Well, good to see you, man. We're gonna get some drinks."

"Sounds good. I'll catch up with you in a bit," Marcus says with a wave, taking off down the grassy hill.

"I'll grab you a beer. Go talk to a girl or something," I tell Cooper.

"Yes, Dad." He shakes his head at me, irritation rolling off him. Then he chuckles and heads toward the fire.

I make my way to the back patio, knowing I'll find a couple coolers full of drinks. I pull two cans of beer out of the half melted ice. Fuck, that's cold. I stand, shifting both beers to the same hand, so I can dry the other one on my sweatshirt. Looking up to make my way back to Coop, my gaze is met with a nice ass in tight blue jeans. Damn.

My gaze shifts upward, and it only takes a split second to realize I know her, which is shocking considering the limited time we've spent together. I haven't seen Maci since the party at my fraternity's house over a month ago, which was the first time I'd seen her since I ghosted her after our date two months prior to that. I felt like such a dick for pretending our date never happened and acting like we'd never met, but it felt like my only option at the time. I didn't know how to explain to her I just wasn't ready. What 21 year old dude is pathetic enough to stay hung up on an ex who couldn't care less about him? What's that expression? The best way to get over someone is to get under someone else. I thought for a split second that might help me, but Maci deserved more than that. She's not rebound material, she's girlfriend material.

I tried to talk to her at the party, but she ran off, wanting nothing to do with me. I can't blame her. I mean, come on, I transferred out of her math class the day after our date instead of being honest with her–like I was a fucking teenager faking sick to get out of a test.

"Maci?" I say as she takes a step away from me toward the fire.

She spins on her heel to face me, surprise written on her face with those same wide brown eyes she had when I showed up on my motorcycle. "Troy? ...Hey. What are you doing here?" At least she didn't tell me to get lost this time.

"I'm here to party?" It was a weird question to ask, but I guess she'd have no reason to know Dean and I are friends, so I add, "I played football in high school with one of the guys who lives here."

"Ooh, okay, that's cool," she mutters, the last word almost cut off with the Truly Lemonade she brings to her lips.

"Yeah, what about you? You're the last person I expected to see tonight."

"Don't worry, I won't be repeating the mistakes I made last time." She laughs nervously.

I expected her to be more relaxed after reading the letter I wrote her. I was flooded with guilt after seeing her and never assuring her that my bailing after our date had everything to do with me. She left the party alone and completely trashed, so I followed her at a distance–like a creep–through the shadows between the street lamps as we walked past the closed restaurants and shops near campus. It wasn't until she was safely inside her apartment that I realized it was really time to get my shit together. It pushed me to grow the fuck up and be an adult who communicates with the level of honesty I want in return. The two mile walk from her apartment to my house in the fresh air and silence helped me find the words for the apology she deserved. I'm hoping now that she seems at least a little more open to talk face to face, an attempt at a conversation might be more successful. "Sooooo, you'll let me talk to you this time?"

"Umm, I mean if you want. But I'm sure whatever we were going to talk about then doesn't matter anymore." Her statement and the way she uncomfortably rocks on her heels makes me think maybe she never got my letter. Carley said she'd give it to her.

My chance to clear the air is now, then. "I guess not, but I did want to explain myself. I figured I at least owe you that."

"It's okay, Troy. Really. Water under the bridge or however that expression goes."

My response is cut off by my name said in a tone I can only describe as *back the fuck away from my girl.* By the time I register Dean has joined our conversation, his fist is reached out, waiting for mine. "Hey, Dean," I acknowledge him as I return the fist bump, letting my eyes drift to his other hand, possessively on Maci's ass. "Ahhh." My thoughts catch up to what my eyes are taking in as Dean kisses Maci's hair. How did I miss she was wearing his sweatshirt, especially when I know his name is printed across the back? When the puzzle pieces are finished locking together in my mind, it hits me how relieved I am about this. Dean's great, and I'm glad she found him. Hopefully he can give her what I couldn't. I smile, genuinely happy for both of them.

Maybe Maci is right, and this conversation that's been weighing on me doesn't matter anymore. Either way, I take Dean's hint and decide to get lost. "I'll see you guys around. Talk to ya later, Maci."

I take off down the hill to find Cooper. Maybe some things work out better than you thought they would. I really fucking hope that's what happens for me when I move to California after graduation.

CHAPTER THREE
LEXY

Ten months later (October)

The clip of my last hair extension snaps in place. I run my fingers gently through the strands, blending it seamlessly with my bright blonde hair, falling over my shoulders in perfect curls. I put a thin line of glue on the edge of my fake lash, blowing on it lightly. While I wait for it to get tacky, I glance sideways at Maci. My best friend stares straight through my TV as some corny reality show plays, her fingers tugging on her straight brown hair mindlessly. She's totally zoned out, the same way she's been for the past month since she and Mack broke up.

I was a little anxious when Mack brought Maci around for the first time–worried I'd lose my best friend. Instead, I gained another. Maci moved to Los Angeles from Oregon four months ago to be with Mack, and it's worked out well for me even if it didn't work out as well for them. We clicked the first time we met. I hate that they broke up because they seemed so good together, but since Maci moved in, I've experienced how soul crushing heartbreak can be. It's another reminder that love is not for me. I'll stick to having commitment free fun.

It's also exactly why we are going out tonight. Maci still hasn't told me what really happened, and I'm trying not to push her, but it's also frustrating. I can see the emptiness in her dark, brown eyes as she stares into the TV. Looking back at the mirror to put my eyelash in place, I see the same vacancy in my bright blue eyes. I'm not in the best place lately either, but right now I want to be the best friend Maci needs, like she's been for me. She may have moved in after the breakup and constantly thanks me for letting her stay here, but she has no idea how much it's actually helped *me* from losing my mind in this city I hate so much.

There has to be something we can do to get her out of her head for a while. "You need to get out of this funk," I declare as I press my other false eyelash in place. I think for a moment. "I have an idea."

Her eyes roll in place of a response.

My mischievous smile makes an appearance as I reach for my light pink lip gloss. "You know that movie *Yes Man*, where Jim Carrey has to say 'yes' to everything anyone asks him? Let's do that. For the whole weekend. You don't have work, and I'm not on the schedule until Saturday night. And you need some excitement in your life."

I can practically see the excuses forming in her mind before she huffs out, "Ugh, how about not? That sounds absolutely terrifying. Plus, I don't know... what if men are involved? I'm not ready for that."

"Maci, I love you, but I don't care. You are choosing to not be with Mack, and you still won't tell me why, which is fine, but I also refuse to encourage you to stay stuck because you aren't sure yet if he's going to be in your future. Anyway, it's only one weekend, and what's the worst that can happen? We will set a few ground rules if it makes you feel better." I've heard the term opposites attract for couples, but I feel like it works for friendships too–at least with Maci and me. She hates getting out of her shell but thrives when I encourage her. I suck at letting people in, and her vulnerability has softened me. I won't go as far to say I believe in the potential of love or hope for happily ever after the way she does, but I'm definitely not as cynical as I used to be.

"Fine," she mumbles, before hopping up and heading to my closet. I still refuse to be all emotional in the way I see some girl friends act, but I secretly like how comfortable Maci feels in our friendship, doing things like stealing my clothes. It makes me feel like I have the sister I always wanted but never got as an only child.

When we get to 3rd Base, we head straight to the cock-tail lounge. The white leather booths lining the far wall are full, as is every seat at the sleek white bar top that wraps around the liquor shelves in the middle of the room. Technically, it's a sports bar, evident by the giant TVs hanging above the alcohol and the room off to the side with stadium seating in front of a wall of screens. It's more upscale than most bars, though.

It's way more crowded than usual, but I'm deter-mined to find a seat for us so we can talk about our epic weekend of what will hopefully be full of a few adventurous yeses. We spot a dirty high top table and wait next to it in hopes we can claim it once it's clean since it's seat yourself.

Maci seems lost in her head. She's leaning against the table, lazily scanning the room as if she's not convinced the answer to all her problems might be floating out there but wants to check anyway. I know a drink will help her relax a bit, so I search for a server. After a moment, my eyes connect with blue ones just a shade lighter than mine. Once I'm certain I have his attention, based on the fact that he's now heading straight toward us, I take a moment to take in the rest of him. His hair is also a similar color to mine, maybe a shade or two darker blond. It's short and styled perfectly in place but not in that overly gelled way that so many LA men wear it. A black dress shirt pulls across his muscles, the sleeves rolled up to his elbows, and his dark jeans hang on his hips perfectly. Damn, he's hot. Even more so with plates stacked up his forearm and three glasses in his hand, something I can be impressed by as a fellow bartender. I send out a silent prayer to the Universe that he asks me something I can say yes to. Anything.

His voice breaks through my heated thoughts. "Do you need a table? I can clean this for you."

Okay, I hoped for something a little more scandalous than that, but it's a start.

Before I can respond, Maci spins on her heel so fast she nearly falls over. Huh. Nothing has pulled her attention that quickly lately. She's gone pale and looks like she's seen a ghost.

The guy starts to speak again, and my gaze is instantly drawn back to the sweet sound of his voice. "Hey, I'm..."

Even though I'm staring right at his lips, it's my best friend's voice I hear match up with them.

"Troy."

My eyes dart to hers. "Troy... like Troy? Math class Troy? Troy who lives in Oregon, Troy?"

She mumbles confirmation to me. Okay, this is weird. I never saw a picture of the guy, and he's not what I expected at all. I guess I assumed she had a type and that he'd look more like Mack. She told me about this guy who took her on a date that honestly sounded like something I would have loved. It was spontaneous, and he seemed sweet. Then he ghosted her, and outside of a few coincidental and short run-ins, never talked to her again. I only know about him because when she was moving into my place she showed me a letter she had gotten from him explaining why he totally bailed on her–something about being heartbroken and not wanting her to be a rebound or something. I almost thought it was considerate, but I was more focused on being proved right once again about the dangers of love.

I'm not someone who feels uncomfortable easily, but this silence is awkward, and I need it to stop. Maci probably needs a moment, and I sure as hell need one to clear my head of the thoughts I was having about this guy a minute ago, ones that no longer feel appropriate. "Yes, please." I motion to the table, answering his initial question about cleaning it for us.

Somehow we ended up in Las Vegas. I mean, I know how–a combination of it being "yes weekend," and my attempt to shake this pull I felt toward a guy I hardly said a handful of words to. I hate being fake, but that is exactly what I was as I feigned excitement about this freak encounter between my best friend and her ex-whatever. Even though they never dated, it feels like I'd be breaking some sort of girl code–something I've never had experience with since I've never had a real girl friend. I remind myself I'm plenty capable of getting any of my needs met, either on my own, or with a different guy.

Each time Troy came back to the table, however, I realized shaking the thoughts about him running his hands all over my body wasn't going to be as easy as I hoped. My solution for this problem happens to be one that might help Maci too. I pushed her toward Troy and us getting away with him and his friend in Sin City. Of course I'm still hopeful she and Mack will get back together, but she's not currently into that idea. Maybe a fling with Troy will help shake her from her mood while simultaneously making him off limits in my mind. Win, win.

Last night was a blast. We went home from the bar to pack and then headed straight to Vegas. We wanted to get the lay of the land and have an adventure, just us, before we met up with the boys. It did not disappoint.

Hands down, last night was one of the most fun nights I've ever had. It was more than enough to distract me from the worry in the back of my mind that I'm lusting for someone I shouldn't.

I stare into the casino bathroom mirror at my best friend. She's wearing my royal blue dress. Even though we are almost identical in 5'6" height and athletic build, my dress looks like it was made specifically for Maci. It's short, with a slit that runs up the side and shows off her perfectly toned legs from all the running she's been doing lately. It reveals just enough of her boobs to be classy and seductive at the same time. I know it makes her a little uncomfortable, but she looks like a total babe standing there twirling a few more curls into her shoulder length chocolate brown hair. I smile, thinking about how thankful I am to have her in my life, before looking at my own reflection.

Personally, I think I look just as good. I'm not conceited by any means, but the only positive thing my mother blessed me with was her good looks. While I would never openly give her the satisfaction or credit, I also refuse to take my good fortune for granted. I have on a simple strapless black dress that hugs my curves in all the right places. After playing softball through middle and high school, there isn't even a chance Maci will ever convince me to go for a run with her. But I do go to Soul Cycle five times a week. It's kind of what women do in Hollywood. Either that or pilates. I'm not usually one to follow the crowd, but I love it. There's something about the intensity that comes from within a dark room and music so loud you can feel it in your soul that helps me get out of my own head. Not to mention, it's what keeps this dress looking this good.

I swipe dark red gloss over my lips before stealing the curling iron back from Maci, correcting a straight blonde hair before we go meet up with the guys. Troy sent a text earlier asking us to meet them at a speakeasy inside the Cosmopolitan hotel. He's bringing a friend who Maci is fairly confident will be a great guy because she trusts Troy enough to keep good company. I've been telling myself the same, in between prayers that it's true. I'm pretty good at convincing other people I'm fun and spontaneous, but I typically have a secret plan for everything and how I want it to go. I like feeling in control since I spent so much of my life out of it.

My plan for this weekend is to get Troy out of my head and into Maci's. That probably seems a little twisted, which is exactly why it's a secret plan. Sometimes I feel like my crazy ideas will only ever make sense to me. My logic is that Maci will either relax for the first time in a month and her heartbreak will fade a little more, or even better, she'll realize how much she misses Mack. Selfishly I'm hoping for the latter because I love my two best friends together. Despite what she revealed to me earlier about their struggles while Mack was on tour, I'm convinced they'll find their way back to each other once Maci fulfills her need to figure out who she is and what she wants outside of a relationship. Either way, if she and Troy have a great time, maybe I'll actually see him as off limits. If he brings a friend even half as hot as he is, it'll be even easier to distract myself.

We finally find the hidden speakeasy, and I push through the door with more force than I intended. I'm both anxious to either get this night over with or mag-ically be overcome by an attraction to Troy's friend. I'm not looking for a boyfriend, but sometimes a girl needs a man's touch. Thankfully, this city screams sex.

TROY

The hotel room door clicks as the girls leave, their whispers fading with them. I fall back onto the bed, noting Nolan still asleep on the other one. Fuck that was a fun night. I can't say I could have ever predicted I'd end up in bed with Maci–and in Vegas no less–but I'd be lying if I said I never thought about it.

As much fun as it was, it'll never happen again. It was bad timing for me when I met her in Oregon and bad timing for her when we stumbled into each other here. But both of us know that even if the timing were better, we wouldn't be right for each other anyway. Maci is great, and if we run into each other again, I'm down to be friends. We just don't have that chemistry, and even if our roles weren't reversed this time around and she wasn't the one getting over a relationship, I'm confident she feels the same. This was meant to be fun–the once is enough kind of fun.

It became evident to me last night I've come a long fucking way this past year. Maci and I communicated like adults about what we wanted–what a fucking con-cept. More than that, I actually trusted her intentions. While I don't have any desire for anything more with her, I have realized I do eventually want more with the right person. It was only one date, but last night showed me I'm ready for what it's going to take to be in a relationship again. Maybe the real reason Maci came back into my life was to help me realize I've been punishing myself long enough.

CHAPTER FOUR
LEXY

Two months later (New Year's Eve)

Reaching for my red, heart-shaped sunglasses I left in Maci's car, I catch Mack's black Jeep Wrangler pull up in front of the apartment. He's already taken the soft top off in preparation for our weekly beach day. I press the manual lock down before slamming the door shut and turn to find Mack has reached across the seat and pushed his passenger door open for me. I slide onto the black leather, turning toward my best friend.

"Hi...iiii" My peppy greeting fades away with hesitation. I follow his flat expression and gaze to where he's staring at the dusty red Corolla. I reach over, my hand landing on his shoulder where his baseball shirt splits between black and gray. "It's just her car, Mack." I squeeze his shoulder before letting go. He rubs his hands up his face before taking off his signature black backward hat. His dark brown hair is a tad longer than usual, and I know it's because he's been distracted lately. He readjusts his hat before turning to look at me, pain evident in his emerald green eyes.

I've known Mack for over two years. Even though I've always lived around Hollywood, I'm not close with anyone from any stage of my life here. Everyone has always seemed fake, pretending to be someone they aren't just to fit in or be loved. I refuse to act like that or associate myself with people who aren't genuine. When Mack moved here from Oregon with his band, he was like a breath of fresh air. He was the first and only artist at Shot in the Dark, the venue where I bartend, to speak to me about more than a drink. I was getting my ass kicked on his first night–a rare occurrence of me being overwhelmed–and he wouldn't take no for an answer when he offered to help. He pulled me out of my bad mood that night, and he's been stuck with me ever since.

I saw that first night the excitement he had for his band's newly secured residency was palpable. It shined through him, brightening whatever space he was in. Even though he was hopeful for his opportunity in California, he's never been naive to the realities of the music industry or idealized this place the way so many people do. Immediately, I could tell something in him had been hardened from his past, and it balanced him somewhere between optimistic and vigilant. We quickly connected on that understanding of life. Until Maci moved here, I considered him not just my best friend but my only true one. Luckily, I still have both of them even if they aren't dating.

He sighs. "It's not the car. Today was her last day of volunteer work in Costa Rica. I *knew* she was going to stay out there longer, but part of me still hoped she'd change her mind."

"It's okay that you miss her, Mack. I miss her too." I confide in him even though voicing any kind of emotional feelings are rare for me. He needs my wall down more than I need it up right now.

"That's different. You don't have to worry about losing her."

"You're not going to lose her. She loves you. She's just working on loving herself which is important too. We both know that."

"I know. God. I sound selfish wanting her to come back before she's ready."

"You're not selfish. But you are depressing me. It's New Year's Eve. I refuse to let you start the new year in this mood."

"Yeah, okay, you're right. Where do you want to go? I was thinking Newport? We haven't been in a while." He looks at his watch. "It's almost three. We could probably make it down there before rush hour."

It's a weekly tradition–whenever Mack isn't on tour with his band–that we go spend an afternoon at the beach. "Mack, every hour is rush hour here. But yes. And then I'm going to talk you into that Irish Pub I love. I bet they have Karaoke tonight too." I flip down the visor and slide open the cover to the mirror.

I love hearing him sing, and the eyeroll I catch in my peripheral tells me he's aware I'm implying he should. "I'm in, but only if you sing with me."

I pull my long, blonde curls back into a tight, high ponytail and slide my sunglasses on, contemplating his request. He knows I don't sing in front of anyone. The only reason he's ever heard me is because he asked for my opinion on lyrics he was writing once, and my suggestion came out more musical than I intended. But he *is* my best friend, and I think it'll help get his mind off Maci being gone. "Okay, as long as I get to choose the song."

"Deal."

CHAPTER FIVE
LEXY

After brushing the sand off my frayed jean shorts, I link my arm through Mack's, leaning my head on his shoulder as we walk toward the bar. He unlinks his arm from mine, wrapping it around my shoulder and giving me a loving squeeze. A shiver runs through me when a cool breeze hits my bare arms. Living in California, I'm almost always good as long as the sun is shining, but it's nearly 9:30 p.m. and way too late for only a tank top in December.

Mack glances at me and pulls away, reaching into his jean pockets and handing me his keys. "Go grab your hoodie, and I'll go order you a shot. What song are we singing?"

I nod, taking the keys from. "Hmmm. Ooh, 'Islands in the Stream?'"

"I'll put our names down so we can get this over with." His words tell me he's annoyed I'm dragging him out, but he flashes me a smile, and I know he isn't really.

"Two shots, please!" I yell over my shoulder on my way to the Jeep.

Tugging my plain red hoodie over my head, I enter the bar. The lights are dim, and the deep, brown wood used for the bar, booths and flooring make it even darker. Regardless, I immediately spot Mack in the back corner by the stage in a circular booth. I slide onto the black leather seat, and he pushes two shots of whiskey toward me. I don't care much for hard liquor. I prefer beer, but I need liquid courage for this. "We are seventh on the list, so you better drink these now."

I shoot both of my shots back quickly, not offering one to Mack. He hasn't had a single drink since he and Maci broke up even though alcohol was never the issue. I'm proud of him for the way he's taking control of his life in every aspect he can.

Mack grins as my shot glasses hit the table. "I can't wait to watch you sing in public for the first time."

"I hate you." While I'm one of the most confident people I know, I'll admit–at least to myself–it's more of a *fake it 'til you make it* kind of thing. It's always worked for me, and I pride myself on my ability to be bold despite any anxiety. But tonight, I'm feeling uncharacteristically nervous.

When it's our turn, I'm hesitant. "You're fine, Lex. You know better than most that everyone here is already drunk, hardly paying attention and probably more concerned with finding someone to kiss at midnight. Let's go!" He seems excited.

"Okay, I'm ready." I shoot back the third shot the waitress just placed in front of me.

Before the chorus even hits, I'm surprisingly comfortable. This is fun. By the time we slide our mics back into their stand and find our seats back in the booth, we both have stupid grins on our faces.

"That's it, next time I go into the studio to mess around, you're coming with me," Mack declares, leaning back into the booth.

"I kind of want to," I admit. "That was fun. Is it weird for you to sing like that?"

"A little, since I'm used to performing my own songs. But I liked it. I needed this tonight. Although I'm sorry I'm the guy you're stuck with on New Year's Eve."

I roll my eyes and rest my chin on the palm of my hand. "I only like two people, Mack, and you're one of them."

"Cynical, as always." He laughs.

Everyone at work has questioned if we were dating at one point or another, probably because I'm so naturally flirty. Despite the fact that I know he'd be an amazing boyfriend from how well he treats Maci, I've never pictured him that way. I'm also not looking for a boyfriend, and I'd rather have a genuine friend any day. Even if I were into musicians, he still isn't my type. I've always found myself drawn to the preppy, athletic guys. Unfortunately for me, at least in LA, a lot of those men don't have attractive personalities. It doesn't matter either way because I don't plan on ever falling in love. I watched my mom do it a million times, and the way it destroyed her life doesn't interest me. "You're an anomaly when it comes to love. Most people who grow up with crap parents end up in dysfunctional relationships. That's exactly what I'm trying to avoid. I have no idea how you're such a romantic."

"Therapy. *Lots* of therapy." His voice is laced with humor, but I know he's serious.

"Yeah, yeah. Alcohol helps me." I push my empty shot glass his way, a pleading and manipulative look in my eyes.

"I'll be right back." He laughs and heads to the bar to get me another drink.

"Beer this time, please!" I yell after him.

I fish my phone out of my hoodie pocket to check in with my other best friend. I don't even get our text thread opened before I'm interrupted.

"Lexy?"

My head spins around, searching for whoever is calling me. My eyes scan the surrounding space until they land on him.

"Troy?" Damn, he looks good, even better than I remember. His blond hair is flawlessly styled, his piercing blue eyes are a perfect match to his t-shirt. The way his dark blue jeans look... whoa, suck on an ice cube, Lex.

"I thought that was you." He smiles, and I force myself to stop imagining what he looks like under all his very well fitting clothes. "I didn't know you could sing."

A wave of fresh heat hits my cheeks, and I know it has nothing to do with the liquor. Embarrassment is not a feeling I'm used to nor enjoy. I shake it off. "You witnessed my debut performance. Lucky you." I shoot him a wink, my *fake it til you make it* confidence in full force.

"Oh yeah? Lucky me." His tone is flirty, but I doubt he's actually trying to flirt with me. Flirtiness is part of his personality too from what I remember. My stomach flips nonetheless. I refuse to give any attention to it.

"Two bartenders, both with a holiday off? What are the chances of that?"

"A miracle, is what it is. Who's here with you?" He must be wondering if Maci is nearby.

Like magic, Mack returns with my beer in his hand.

He looks at Troy, his surprise evident. It's rare I give any guy the time of day, unless I'm in the mood for a hookup, and he knows it. He directs his gaze at me with a smirk. It took me 21 years to find someone I connect with well enough to be such good friends, but the way he can read me feels like a curse right now. I ignore him.

"Mack, Troy. Troy, Mack." My hand bounces between them with the introduction.

"Hey, man." Troy reaches out to shake Mack's hand, his gesture returned. "You guys were great up there." He nods to the stage.

"Thanks. How do you two know each other?" Mack flicks his finger between the two of us.

I speak before Troy has a chance to. "He works at 3rd Base–that place I go for Happy Hour sometimes."

"Oh nice." Mack moves to sit down in the booth, on the side opposite where Troy stands.

I shift my focus back to Troy. "Who are you here with?"

He chuckles, leaning against the dark wood frame of the booth. "No one now. Nolan took off an hour ago with some chick."

"Figures." I laugh. Nolan is an even bigger flirt than I am. We had an unspoken mutual agreement of just having fun and sex in Vegas, and it was everything I needed to forget the weird feeling I had around Troy. I never thought I'd have to see him again after that weekend.

Mack clears his throat, and my attention goes back to him. I'd completely forgotten he existed. "Umm, I totally forgot I have to get to the recording studio early in the morning. I should probably head out soon."

"Oh, umm yeah. We can go." I glance at Troy before meeting Mack's gaze. It's then I realize he doesn't have to go to the studio tomorrow. There's no way. Mack's eyes flash to Troy so quickly there's no way anyone else would have caught it. He's trying to wingman me.

Troy's voice comes from behind me. "I can give you a ride home, if you want to stay."

"Uhhh." Mack kicks me under the table. I must have been expecting it because I didn't even flinch. "Yeah, sure, that would be great. Thanks."

Mack stands, taking a sip of his water and setting it back down on the table. "Nice to meet you, Troy. I'll see you tomorrow, Lex."

CHAPTER SIX
TROY

"Solid wingman you have there." I chuckle. I will give it to the guy, he was subtle. I've just been playing that game with Nolan for long enough to read the signs.

Lexy laughs like she's not embarrassed in the slightest I caught onto what was happening. "He means well. I don't give attention to someone unless I think the reward will be worth it, if you catch my drift. He must have thought that's what was happening." She chuckles to herself like us together is a ridiculous notion then casually takes a sip of her beer. Anyone would be insane to deny it wasn't cute as hell.

"I see, and how do you determine who is worthy?" I play into her game.

"Eh, it's typically based on my mood more than anything else. A vibrator can only do so much for a girl."

I nearly choke on my beer. I can't tell if she's drunk or if this is how she is, but it's not what I expected. Not that I would have known what to expect. I haven't spent any real time with the girl and only had a handful of conversations with her over two months ago. I only came over here because I was trying to escape a girl who was attempting to hit on me with an annoying one-sided conversation. Also because she's really hot.

She shrugs, a sly smile on her face, like this conversation is as plain as talking about the weather.

"Well alright then. Sounds like you're not the kind of girl who needs a wingman."

"Definitely not. Mack knows that. If I want something–or someone–I'm more than capable of getting it on my own. He mistakenly assumed what I wanted was you."

"You sure know a way to a guy's heart, don't ya?" I joke.

"Nope. Just the way to their pants, and that's a totally different game." She smirks at me. She's not completely wrong.

I change the subject before we get too far down that path. I do not need to think about sex with anyone complicated. "Doesn't Mack know us hooking up might be weird considering we've both fucked the other's best friend?"

"Yeah, he's missing some key information." Her smirk falters for only a second, but I catch it. I wonder what thought crossed her mind.

My memory flashes to Vegas, my eyes drifting to the corner of the room. I replay hooking up with Maci with a view of the Strip. That was a fun night.

"Ewww, can you not think about fucking my best friend right now." Lexy's mocking voice pulls me out of my head.

I laugh and give her a dramatic eye roll that lands on her. "Hey, from what I heard, I wasn't the only one who had fun in Vegas." I add a wink for effect.

"Life is too short not to have a good time or be one." She leans back in her seat and drinks the last sip of her beer before setting it on the table.

Sounds like something I would say, at least ever since I got over Emily.

"You two want another round?" The waitress saves me from the downward thought spiral I do not need.

I wasn't planning on staying much longer. The way girls are on the prowl for midnight kisses tonight is such a turn off. Desperation is unattractive. Sometimes I really hate California. I'm sure someone would be offended if I lumped all Californians together, but overall the people in Oregon are higher quality, at least from what I've seen.

I look over at Lexy. This night has definitely started improving. She's a lot spicier than I realized. It's fun. "One more?"

"As long as you're good to drive, yes."

I nod at the waitress. "One more round is good, thank you."

When she walks away, I turn back to Lexy. "I would have thought you'd have some wild plans tonight."

She laughs like I'm joking. "Holidays have never really been my thing. I usually have to work anyway. Plus, Mack is a heartbroken mess." She sighs, and I can tell it upsets her. "I'd rather get him out of the house than make superficial plans with people who only care about me because I know how to party."

This girl may be fiery, but she's also a little cynical. It might come off depressing to someone else, but I relate hard to her. Ever since my relationship with Emily blew up in my face, my willingness to trust anyone's sincerity is a rare occurrence. "Sounds like you're a good friend."

She shrugs. "Mack would do the same for me. Not like he'll ever have to."

"Because you have an amazing boyfriend who would never break your heart?" I know that's not what she's saying, but she's kind of cute when she's annoyed.

She rolls her eyes. "Smooth. Hard pass on the boyfriend thing. What about you? Were you naive enough to think Nolan wouldn't ditch you at some point?"

"Nah, I knew he would. I figured I'd make some new friends or go home whenever he did."

"To your girlfriend?" she asks jokingly, but I don't miss the hint of curiosity in her tone.

"Hard pass on relationships for me too. Especially in California."

"I feel that," she mumbles under her breath as our waitress comes back with our beers.

I reach for my wallet. I noticed earlier this lady was running circles around this bar trying to take care of everyone. The last thing she needs is to make an extra trip back to our table. As I flip my wallet open, Lexy's hand covers it. "I've got it. Thanks for giving me a ride home in advance." She pulls out two twenties from the pocket of her jean shorts and holds them out toward the waitress. "We can cash out now, I'm sure things are going to get wild in here soon with it being fifteen minutes until midnight. Keep the change." She smiles warmly when the waitress thanks her and scurries off.

I'm more turned on by her interaction with the waitress than when she was talking about her vibrator.

How someone treats restaurant staff is a true judge of character in my book and an attractive quality to me. Not that Lexy turns me on or anything. Okay, maybe my dick twitched a little at that vibrator comment, but what guy's wouldn't? Especially coming from a hot woman. Now that I'm looking at her for the first time without the shock of running into a blast from my past, I've noticed she's really fucking pretty. Her long, blonde hair looks salty and windblown, leaving her tangled curls falling over her shoulders. The blue of her eyes is much richer than mine which tend to look gray more often than not. But it's the red hoodie that matches the red heart sunglasses on her head that's doing something for me. Red is definitely her color.

Get a fucking grip, dude. You're only doing hookups unless the perfect person comes along, and hooking up with someone you're kind of friends with isn't how you keep things from getting complicated.

Her voice pulls me out of my thoughts. "So, how did you end up in California?"

That's a more loaded question than she thinks it is. I stick with the short version. "My cousin lives here, and I wanted a change in scenery, so I thought I'd give it a try."

"Do you like it?"

"Don't think I'm crazy, but I don't like it as much as I thought I would."

"Oh yeah? How come?" I can't tell if she's judging my opinion or not.

"Partially the people? Mostly the–"

"Vibe," she says at the same time the word leaves my lips then laughs. "I knew you were going to say that.

Maci says it all the time, and no one I've ever met here uses that word."

I can't help but smirk. "It's an adjustment living here for a lot of reasons."

"Are you going to move back?"

"Not sure yet. I don't hate it here, so I'm trying to give it a real chance. It's only been a few months. Depends on the opportunities that come my way. What about you? Have you always lived here?"

"Yup. I've been here my whole life."

"Do you want to stay here for the rest of it?"

"I don't want to die in LA, but I'm too comfortable here to leave."

As I'm about to comment, the music shuts off. Someone turns on the television, the wind-chilled voice of the announcer on the replay of the ball drop in Times Square crackling through the speakers. I forgot for a second it was New Year's Eve, we are in public and that there was anyone else around.

"10...9...8..." Everyone in the bar chants loudly, overpowering the TV.

I glance at Lexy, and an unexplainable force draws me to her. I slide across the three inches of black leather seat that separates us. We must have been inching closer together as we were talking because I'm confident I did not sit this close to her initially. Her blue eyes fill with both confusion and curiosity at my movements. I don't know. I seriously don't have any fucking clue.

"3...2...1..." I lean in and kiss her. Apparently that's what I'm doing. I feel her tense up and immediately pull back.

Her gaze is locked onto mine. "What was that?" She says it softly, but there's demand in her voice.

Seriously, what the fuck was that? I shrug. "I think it's pretty cool you chose cheering up your friend over a date tonight. You shouldn't have to miss out because of it." I wink at her.

She hesitates for a second as if she's contemplating her response. "Okay, well that 'catch me by surprise thing' was not cool."

I can't tell if she's truly mad. I start my apology, but she cuts me off.

"I can't have you misjudging my capabilities." I catch her smirk right before her lips collide with mine again.

This time she's less tense. She's so far from tense it feels like she's melting into me. It's sweet. For a second. Then her hand grips my neck, drawing us closer together. She takes over the kiss, her tongue finding it's way to mine as if she knows it's what I want; it's sexy as fuck. My hands reach for her hips, middle fingers sliding through the belt loops of her shorts and pulling her closer to me.

Her fingers run up my neck, through the short tips of my hair. As fast as they found their way there, they disappear. The rest of her pulls back too, leaving me stunned. "Much better." She smiles innocently at me like she wasn't just trying to seduce me. "Are you ready to go?"

It takes me a second to find my words. "Yeah." I clear my throat. "Let's go."

CHAPTER SEVEN
TROY

Pressing the button on my key fob, I hear the door of my white Honda Civic unlock right before Lexy's voice cuts through the cool night air.

"Wait, is this what you drive?"

"Umm, yes?" I chuckle and pair it with a look of confusion in her direction.

"Oh, I thought you had a bike."

"I do," I say with hesitation. "I left it in Oregon with my buddy Cooper."

"Why?"

"I couldn't drive both down here at the same time, and I thought a car would be more practical." I open my door as Lexy's swings open, and we slide onto my black leather seats simultaneously.

"Oh, ok, that makes sense." She sounds almost... disappointed.

I start the engine and shift into reverse. Before I switch to drive, I hand her my phone.

"You want to put your address in?"

She takes it from me, the navigation screen of my car showing the directions a few seconds later. I reach back over for my phone, but when it doesn't land in my hand, I glance her way. She's scrolling through it. I'm about to ask her what she's doing–more out of curiosity than actually caring–when my favorite Every Avenue song comes blaring through my speakers. Whoops, I probably should have turned my stereo down, but it's never loud enough for me.

Lexy seems unaffected by the volume as she continues scrolling through my Spotify. I can see her clicking to add songs to the queue out of the corner of my eye. I stay silent, drumming my finger on the steering wheel, curious to see which song she plays next.

It's Fall Out Boy. Circa 2005.

I won't deny this girl is hot, even more so because of her taste in music and the look on her face when she wished I had my motorcycle with me. I have missed my bike but not as much as I do right now. I've always known it could easily be a chick magnet, but I've never cared about that before. Again, desperation isn't a good look on anyone.

Lexy doesn't seem to possess that emotion. She wasn't kidding when she said she just takes what she wants. The way she took control of the music and the way she's turning the heater up right now without even bothering to ask... Some might consider it rude, but something tells me she doesn't mean it that way. I get the impression she's always had to look out for herself to get by, like she's had no other choice but to take what she wants or she'll never get anything. But what do I know about her or what she wants?

Like that kiss. For a second I thought maybe she actually wanted to kiss *me*, but I'm sure it was all part of her game. It's a game I understand well, especially after these last few months in California. It's not that hard to figure out what kind of person you need to be to make someone interested. I wouldn't consider myself a player, like Nolan. If you base it on how many hookups I've had in the past year, you might think so, but unlike my best friend, I'm always upfront about what it is. I would never mislead anyone, not after what happened with Emily. Maci back in college was the exception to that, but I was so fucked up. It's not an excuse though, and I still feel bad about it.

Would Lexy even consider hooking up with me since I slept with her best friend? Does that break some kind of girl code? I know for sure Nolan wouldn't give a fuck, and this is a totally different situation than Emily, especially since Maci and I didn't even date. Why am I even thinking about this? Fine, my dick practically sprung to life when I turned around, struck by that sweet but spicy voice singing the chorus of "Islands in the Stream." Fun and flirty emanated out of her. One of her hands was curled inside her sweatshirt sleeve, the end of it balled in her fist while the other held the microphone. Her beach wavy, blonde hair was tied in a loose ponytail with her sunglasses woven through the strands to keep them on her head. The smile on her face made it evident she was having a blast. It was cute as hell. And her legs in those cutoff jean shorts... I adjust my jeans after turning my blinker on and making a left turn, hoping the darkness of the night keeps her from noticing.

What the fuck. Hopefully I'll shake it off by tomorrow. Sex was in the air tonight, so surely Lexy's allure was simply a product of that. Maybe I'll text Lauren. She's been wanting to hang out and she knows what's up. I probably just need to get laid to get these thoughts out of my system.

We don't talk the entire drive to her apartment. It's not that I would mind a conversation with her, but this is how I prefer to drive, with nothing but the right music. The playlist she created cycles through mostly Escape the Fate, A Day to Remember and Taking Back Sunday. As we pull into her apartment complex a Straylight Run song plays, and I catch her silently singing along even though she's leaning against the car window with the hood of her red sweatshirt pulled up. How does she even know this song?

I park in a space in front of her building but leave the car running. She reaches my phone out to me. "Thanks for the ride." She half smiles before opening the car door, the interior lights illuminating her pretty face.

"Thanks for the kiss." It comes out before I think about it.

She steps out of my car, but I catch the edge of a smirk.

"Hey." I get her attention, and she sticks her head back inside my car. "Where do you work?"

"Shot in the Dark." Her bright blue eyes hesitate on mine. "See ya, Troy." She closes the door and takes off in the direction of her apartment.

I follow her movement until she safely disappears to the other side of the door, wondering what it is about this girl that blurs my ability to read a situation.

CHAPTER EIGHT
LEXY

Thank God I'm not hungover. By the time Troy dropped me off last night, it was only 1:30, which is early for me considering my bar doesn't close until 1 or 2 a.m. I could have stayed out longer. Driving around listening to music is one of my favorite simple pleasures. I had a used car for a few years when I turned 18. I saved all my money from makeup gigs as a teenager so I could stop taking public transportation. That sucked.

About a year ago, my car finally crapped out on me, but luckily I had already moved into a new apartment close to work. Mack has always let me use his Jeep when he's out of town, and Maci left her car with me when she went to Costa Rica a couple months ago. Damn, I have good friends. LA would be unbearable without them. I don't even know what I did before Mack. Partied a lot. Drank a lot. It wasn't great, not that I could admit that to myself at the time. No matter how much I hated the people I was hanging around, I kept going out with them.

I have a feeling if Mack and Maci get back together, they will move back to Oregon. I'm not quite sure what I'll do when that happens. As much as I don't think I'm as happy as I could be in California, I've never truly considered leaving. Since Maci started suggesting it frequently, it crosses my mind on occasion, but making such a big shift would be terrifying. It would change every aspect of my life I do enjoy–a good paying job I'm great at, a city I know my way around, a gym and restaurants I love, easy access to the beach. Plus, I've never even been to Oregon. Hell, I've never been outside of Southern California except for that one trip to Vegas.

Vegas.

Thoughts of Troy sneak into my mind. Last night when he brought up sleeping with each other's best friend, I couldn't help but recall my night with Nolan. We were exhausted from dancing until the club kicked us out, only stopping for fresh drinks and sex in an exceptionally dark corner of the club. It was almost 5 a.m. when we snuck into the hotel room. By the way clothes were thrown everywhere, I knew Maci and Troy had sex too. I practically forced her on him, so it wasn't unexpected. But seeing the moonlight cast across them tangled together in the sheets as they slept pulled my exhibitionism high right out of me. I blamed my churning stomach on too much alcohol, but I know that was the silent, jealous rage talking.

Then last night, it was like a delayed "yes weekend" wish coming true. The whole time I was with him was too good, too easy–the banter, the closeness, the touching, the drive. I like driving alone, but being with him, as he drummed his finger on the steering wheel, listening to music in silence with me, it was better.

What.

The.

Actual.

Fuck.

This will not be a thing. My traitorous mind dares to suggest that I didn't want to leave Troy last night, which is the most absurd thought. I'll likely never even see the guy again.

Although that's what I said when we left Vegas.

I yank open the door to Soul Cycle with so much force the receptionist looks up, startled.

"Hey, Lexy." She smiles at me through tired eyes.

"Hey, Hannah. Looks like you had a fun night," I comment with a chuckle.

"The morning after always tries to convince me it wasn't as great as I thought." She groans.

"I feel that. Seriously. Please tell me it's Jared's class this morning. I need a good ass kicking."

"You're in luck." She holds out a clean towel for me.

"Thanks."

She focuses back on her book, and I head into the cycle room. It's almost completely dark in here, except for the strip of neon purple lighting where the top of the wall meets the ceiling. The class is surprisingly full, almost all the bikes in the eight by five rows filled. Yeah, it's day one of New Year's resolution season, but it's only 8 a.m., and we are in the heart of Hollywood. I can guarantee some of these people haven't even been to sleep.

I find an empty bike in the front row, off to the left. Perfect. I've been coming here long enough Jared knows I like all the tough love, and he's more than happy to direct it straight at me, especially when I'm in the front.

I tug my black, off-the-shoulder sweater over my head and toss it on the floor near my bike. Maci got me a set of sports bras for my birthday this year, and

I'm obsessed with them. They have criss-cross straps across my chest. I'm wearing the black one today along with plain black leggings because that's a thing girls do, wear cute outfits to have a better workout. And I need a good workout today. I need to pedal any thoughts of Troy out of my head.

I finish adjusting my bike and get on as Jared comes onto the small stage at the front of the room. "Got something fun planned for you guys today. Picked my favorite song from each of the past 15 years. I thought a nice trip down memory lane might help you forget that I'm killing you." He says exactly what I want to hear.

This is the reason I cycle. The dark. The music. The endorphins. It consumes me in a way that allows everything else to fade away. Twenty minutes go by, and I've already pushed myself so hard, all my baby hairs are wet from sweat and fraying out of my ponytail. I like it here because I feel in control of my body in a way that helps me control my mind.

"Shake It," by Metro Station, blasts through the speakers. Jared yells through his mic over the music that it's time for a round of HIIT, 30 seconds of pedaling fast, with hard resistance, alternating 30 seconds of recovery. I push hard for the first 30. When the recovery starts, he turns the music down a notch so we can hear him.

"Let's talk about comfort zones. Who wants to get the hell out of theirs this year?!"

Half the room cheers. The other half of the room, me included, doesn't. I don't like where this is headed, probably because I need to hear it and don't want to.

"Your comfort zone is just a psychological state where you feel safe and secure." Jared's tough voice echoes through his mic. "But here's the kicker. You can choose what things make you feel secure, if you're willing to shift your mindset."

I'm all for fun, spontaneous, adventures, which might make some people uncomfortable. Not me. I'm that girl who is uncomfortable in the kind of situations that bring others a sense of calm and excitement, things like relationships and reaching the next level of success. I'm more of a live day to day kind of person. Thinking beyond that causes all sorts of discomfort, and I avoid it at all costs.

The next 30 seconds of intensity hits, and the music volume increases. I turn my resistance all the way up, pushing until my legs burn.

When we switch to recovery, Jared's voice overpowers the music again. "If you wanted to stay in your comfort zone, you wouldn't be here."

This kind of stepping outside of comfort is easy for me. It's the emotional stuff that gets me. As if he's reading my mind, Jared adds, "If you're thinking, 'but Jared, pushing yourself physically is different than pushing yourself emotionally,' you're wrong. The two are intertwined. Pick up the pace, one more sprint. Add another half turn. Push yourself. Your body is capable." He pauses as we do as we're told. "I just looked around the room, and every single one of you made that turn to the right. You did that because you decided your body was capable, and if you were unsure, you chose to at least try."

Oh. Fuck.

"10 more seconds. Let's go." He's quiet until we hit recovery, allowing us to focus, to push.

"Back it off." I turn the resistance down and grab my water. "If you can push yourself in this room, you can push yourself in life. It's not more complicated than simply making the decision that you believe in yourself, or at the very least you're willing to try and find comfort in that. Alright, uphill climb for this next song. Resistance back up. Get out of the saddle."

"I Gotta Feeling," by the Black Eyed Peas, plays next. I'm instantly transported to Vegas and being in the club with Maci. My mind wanders right back to Troy. It keeps fucking doing that. We walked into that Speakeasy, and I was immediately taken aback by my attraction to him. Thank God I snapped out of it in the second it took Maci to slide in the door behind me. I practically threw myself into Nolan as a distraction. This stupid pull I felt toward Troy was so strong that at some point I had to physically get away from him.

Don't get me wrong, I had a blast with Nolan. He's a good time, but my mind kept wandering back to Troy. For no fucking reason. Like it is now. Maci made some offhand comment on the drive home about how Troy and I would probably be great together. That was the last thing I needed to hear after making him off limits in my mind.

I doubt I'm even going to see him again, so none of this matters. I turn the resistance up another half turn.

CHAPTER NINE
TROY

"I can't believe it was so busy," Lauren says as she hands me half of the tips we made tonight.

Not all the bartenders here split evenly. Most of them take their own sides of the bar and whatever cash comes with that. When Lauren and I are the only ones here, we have our own arrangement, one of two that works well for us. We communicate, we work hard, and we have a system for making the most each night. It mainly involves a lot of shameless flirting with the people who want it and toning it down for those who don't. It seems contradictory to my new life motto of honesty first, but bartending is its own ball game, and I'm just here to give the people what they want.

"Yeah, I thought everyone would be too hungover from New Year's Eve last night. What did you do?"

"I tried out this new club in Hollywood with a couple of my girl friends. It was pretty cool."

"No ending the year with a bang?" I tease, and Lauren looks up in time to catch my smirk.

"Oh, God no. Men were on the prowl last night like it was the end of the world instead of the end of the year."

"The level of desperation was off the charts. New Year's Eve is not the same here as it is in Oregon."

"Left unsatisfied too?" she jokes.

"Something like that." I turn away from her, loading the last few glasses in the dishwasher behind the bar.

"What does that mean?"

"Nothing." I need the image of Lexy out of my head, not to recall it. "You have plans tonight?"

"Just you, if that's what you're asking."

"I was thinking we should remedy the dissatisfaction from last night," I flirt.

"Yes, please. My roommate is hungover and whiny as shit though, so your place?"

"Yeah, I'll meet you there."

Lauren and I have an agreement outside of work too. We're basically fuck buddies. After one of my first shifts working with her, we got drunk together and hooked up. We realized immediately that while the sex was good and we enjoy each other's company enough to hang out, it'll never be more than that for either of us. She's stuck somewhere between looking and not, and I have no desire to be in a relationship again unless the right person magically walks into my life which I doubt will happen while I'm in California. So, when this opportunity fell into our laps, we created a mutually beneficial arrangement.

Part of our deal is that if either of us happens to meet someone with dating potential, even if it's on a night we are together, we get an out, no questions asked. She's used her out three times in the past three months. The hall pass I took for Maci is the only time I've used mine, but I knew it was only a one time pass going into it.

By the time we both pull into my complex, it's almost 3 a.m. By the time we've reached every level of satisfaction we both missed out on last night, it's a little past 4.

"Am I more tired? Or hungry?" Lauren ponders as she comes out of my bathroom, towel wrapped around her from her shower.

I'm starving. "I think I have a frozen pizza." I slide off my bed to head to the kitchen.

"I'll put it in the oven while you shower." With that she takes off, still only in a towel. I won't deny Lauren is hot, and she's fun in bed. If I had any sort of romantic feelings for her, I'd date her, but I don't. I didn't think friends with benefits could actually be a thing that works, but it really does for us. We wouldn't click in a relationship, or anything more than what we currently have. No sense in ruining that.

By the time I get out of the shower, Lauren is on my bed sitting criss-cross in one of my t-shirts. She usually spends the night if she comes over after work since we close so late. It doesn't bother me. She doesn't want to cuddle or kiss me goodnight or anything relationship-y. She just doesn't want to drive home in the middle of the night, especially after I've completely exhausted her. Can't blame her for that.

I pull on my sweats and join her on the bed, leaning against my headboard and reaching for my phone while the pizza bakes. I rarely scroll Instagram, but my curiosity gets the best of me, and I pull up Lexy's page. I started following her after Vegas last year but haven't given her a second thought until last night. I was a little preoccupied finishing what I started with Maci.

There isn't a lot on Lexy's Instagram, just a few pictures with Maci and a few with Mack, separated by pictures of the beach, and a stage I'm assuming is from the bar where she works. Each caption is a song lyric, most of them I know. I scroll back until I get to pictures from October and see an escalator selfie of Lexy and Maci. Don't get me wrong, Maci is pretty. But Lexy, fuck. This must be from the night before Nolan and I got there. Lexy is wearing a silky red dress, her blonde curls falling down her back, giving me a perfect view of her chest and shoulders. The thin straps and low cut in the front leave little to my imagination. I'm still imagining anyway.

"Ooooh, who is that?" I didn't realize Lauren was standing next to my bed, looking over my shoulder until she spoke. I look up, and she's holding two plates of pizza.

"No one." I swipe out of the app and put my phone on the nightstand before taking my plate from her.

"Well 'no one' is really fucking sexy, Troy."

"Yeah." I take a big bite of my pizza, hoping to avoid the rest of this conversation. Shit, that's hot.

"Nope. You're not doing that." She catches onto me. We might not be in a relationship, but after three months of fucking consistently and working together almost every shift, you pick up on a lot about another person.

After I finish chewing, I start to talk, but she cuts me off. "Do not tell me it's nothing. I literally watch you around girls all day. I can read your damn face, so don't act like I'm stupid." She's being sassy. It's not as much fun when it's not in bed.

I cave. "Remember when I went to Vegas?"

"With Nolan? Yeah. Oooh is that hall pass girl?"

"Depends which girl you're talking about."

"I mean, they are both pretty. But that girl in the red dress is who I know you were looking at."

"Yeah, hall pass girl's best friend. Lexy."

"Dang, she even has a sexy name. So, what's the deal?" She moves to sit on my bed, cross-legged in front of me like she's waiting for a damn story.

"I hardly noticed her in Vegas. But I ran into her last night at that Irish bar I like in Newport."

"And?" she asks when I don't add anything else.

"And nothing. She's hot. I gave her a ride home."

"And you wanna have sex with her." She wiggles her eyebrows at me.

"You're hot. I can have sex with you."

She sighs. "Look. As much fun as this is." Her finger draws a circle in the air between us. "We can't do it forever, Troy. I don't want you using this agreement we have as an excuse not to find someone. You're not going to believe anyone is different from Emily if you don't give them a chance." I cringe at the sound of my ex's name, but I know she's right.

"Yeah. I know that," I say with a hint of frustration, "but she's just some girl, Lauren. Seriously. She doesn't want a boyfriend, and she only kissed me because it was New Year's Eve."

"Whoa whoa whoa. Back up. Who kissed who?"

I roll my eyes at her and set my plate of pizza on the nightstand next to my phone. Apparently, we are not eating right now. "I kissed her. For like one second. It was New Year's Eve."

"And she kissed you back?"

"Not the first time."

"Umm, there was more than one time?!"

I stare back at her. "She said I caught her off guard, and she wanted a redo."

"Did you like it?" She's acting like this is a big deal.

"It was a kiss, Lauren. I kiss you all the time."

"Ummm, you don't actually. Which is fine, and I don't care. Just doesn't seem like your thing." She shrugs.

I shrug back and reach for my pizza again. She's not wrong. It's not that I don't enjoy kissing. I just don't tend to initiate it or focus on it. "I think you're reading too much into this," I say before taking a bite.

"I think you're not reading *enough* into it."

"You know, if you want out of our arrangement, you can tell me," I tease.

She takes my plate out of my hand and sets both of ours on my nightstand before she straddles me, her hands on either side of my head pressed into the headboard. "Troy, I like our arrangement. You know if I wanted out, I'd tell you."

My hands fall to her hips, but I don't say anything.

"Tell me you don't wish Lexy was here instead of me." There's no spite or jealousy in her voice, just a demand to know she's right.

I know she won't be offended no matter what answer I give her, so I might as well go with the truth. "Fine. I do wish that, but I have no fucking clue why. I hardly know her."

"It's called chemistry, Troy. That thing you and I don't have."

"Our relationship is fucking weird." I laugh.

She shrugs again as she climbs off me.

CHAPTER TEN
LEXY

Mack approaches my bar now that he's finished setting up for his show. "Hey, how was the rest of your New Year's Eve?" It's been two days since our karaoke adventure.

I roll my eyes at him. "You totally ditched me."

He laughs and reaches into the open bag of gummy bears I've been snacking on while I prep the bar. "You're more than capable of fending for yourself. Plus, you had sex written all over your face. Kind of looked like more than that even." He grins as he pinches the sleeve of his baseball shirt, tugging it up slightly.

I stare back at him. Damn. I thought I had my thoughts totally under wraps. What the hell is wrong with me? Usually my emotions are more in check.

"Chill, Lex. I doubt he noticed. I'm just skilled in reading the many faces of Lexy."

I release a breath.

"Wow, he's got your panties all in a twist. Who is this dude?"

"Gross. Don't say panties, Mack. He's no one, okay. Just a friend. Not even that. Let's drop it. What did you end up doing? Have you talked to Maci again? I meant to text her last night."

The color drains from his face. That can't be good.

"What is it?"

"She's with Dean." Anger flashes in his eyes, but he takes a deep breath and they clear on his exhale.

"Like her ex Dean? How is that possible? She hasn't seen him since... before you two got together?"

"Yeah, until yesterday. She literally ran into him on the beach. What are the fucking chances of that? Do you think she knew he'd be there or went looking for him?"

"No." I answer immediately because I know Maci well enough to know she wouldn't plan something like this. "The girl is just drawn to coincidence. She definitely didn't cross his path on purpose." So weird. This is even more trippy than when we ran into Troy. I pull myself back from thinking about him again when I see the devastation on my best friend's face. "Mack, take a breath. It's okay. She's only going to be in Costa Rica for a few more days, and when she eventually comes home, she's coming home to *you*."

"Yeah, I know." He seemed to lose all his confidence in the weeks after he and Maci broke up. Since he's been going to therapy, it's a little better, but it comes in waves.

The doors to the bar open, and the line of people from outside starts to filter in. "Seriously, Mack. You're such a catch. You're the nicest guy I've ever met. You're smart. You're talented. And you're sexy as hell up on that stage, which is where you need to be right now. So go, get out of here." I wave him off.

"Yeah, yeah. Thanks, Lex. Have a good shift."

This dude is such a tool. For starters his name is Todd. Everyone named Todd is a douchebag. This particular Todd thinks he is hot shit and entitled to priority treatment, and yet he doesn't even have the decency to tip me. Ever. When I realized that's how it was going to be, I stopped giving a fuck. To get my attention, he likes to wad up straw wrappers and fling them at me. It doesn't bother me enough to make security kick him out, and his friends always tip at least. Still, it's obnoxious.

I turn slowly to look at him, making sure my annoyance is evident.

"Hey, sugar, you got something sweet back there, just for me?" He winks, and it makes me want to gag. He thinks he's being flirty, but he also wants a Malibu Sunset. Short of drizzling some simple syrup on top–which he has actually asked me to do before–it doesn't get much sweeter than that. It's gross. Just like him.

I pour orange juice over ice and top it off with a splash of grenadine and a tiny shot of Malibu. I don't even bother adding the cherry before I slide it across the bar top at him.

"That wasn't very sweet, *sweetheart.*"

"Neither is not tipping me." I shrug. As I turn toward the group of girls who are clearly here for a 21st birthday–based on the black and hot pink sashes they are wearing–I catch him reaching across the bartop and grabbing a handful of cherries on his own. God, I hate this guy.

Shaking him from my head, I give my full attention to the girls who have zero clue what they want to drink. They must all be newly 21 and new to drinking. While they debate, I yank the elastic out of my fallen blonde ponytail, gather my hair up and re-secure it. "How about I make you all something special?" I offer since they still haven't decided.

A few heads nod as I line up five glasses in the well. After dumping a scoop of ice into all of them, I turn to reach for the Blue Curacao, catching a glimpse of blond as he walks through the door. My heart thumps in my chest the way it does when I'm stressed, but I've managed to stay calm throughout the chaos of this shift up until now. It's not that it didn't cross my mind when he asked me where I worked, but I didn't actually expect him to show up, especially so soon. I should not have kissed him again. I know better than that. I'm partially convinced that I just need to sleep with him and get this out of my system.

I turn back to the well, scooping ice into the glasses. What the fuck am I doing? I already did that. I tip the first glass to dump some of the cubes out before grabbing the vodka and tequila in one hand and the gin and rum in the other. I tip them all upside down, letting the alcohol pour out of the spouts as I drag it along my row of glasses. Using the soda gun, I add just enough Sprite and sour mix to make the drink tolerable before topping it off with Blue Curacao and moving the drinks to the bar space in front of the girls.

There's a reason I have so many regulars and make the kind of money I do. I might not love LA, and bartending isn't something I want to do forever, but I'm very good at my job, and outside of the assholes, I enjoy it.

By the time I turn to put the Blue Curacao back on the shelf behind me, I can't see Troy anymore. When I twist back to the well, he's standing in front of me. He leans in ever so slightly while pushing up the sleeves of his black sweater before leaning his forearms on the bar, his muscles on full display. His blond hair is perfectly in place, and his smile reaches his gray-blue eyes. Is it hot in here?

"Hi." My arousal fades when I notice the perfect strawberry-blonde next to him. Her little black fit and flare dress makes her boobs look great, and her green eyes contrast both her outfit and her curls perfectly.

"Hi. We'll have two of whatever you made all those girls, please." I nod, turning back to get what I need again. "How's your night?"

"Better now that I picked all of the wadded up straw wrappers out of my cleavage." I laugh in an attempt to appear unbothered by Troy's arrival. Todd may be a douchebag, but he has good aim. I'll give him that.

He immediately knows what I mean. "Last week, a girl tried to get my attention by sticking her hand up the back of my shirt while I was at the table next to hers."

The girl with him chimes in. "At least your bar is enclosed so they can't get to you." She's got a peppy voice, but it's friendly rather than annoying. Ironically I'm annoyed by that. She must work in the industry too.

"Doesn't mean they don't try." I shake my head recalling the time Todd tried to hop over the counter to "help me out" after his drunk ass flung his drink onto the floor behind me.

She smiles sweetly at me as I hold their drinks out for them, and Troy makes eye contact with me. "Keep my tab open?"

"Yeah." I turn to my next guest as they walk away but not quickly enough to miss his hand falling to her lower back as they do.

CHAPTER ELEVEN
TROY

When I showed up to the bar where Lexy works, I was a little hesitant. I've driven by this place before but never stopped because the building looks like trash. The black paint is faded. The marquee sign is rusted, and the clear plastic tiles spelling the name of the band for tonight are chipped at the corners. But inside is a completely different story. The square black bar is sleek and sexy, trapping both the alcohol and a beautiful blonde inside it. The crowd is still a manageable size, the cement floor yet to be covered in bar napkins and straw wrappers. The band sets up to play on the polished wooden stage that takes up the entire length of the room.

I will say, overall the music scene is much better in California than it is in Oregon, where there aren't a ton of options for places that hold a stage bigger than the back corner of a bar. Nolan and I go out a lot, so I'm surprised we haven't tried this place. Lauren hasn't either, but she's easy to convince.

I texted her this morning when I woke up with Lexy already invading my thoughts, conceding to her accusations from the other day that maybe I might be a little interested. She insisted we come here so she could assess the situation herself.

The second I saw her, my mouth went dry. She's fucking hot, with her perfect ass in cutoff jean shorts and a tight black tank top that I want to rip off to reveal the lace bra peeking out. She mentioned her cleavage, and now I can't stop imagining her perky breasts in my hands. Her blonde hair is pulled back into a spunky ponytail that skims across her bare shoulder every time she turns her head. She's wearing a lot more makeup than she was the other night. She doesn't need it, but that's not the kind of naked I'm daydreaming about. Fuck. I drag my hand across my mouth at the thought of her under me.

"Troy."

Lauren pulls me out of my thoughts. "Hmmm?" I hesitantly meet her gaze.

She laughs. "You're a goner."

"Huh?"

"I've never seen you check out a girl like that. That says a lot considering we're together all the time. Thank God I'm not your girlfriend." She laughs again, and I roll my eyes. I'm irritated. Yeah, Lexy is hot, but she's clearly not interested in me. Even if she was, the whole situation feels complicated even though I know Nolan and Maci wouldn't care at all.

Lauren's hand squeezes my forearm playfully. "The thought has never crossed my mind I'd go home unsatisfied after we hang out, Troy, but that girl needs you to fuck her a hell of a lot more than I do." She smirks.

"You don't even know her. We're just friends, if we are even that. And you know I'd never leave you unsatisfied." I wink for good measure.

"While I appreciate the sentiment, I'd be a bad friend if I didn't inform your blind-ass that girl was eye fucking you harder than I ever have."

"Hey!" I tease. I'm not offended at all. I know for a fact Lauren is as physically attracted to me as I am to her.

"And you were looking at her differently than you've ever looked at me." There's no jealousy or spite in her voice, like there wasn't the other night. That's why I love my deal with Lauren. I don't have to worry about feelings. Feelings inevitably lead to problems.

"Why would I fuck someone else who could turn complicated when I could just take you home and keep it simple?" I'm joking, but I'm also in need of a real reason for it to be worth it.

"We already went over this. But fine, let's make a deal." She continues. "I'm going to leave right now. You're going to stay. I'll text you in a few days and see where you stand. If you're still thinking about her, you have to promise me you'll at least try to pursue her."

"She doesn't do relationships. I don't even know if that's what I want. I don't even know her."

"Everyone does them if they find the right person, and the right ones almost always start with good chemistry. You won't know if you don't try." With that she leans in for a hug. I wrap my arms around her neck, kissing the top of her strawberry-blonde hair. I've always been attracted to Lauren, enough that I want to rip her clothes off when she's in my bed, despite our lack of chemistry. But right now, with my arm around her, I've never wanted to rip the clothes off someone else more.

I haven't heard of Mack's band before. I'm pretty sure that's his name. They are good, but it's not like I'm paying much attention because my focus is entirely on the badass working the bar like she's superhuman. The restaurant industry gets a bad rap for being a low class job but only by those who have never truly lived it or mastered the art of serving. Especially when you're working with alcohol, you're constantly surrounded by a lot of the worst kind of humans. Even good people can be unpredictable with a few drinks in them. You have to master multitasking when it's so busy you can hardly think and constantly have someone demanding something from you. You need to be able to remember and read people, keep them all happy, and find the balance between the line of staying professional and working for your tips. It's not something a lot of people do well.

Lexy was *made* for it. I'm decent at my job. I can put on a show, twirling alcohol bottles and lighting shots on fire, but I like to talk too much, and girls usually like to talk back. Lexy, however, doesn't waste her words. She's calm and focused on whoever she's helping as if she doesn't have eighteen other things she needs to be doing, yet somehow still gets it all done. Anyone else would have a line around their bar, but the girl is as efficient as they come. When I got close enough to be able to hear her, I realized she was also complimenting almost every girl and shamelessly flirting with every guy. She knows exactly what she's doing. The compliments seem genuine, though.

I'm torn between being worried she'll catch me staring and wanting her gaze to meet mine, but neither happens during the hour I spend stealing glances her way like a creep. Now that the show is almost over and most people have cashed out their tabs, I snag a bar stool by the well while she closes.

I slide on the black leather seat, but Lexy doesn't notice because right then another wadded up straw wrapper lands right between her perfect breasts. My eyes follow the direction it came from to the douchiest looking dude I've ever seen. That says a lot considering I spent four years of college going to fraternity parties. He's wearing a red muscle shirt–if you can call it a shirt considering the arm holes are cut out so much I can see his nipples. His cargo shorts are tan and his hat rests tilted to the side on top of his hair. Yes, his hair. How it hasn't fallen off is beyond me.

"Hey, baby. So, I was thinking," he says lazily, drunk.

She cuts him off, not even bothering to turn toward him as she swipes someone's credit card. "That's a thing that you do?"

He ignores her statement. "Maybe just tonight you could break your boss's rule about hanging out with customers." Lexy turns toward him, and he reiterates himself. "Hang out." He winks as he says it the second time. This moron believes that's a rule? I can't help but chuckle. Lexy isn't facing me, but for some reason I know she knows I'm here. She smirks at the dude.

"I have to close the bar. I don't have time for your crap."

"You're almost finished. Perfect timing."

"Sorry, I meant I don't have time for you, Todd. Even if I have nothing else to do."

"What could you have to do that's better than this?" He takes a staggered step away from the bar, waving both his hands slowly up and down his body. He looks like a desperate college girl trying to make a fraternity brother realize what they are missing out on by showing off the goods. It rarely worked for them, and it sure as hell isn't working for Todd.

"I would rather pick up the used condoms on the floor with my bare hands than spend time with you." Lexy's attitude is working for me. Fuck, she's sexy when she's sassy.

She forcefully puts a receipt on the bar in front of Todd, and he finally takes the hint. He signs it, without adding a tip, and shoves it forward into a wet spot, soaking the paper. What a dick. Overly aggressive thoughts invade my mind. The possessiveness I feel for this girl is absurd.

I shake the thoughts from my head as Lexy cashes out her last few customers and reaches into a soapy bucket for a rag. Seems like she's almost finished for the night, and the show only ended a few minutes ago. It was busy, and she was the only one working. I'm impressed.

By the time she makes her way to the bar in front of me, only a few stragglers are left. She tosses her rag back into its bucket before grabbing her cash bag and opening the register to pull out the drawer. She sets them in the space between us.

"What's up?" she questions me.

"I forgot to cash out earlier." The way she's already counting her till makes me think she didn't even start my tab. Watching her multitask like a rockstar all night, it doesn't seem like something that would slip her mind, but the look she's giving me contradicts that thought.

She takes the two steps to the computer behind her and punches in a drink before printing a receipt and holding it out for me.

She only charged me for one drink. I pull out my card, our fingers grazing as she takes it. Shit, that contact was enough to make me want to grab her hand and pull her to me. I can't remember the last time I've been this attracted to someone, if ever. I'm not going to be able to drop this until I have her. Hopefully I can convince her.

While she runs my card, I reach for the pen on the counter and scribble a note on the itemized receipt she gave me. She sets my card on the counter, and I sign the receipt, making sure to slip her a twenty when I hand it back.

I watch her as she turns back to her register to close out my check. From where I'm sitting, I can see her perfectly from the side. She notes the tip free slip and slides it to the back of the stack, smirking at the $20 under it. When she looks at the last receipt, noticing it's the original itemized copy, she moves to crumple it, but pauses mid scrunch when she sees the writing. She stares at it for a second, confusion flashing over her features for only a moment. Then she folds it in half and sticks it in the back pocket of her shorts before turning back to me.

"Where's your date?" she asks, nothing telling in her tone.

"Lauren. She's a friend." I eye her for a reaction, but she gives none.

"Mmm. Well her boobs looked great in that dress. She's gorgeous." She's not saying it with malice. I think this girl just shares whatever thoughts pop into her head. I like it.

"So are you."

Her eyes flick from the money she's counting to my gaze. "Thanks." I earn half a smile for that. She's going to be hard to crack. It's like she shares all her thoughts freely, but I have no idea what the fuck she's actually thinking.

"Looks like you do well here."

"Not bad." She has at least a couple hundred in cash in front of her.

"It'd be even better if assholes like Todd actually tipped."

She rolls her eyes. "Yeah, he's a dick who can't take a hint that I'm not interested, or that no one is for that matter."

"You handled it better than I would have. I wanted to punch him."

"Why didn't you?" She stops counting again and looks up.

I hold her gaze. "You don't seem like the type to want someone swooping in to save you."

She doesn't say anything, but I swear I see a glimmer of appreciation in her bright blue eyes. Is she just a challenge to me, or do I genuinely want to figure out what makes this girl tick?

The ball is in her court now if she figures out what my note means.

"Well, I'll let you finish up here. I'll see you later, Lexy."

"Bye, Troy."

As I push through the exit, I look back to see her staring down at my note again.

CHAPTER TWELVE
LEXY

This is totally not a big deal. I was going to bars by myself for a couple of years before Maci was here, and I've been doing it since she left two months ago too. 3rd Base LA has been one of my go-to places for a while. They have the best happy hour and the local beer I like on tap. It's surprising I haven't run into Troy more since Vegas. Maybe we have the same work schedule.

I find an empty stool at the sleek white bar, not knowing whether Troy is bartending or serving tonight. Maybe he's not even working. I'm only assuming he is since he's already had two nights off this week–New Year's Eve and when he came into my work two nights ago. I adjust myself on the hard black plastic chair, setting my red heart sunglasses on the bar.

"What the fuck happened to your phone case?" He startles me, pulling my phone from my hands to examine it.

"Yeaaaah, it's seen better days." I cringe. The screen protector is cracked, and the case has a chunk missing from the side from when it flung out of the back pocket of my shorts when I was getting ice one day, and then it got caught on the drain grate. Not my best bartending moment.

"It's on its last leg for sure." He laughs.

I shrug. "I'll get a new one eventually."

"Sooooo. What can I get you?" He holds up his hand. "No, wait, let me guess."

I stare at him. He looks sexy as hell in his dark blue jeans and untucked black button up shirt, like the first time I saw him.

"You strike me as a beer girl."

"You think you know me already, don't you?" I deadpan. He smiles. It reaches all the way to his gray-blue eyes. Do not get lost in them.

"Nah. I'm just good at my job too." He shoots me a wink. "What do you like?"

"Mango Cart, please." It's one of the reasons I come to this specific bar. It's one of the few that have it on tap.

He returns with my beer, slinging a coaster to the space in front of me before setting it down. "Wouldn't have guessed this. Seems a little too mellow for you."

I hide my smile in my sip. I'm satisfied with his perception of me. It's much better than him sensing I want him to rip my clothes off on top of this bar. With anyone else I'm attracted to, I'd make it clear if that's what I wanted. But the way Troy has worked his way into my thoughts–more than just how attractive he is–makes that a big no-go for me. I won't deny I want the sex, but not until I can get rid of any potential feelings that would complicate it.

"It's my favorite. My first legal job was waitressing at Pub at Golden Road when I was 18. I worked there until I turned 21 and switched to Shot in the Dark because living on your own in LA kind of costs a lot." Not that I know any different, but it *has* to be cheaper to live somewhere else. If I wasn't so good at bartending, I don't know how I'd afford it.

"Yeah, it's amazing you do it on your own. I'm lucky my cousin owns our condo, and I just pay utilities. How old are you?"

"Older than you." I'm guessing anyway. He graduated with Maci so I'm assuming he's 22 as well, so two years younger than me.

His eyes shift toward the couple that just sat a few seats down from me. I nod in their direction.

"When I come back, be prepared to tell me why you clarified it was your first legal job." He looks at me curiously before grabbing two coasters off the bar and tossing them in front of the new guests.

It's another half hour before he comes back. The way he works is mesmerizing. Anyone would be lying if they said they weren't impressed. I pride myself on being able to multitask better than any bartender I know, but I'm not fancy like this. At one point there was a bottle twirling through the air. He caught it perfectly before pouring dark rum floats onto a couple of Mai Tai's. I'm impressed. Or turned on. I don't know.

Now he has two half full beer glasses next to a couple of shot glasses. He fills them with Amaretto and tops them off with 151 proof rum. He sends a sly wink my way before lighting the shots on fire and dropping them into the beer before pushing them toward the two girls in front of him.

A few minutes later, he's back in front of me.

"So, tell me about all these illegal jobs you had."

"I meant under the table. When I was a teenager I did makeup for C-list celebrities for parties and events."

"Impressive. And your parents let you do that?"

I can't help my humorless laugh. "Never met my dad. Wish I'd never met my mom. She couldn't have cared less about what I did." It's not a secret my mom is a total deadbeat. I'm not ashamed of it. It's not my fault. It's just that not many people know because no one ever asks. That and I don't like most people enough to share anything personal about myself with them.

There's always instant pity in the eyes of anyone I confide in, and it drives me nuts. I don't need anyone's pity. I manage fine despite my mother's absentee parenting. One of the reasons Mack is my best friend is because he understands. We are in the crappy parent club together.

When my eyes meet Troy's, I instantly know by the lack of pity staring back at me that he's part of the club too. He doesn't even apologize, which is noteworthy because that's everyone's go-to.

I take a slow sip of the new beer he brought me, hoping he doesn't press further. He doesn't need to hear about my commitment issues yet.

He takes the hint. It's like he can sense the type of response I want. "One time, my mom spent her entire welfare check in a day. Half of it she used to get her hair and nails done. The other half she blew on pot. She made like four pans of weed brownies, and since she spent all her money, it was the only food in the house. She was so high–not just on weed–when I asked for dinner, she gave me one." He chuckles recalling the memory. "I was so excited I got dessert for dinner."

"Oh my god." I stare back at him in surprise. "How old were you? What happened?"

"I was ten. I ate the whole thing and snuck another. They were so strong. Luckily the neighbor came over for some reason. He found me sick on the couch and took me to the hospital. They called my uncle who lives here. He flew to Oregon that night."

"What happened to your mom?"

"Nothing." He shrugs. "She didn't even show up to the hospital. My uncle didn't let me go home, and she never came looking for me as far as I know. I've only seen her a few times since. My uncle stayed for a few weeks and arranged for me to stay with my buddy Cooper and his family."

"He didn't want you to move here?"

"Nah. I mean he would have let me, but he figured I'd been through enough and didn't want to tear me away from my school and friends. He has a cabin a couple hours from Eugene and comes to visit every summer, though."

"Wow. I'm..." I almost say I'm sorry but catch myself on how little that helps. "Glad you got out of there."

"Yeah, I'm lucky. Somehow I only ended up a little fucked up. And with a motorcycle. It's a win if you ask me." He reaches over for the empty beer glasses from the guests who left and sticks them upside down in the mini dishwasher at the end of the bar.

"How are those two things connected?" My face scrunches in confusion.

"They aren't really. My uncle helped me buy it. I just wanted to watch you light up again when I talked about my bike."

I roll my eyes. "When I go to Oregon someday, you owe me a ride for that comment."

"Okay." He doesn't hesitate. Maybe he doesn't think I'd ever go to Oregon. With Mack and Maci likely ending up back there one day, I'm sure I will, at least to visit.

"I'm holding you to that."

"I'm counting on it." He stares back like he's daring me.

Okay, I'm not an idiot. Flirting is all but an official job description as a bartender, but I'd be willing to bet at least the $20 I'm going to tip him that he's picturing fucking me on his motorcycle too. "As much as I'd like to ride your bike, I have to be up early for class with a real bike tomorrow."

"Huh?"

"Soul Cycle."

"Ahhh, that's why your legs look so good in those shorts," he says, as if it's more of a realization to himself than a response to me. He slides me the check he's already printed with only one of my three beers on it. He runs my card as soon as I hand it to him and walks away begrudgingly when a man sits down a couple chairs from me. I sign the slip, pulling a $20 from my red wristlet and sliding my card back in its place. It could very well be the same bill Troy gave me a couple days ago. Even if I had charged him for both of his drinks, it still would have been an excessive tip. God, good tippers are sexy as hell. It's probably because he's in the service industry, but still.

I didn't understand the note he left on his receipt the other night even though it should have been obvious. *Wondering "what if" is the worst thing there is.* It wasn't until I was pulling into my complex that night when my favorite Straylight Run song came on–this bridge in the opening verse–that it made sense. It's the song that was playing when Troy dropped me off too.

I wouldn't read into it, but how else am I supposed to take that? I can't do anything with feelings attached though, so unless that's crystal clear, I won't be making any moves. I glance up to see Troy pouring a beer out of the tap and pick up the pen again to write the changed lyrics from the second bridge.

"Giving in" is the worst thing there is.

CHAPTER THIRTEEN
TROY

Reading the note Lexy left on her receipt was a gut punch. On first instinct, it was a total rejection. But then I did that thing girls do, where they read way too much into everything, and decided maybe it wasn't a *total* dismissal. She took the time to not only write a note but knew what mine meant and played my game back. That and leaving her sunglasses when she came to my work was enough to convince me I still have a shot. Since I don't have her phone number, I only have one option.

So, I find myself standing in front of her apartment door–at least the one I'm pretty confident is hers. It was dark when I dropped her off last week. It's almost 10 a.m., and I spotted Maci's car in the parking lot, so I'm guessing she's back from cycle class. I'm praying she lets me in before she's changed out of her leggings–and that she opens the door for me in the first place.

I knock.

A few seconds go by, and I hear the chain lock being unlatched from the inside. There's a pause before she slowly opens the door, like she's debating.

"Troy, hi," she says when the door stops half way open. I scan the length of her, unable to help myself.

Fuck me.

Figuratively and literally.

She is still wearing her leggings–tight, black and cut low enough to show off her toned stomach–with a red sports bra that does some criss-cross thing over her chest. God damn, this girl is hot. "What are you doing here?" Her voice pulls me out of the fantasy that was forming in my mind.

"I came to make a deal with you." I smile and step forward, leaning against her door frame, my ankles crossed and my hand in my pocket.

She fights a smile and opens the door a little wider. "Oh yeah? What kind of deal?"

"I'll give you these..." I pull her sunglasses from my pocket. "If you get ice cream with me. Right now."

"It's breakfast time."

"Are you a rule follower?" I ask daringly, highly doubting she is.

She pauses in thought for a moment. "I just got back from the gym. Can I shower first? Twenty minutes?"

"Take as long as you want." Cooper's mom, who I claim as my own, taught me young that the most intelligent thing you can do is give a girl as long as she needs to get ready. I trust her advice and don't argue.

Lexy opens her door, stepping back to allow me to enter. Her apartment is nice. There's a closet door right in the entryway which continues on to a small kitchen on the right and a living room on the left. She nods toward the coffee table, completely clear besides a remote. Her whole place is surprisingly uncluttered. There's nothing on the walls, not a single shred of anything remotely sentimental. I can already tell she is unlike any girl I've met.

"You can put something on the TV if you want. I'll be out soon." With that, she disappears through a door on the other side of the living room, and I take a seat on her couch. A few moments later I hear the shower turn on. I pull my phone out of my pocket to keep my mind from wandering into the steaming water with her.

Me: *Have you rented out my room yet?*

Cooper: *Not yet. You had to be a dick and leave right before the quarter started when everyone had housing already.*

Me: *Must be hard having the whole place to yourself while half the mortgage is still being paid.*

While I'd been waffling on the idea of moving to California for over a year, it wasn't until my cousin got some fancy job where he's gone most of the time on business that I actually committed. He's letting me stay at his place for free as long as I water his plants and bring in the mail. I've still paid for the house I split with Cooper in Oregon the past few months to give him time to find someone even though he recently bought the house we rented in college.

Cooper: *Maybe if Sophie would pull her head out of her ass.*

Me: *Still doesn't believe you two are end game?*

Cooper: *Your guess is as good as mine. What's up?*

Me: *I was thinking I'd come home for a few days next month. I need some smog free air and my bike.*

Cooper: *Your room is all yours. Let me know.*

I check flights for the next twenty minutes. I haven't requested a day off work since Nolan and I went to Vegas in October, and I'm due for a break. I swipe out of Google Flights when I hear the doorknob turn.

Her gray cut off jean shorts sit right at her hips, and a loose black sweater hangs off her left shoulder. A sliver of her stomach shows when she reaches her hand out, demanding her sunglasses, and it takes everything in me not to let my eyes linger.

I pick them up off the coffee table and hand them over. She slides the red frames casually into her blonde hair, full of loose curls. She's wearing a little more makeup than she needs. I can say that with certainty now–based on that post workout glimpse I got of her earlier–but either way she looks cute as fuck.

"Alright, let's do this."

I'd rather stay here and do her.

LEXY

"Thanks for bringing these." I glance over at Troy as he starts his car, and I slide my sunglasses onto my face.

"Thank me by playing DJ?" He grins and hands over his phone. "Seems we have the same taste."

I wasn't a hundred percent sure he was into the music I queued up when he drove me home. All the songs came from an untitled playlist he had, but it very well could have been created by someone else. He didn't stop me, so I picked my favorite tracks and went with it.

"Don't think I didn't see that playlist full of that new crap they call music these days." I don't even know how people listen to it.

He chuckles. "Don't hold it against me. Someone in my fraternity made it."

"I'll let it slide this time." I click shuffle on Good Charlotte's *Young and the Hopeless* album and set his phone in the center console.

"An oldie, but a goodie." He licks his bottom lip and bites down on it like he's trying to stop a grin. His fingers drum on the steering wheel as "Riot Girl" blasts out of the speakers. I wonder if he knows he does that.

"It's my favorite."

He reaches over and turns the volume down a bit. "Oh yeah? You must have only been like seven years old when this came out."

I decide to throw him a bone so he can figure out how old I actually am. "Eight. It was my first CD."

"You've listened to pop punk since you were eight?"

I shrug. "Yeah. It was an accident. One of my mom's boyfriends was trying to make a 'good impression' on me." I do air quotes for the full effect even though his eyes are on the road. "He brought it in from his car and gave it to me."

"I'd say he sounds like a loser, but you kind of won in that situation."

"Exactly. Guess I got hooked, and there was no going back. What about you?"

"Similar, but less tragic story. I was only six when this album was released, but by the time I was like 12, my cousin was ready to hand over his entire CD collection."

"Well, your cousin has good taste. He lives here right?"

"Yeah, I live with him. Sort of. He's never there. I basically live alone."

"Must be a huge change from living in a frat house."

"Eh. I only lived there for a year, then my buddy Cooper and I got our own house. I can party, but no one needs to party that much."

"You came to the wrong city for that mindset." I laugh.

"I think I'm in the right one." He glances over, and his eyes meet mine for only a second before they are back on the road. I'll give it to him, the guy is smooth. He's also extremely attractive in his dark blue jeans and light blue button up rolled to his elbows. Damn those forearms. Maci told me he played football in high school. I'd do something shady in trade for seeing him in his old uniform. Ugh. The effect he's having on me is terrifying.

He pulls into one of the parking spaces outside a strip mall. I look up and see the worn white sign. It says *Mashti Malone's* in green capital letters on top and *Ice Cream* in red below it. There's a four leaf clover on the side. "Irish ice cream? Is that a thing?" I say it more to myself, but Troy answers me as he pulls the key out of the ignition.

"No." He laughs. "I mean, maybe. This place is actually Persian, but when the owner took over this space to open his shop he could only afford to change half the sign. It's been around since the 80s."

"Look at the outsider teaching me new things about my city."

"I could teach you a lot of new things." His response is quick and laced with everything but innocence. He's playing my game, and being on the other end of it is torture. I ignore him and the desire between my thighs begging to know what exactly he means.

A glass display case filled with twenty colorful tins of ice cream is to the left when we enter, and I can already tell they aren't typical flavors. Fine by me. I tried a lot of weird foods at celebrity events when I did makeup. "Are you picky?" Troy questions.

I chuckle at our parallel thoughts. "Only with men."

He doesn't seem phased by my comment. "How do you feel about me ordering and us sharing?"

"I don't want your cooties, Troy," I tease.

"Wouldn't be the first time you had them." The direction he's headed is clear, but what his aim is, I have yet to figure out. "And it won't be the last." The words sound playful, but his voice is steady and serious.

Our eyes lock, and the moment we share makes my stomach flip. I think it's sexual tension, but whatever it is makes me uneasy.

"You can choose the flavors." I leave him at the counter to escape the tensity and find a seat at one of the two round metal tables outside.

A few minutes later, Troy joins me. He sets a single clear plastic to-go container between us. There's a big, sticky cookie on the bottom. According to the sign inside, they make fresh middle eastern pastries with honey and rosewater. I'm guessing that's what this is.

"I got saffron rosewater with pistachio and persian cucumber. Whatever the hell that is. I like to live on the wild side." He holds out a spoon to me.

I dip my spoon into the bright yellow ice cream, and as I'm bringing my bite to my mouth, Troy's phone vibrates on the table between us. It's face up, and I can't help but look at it. The table is small enough, and we are sitting close enough that it doesn't take much straining for me to make out the notification on the front of his screen.

Lauren: *What's the verdict? Are you coming over tonight? Or never again?*

There's a winky face emoji at the end.

I'm pretty sure it's the girl from the other night who he claimed was *just a friend*. That text doesn't exactly scream friendship.

I finish my bite, the cold cream exploding my taste buds with floral flavor. Damn, this is good. I go back for a second bite. I don't care about whoever is texting him. If anything, I only want sex from Troy–to fuck any non-platonic thoughts out of my head. I've only slept with one person since Nolan. I'm due for some human contact. He's just an itch I need to scratch.

When he speaks, it startles me. "Lauren is my friend you met the other night."

I take a second to respond, diving in for a bite of the persian cucumber, the sweet and crisp flavor drastically contrasting the first one. "She seems cool." I mean it.

"She is. She said the same about you."

I lean back in my chair and study his face, trying to decipher those words. It's unlike me to attempt to read more into anything a man says.

"I am pretty cool." I shrug and rip off a piece of the sticky cookie. I shake my head and lick my fingers. Troy's gaze follows my actions. Damn. I thought I was good at reading people, but there's no way he's thinking the thoughts it looks like he's thinking.

"Lauren and I are just friends," he reminds me. "Well, that's not really true. At the risk of my honesty backfiring here, she and I have an arrangement."

I'm intrigued, but I don't tell him as much. I take another bite of persian pastry and feign indifference.

"I could try to make it sound better than it is, but long story short we're fuck buddies."

Huh. I wasn't expecting him to say that. "The directness is refreshing, although I'm not sure why you felt the need to tell me."

"Part of our deal is that we can call each other whenever, but if we meet anyone else we are interested in, we get an out with no complications."

"You're trying to tell me you found a girl you can screw whenever you want, who will also give you any freedom you want, and you won't get attached to her?"

"That's the part you picked up on?" His brows push together in confusion. "But yes, that's the general idea." I can tell he's trying to read me.

"Damn. That's a way better deal than the deal I have with my vibrator." A smirk finds its way to my lips, but I hide it with a spoonful of ice cream. He wasn't expecting that response, and his eyebrows shooting up in surprise is more satisfying than I would have thought.

"I would assume orgasms from actual people would be better," he counters, equally as unphased by this conversation we are having in public.

"I wouldn't really know." I shrug.

This catches him more off guard than the vibrator comment, his spoonful of ice cream freezing mid-air as he stares in shock and confusion. It would be amusing if it wasn't a semi-accepted annoyance of mine. "Wait, what do you mean? You're telling me the guys you've been with don't get you off?"

"Sometimes. Rarely. It's fine. I'm better at it myself." It's true. I still think sex is fun, and it's much less frustrating now that I've taught myself some tricks.

He doesn't respond. He's staring back at me like I told him I believe in aliens. I kind of assumed most girls don't orgasm often, and it's not like I have many girl friends to compare notes with. It doesn't seem like he has anything to add, so I change the subject. "Sooooooo, you really think Lauren won't fall for you?" I highly doubt that. Most girls can't detach that way.

"Kind of sounds like you think I'm a catch."

"Don't flatter yourself. Most girls just get attached too easily."

He hesitates as he contemplates his next words, finally eating his first bite of ice cream. "Well, I'm positive she won't. I wouldn't have made a deal with her like that if I wasn't confident. I know this might sound fucked up–"

I cut him off. "It doesn't. I think it's rare that people are on the same page, or willing to talk about sex in the way they should. I actually think it says a lot about the kind of person you are that you want to be upfront about things with her."

He looks shocked by my opinion. "It's important to me." It feels like there's more to that comment, but I don't ask, and he continues. "But this really isn't about her."

I stare back at him, not knowing where he's going with this.

"I'm interested in you."

"What kind of interested?" I ask slowly as if it'll give me time to process.

"Can I ask you something?"

I nod, breaking his eye contact to get another bite of ice cream.

"Is it a deal breaker for you? That Maci and I hooked up?"

"A deal breaker for what exactly?" I assume he means sex.

He waits until I finish my bite and meet his gaze again. "Sex," he confirms.

"I don't mix sex and emotions, Troy. I couldn't care less who you've been with. It's just sex."

He eyes me like he's trying to see through the wall I like to hide behind, but then his face softens. "I didn't hear 'I have no desire to have sex with you' anywhere in there." He smirks, and his confidence is so sexy, I'd let him rip my clothes off right here.

I lean forward on my elbow, my opposite hand reaching out for another spoonful of ice cream. In the most nonchalant tone I can muster, I admit, "I'm down."

He stops the pastry right before he bites into it, his eyes widening in surprise for a moment before he recovers. "I'm really fucking attracted to you, Lexy."

Damn, if the way he says my name doesn't make me want to hear it a hundred more times. Preferably, in his sex voice. But that's all this can be, and I need to be clear about this. "This is only sex, just clarifying."

He studies me, but doesn't respond.

"Troy."

"We'll see."

"What does that mean?"

"It means I don't know, and I don't want to commit either way yet."

"I don't do boyfriends. I don't do feelings."
"Noted."
"If we do this, it's just for fun."
"Can we start right now?"

CHAPTER FOURTEEN
TROY

Not that I was trying to play some game or work her over, but I can't believe that worked. I didn't expect her to respond to my directness so receptively. There's the slight issue of her being convinced this will be just sex, but my gut tells me it could be so much more. I wasn't super confident at first, but the second she said she was in, without a fight, I had the urge to text Lauren and put an end to our deal. That told me what I needed to know right there. I don't want a comfort fallback. Lexy is the first girl I've been interested in getting to know since Emily. I can't not pursue her, and I refuse to half-ass anything.

I open the car door for Lexy, and she looks at me like my chivalry annoys her. I chuckle as she slides in the passenger seat. Shutting the door, I feel my phone vibrate in my pocket and glance at it before sliding into my seat. I have another text from Lauren.

Lauren: *Don't fuck this up.*

I roll my eyes and shove my phone in my pocket, annoyed at her accurate assumption based on my lack of response. Lauren knows I have more than enough confidence in the bedroom, but I am worried I only have one shot at this. I'm fully aware my arrangement with Lauren isn't typical, but it has been working for me. She thinks she's going to meet her true love every other week, but I've never wanted to end our hookup arrangement until now. Catching feelings wasn't even on my radar, but there's something about Lexy that makes me want more, and we haven't even had sex yet. That's the crazy part. What the fuck am I going to do when she rocks my world and wants it to be a one and done?

"Do you work tonight?"

"Yeah, at 8. What about you?" She looks at me like she knows why I'm asking.

"My shift starts at 6." I glance at the clock on my dashboard. It's only a little after noon. I don't bother asking her and get off the exit for my place, which is two before hers.

I glance over and catch the mischievous glint in her eyes. If I was trying to hide my impatience for having her, I wouldn't be doing a good job. Luckily, she says she likes direct and honest, and that's exactly what she's going to get. I hope she means it.

I pull into the parking garage of my complex. Before I unbuckle my seat belt, I turn to Lexy. I know I want this. She doesn't seem like the type to agree to something without being sure, but I still want to double check. She's already getting out of the car and looks back when she notices I haven't made a move. "You coming?" She's sassy as fuck. I love it.

"Yes. Like you will be soon."

Thank God I was blessed with quick wit because the way I watch her eyes light up with fire at my words... fuck. If I wasn't turned on by her enough already, I sure as hell am now. She steps out of the car, and by the time I get my door shut and hit the lock on my key fob, Lexy is waiting by the elevator a couple of spaces down. She pushes the button as soon as I reach her. Turning back to me, she takes a step closer, her hands smoothly sliding under my shirt, running up my abs. She locks her eyes with mine, her hands making their way to my back, where she digs her fingers in slightly. "Just getting a feel for what's in store for me." She answers a question I didn't ask with so much confidence, and I finally get a glimpse of her excitement. For the first time, I feel like there's a chance she might be as into this as I am.

The doors open a second later, and she pulls away from me so we can step inside. There's no way she doesn't feel whatever the hell is between us. If air could literally get thicker with tension, that's what would be happening in this elevator as the doors close. It's taking all my self-control to not push the emergency stop and fuck her right here, but if there's even a chance that this might only happen once, I'm doing it right. I'm going to take my time.

I glance at her, and right as I do, I watch her eyes shift toward the red button. Fuck. I don't even think about it. I push on it. In the next second my mouth is on hers like that's the emergency.

Her arms are around my neck, her fingers running through my hair at the same moment as I lift her, pressing her body against the wall of the elevator, her ass resting slightly on the handrail. My hands run up her thighs, sliding against her soft skin, under her cutoff jeans shorts. She pulls me closer, her tongue tangling with mine. I grind against her, already getting hard. I.Can't.Stop. I want all of her. Right fucking now. I press into her harder, shifting my hips until a moan escapes her, and I swallow it in a kiss. We're aligned perfectly as I rock into her. Her legs wrap around my waist, linking behind me, begging for more. I wish there weren't clothes separating us, but I can't pull myself away to change that. I feel her shake around me, and all of a sudden she breaks our kiss, her mouth falling to my shoulder, where I feel her teeth bite into me. Fuck me. Didn't she tell me it's nearly impossible for guys to make her come? I've hardly even touched her. The way she's falling apart is a huge stroke to my ego.

She squeezes her legs tighter around me as she climaxes, right before she unlinks them and they start to fall, like she doesn't have the strength to keep her legs wrapped around my body any longer. I adjust my hands, guiding her feet to the floor as I press into her more, my dick begging for the same release. I move one hand up her body to bury it in her hair and pull her head back enough to kiss her again. My lips move to her ear. "Tell me what you want," I demand.

"Do that again," she mumbles breathlessly.

I step away from her just enough to release the emergency stop then slip my finger into the top of her shorts and tug her back to me. "As many times as you want."

She gives me a new smile I haven't seen yet, and I can't help but grin back at her. I reach up, running my fingers through her hair on either side of her head in an attempt to fix her curls. Not that it'll stay that way for long.

The doors open onto the fifth floor. I link her fingers with mine, and I walk backward toward my condo two doors down. She follows me in silence, her eyes never leaving mine. I reach over, sliding my key into the lock and turning the knob all without taking my gaze off her. I don't want to miss a second of her looking at me like she wants to rip my clothes off.

As soon as I push the door open, she shoves me through it and closes it behind us. I bite into my lip to keep from smiling too hard at her eagerness.

"What?" She catches it anyway.

I debate teasing her, but decide against it. I shake my head. "Nothing." Her loose black sweater is hanging off her shoulder enough that I can see the lace of her bralette underneath. "Just can't wait to see what I can do with your clothes off."

She grips the bottom of her sweater, pulling it over her head in one swift movement before tossing it on the ground beside her. I reach my arms for her waist, and she reads my mind. I catch her when she jumps, linking her legs around me. Her hands are in my hair, and I groan into her kiss. We haven't done anything yet, we haven't made it through the entryway, and I can already tell one time is not going to be enough with her. I can't even decide what I want to do to her first.

I walk her straight through my living room, kicking my bedroom door open with my foot when we get to it. She breaks our kiss to glance behind her, loosening her grip on me just enough. I grab hold of her hips and toss her backward on my black comforter. She smiles playfully at me when she hits the bed, and it's enough to make me want to fuck her right this second. But the way she came undone in the elevator, after assuring me that wasn't common for her, all I want is to watch it happen again at my hands. And my mouth. If she thought what happened in the elevator felt good, she's going to love what my tongue can do.

As soon as I straddle her, she sits up just enough to link her hands around my neck, pulling me to her. I keep myself far enough away from her, with one hand pressed into the bed, that I can run the other one up her stomach. She lets her hands fall to my chest, making quick work on the buttons of my shirt while keeping her lips locked with mine. When she gets to the last one, I lean back, pulling my shirt off and tossing it on the floor. She whines at the loss of contact, but I take the moment to stare at her instead of giving her what she wants. "Fuck, you're sexy." Her blonde curls are spread across my pillow, her black bralette cuts low in the front, hardly covering her nipples and her jean shorts... they need to come off immediately. She relaxes into the bed and smiles up at me, letting me appreciate her.

I watch her gaze rake over my abs slowly, but they shift to my fingers when she realizes I'm undoing the button of her shorts. Once I tug the zipper down, she lifts her hips enough to help me pull them off, revealing a black lace thong that perfectly matches her bra. Is that a thing girls do even when they don't expect anyone to see them? Because there's no way she was expecting us to hook up.

She reaches for the button on my jeans, and it refocuses my attention. I push her hands away, by grabbing both and moving them until they are pinned above her head. I catch the heat in her eyes as I kiss her, only once, before whispering against her lips, "You told me to do that again, I get to choose how." Her breath catches at my words, chills instantly cover her body, and I attempt to stifle my grin at my affect on her. I release her hands so I can trail my fingers and mouth down her body. My lips meet the edge of the lace, my fingers hooking on it and tugging them off. When I kiss her inner thigh again, she squirms a little, and I glance up. Her eyes are wide, and she's nervously biting into her lip. She has no reason to be nervous around me. There isn't anything I want more than the girl under me. I reassure her with more light kisses against her silky skin, working my way slowly toward her center. When I sense her tension has melted away, I look up. This time I'm met with bedroom eyes, letting me know she's ready.

I shift to the end of my bed before wrapping my arms around the backside of her legs and pushing them apart with my shoulders, burying my face between her thighs. I planned on teasing her, but I can't help myself. I press my tongue flat against her center and glance up to gauge her reaction. If there was any more heat in her eyes, they'd be on fire. She's biting into her lip as if she's trying to keep herself quiet. "Don't stay quiet on my account," I say with my eyes locked on hers before I nip at her inner thigh. She relaxes into the bed on a heavy breath like she's surrendered all control to me, and I want every bit of it.

On a mission to discover everything she likes, I start with small strokes, barely dipping inside her. Fuck, she's already so wet for me. I unhook one arm from around her leg, so I can slide a finger inside her. I withdraw it slowly before sliding it back in at the same pace, matching the swipes of my tongue. Her fingers run through my hair, and she tugs at the strands. I gently suck when I find an overly sensitive spot, noted by a moan finally escaping her. God, that sound does something primal to me.

"That's it, baby. Come for me," I breathe against her wet skin before touching my tongue to her again. I can tell she's close. Her hips press up in an attempt to get closer to me, and I give her exactly what she wants, my tongue diving back inside her as I pull my fingers out, digging them into her thigh, pushing her legs wider instead. She shakes as her orgasm rips through her. Her grip on my hair tightens, as if to keep me there, but the rest of her tries to squirm away from me, sensitive to my touch. I hold her still, flicking my tongue against her faster a few times before taking a slow drag that dips inside. I don't pull away until I feel her body relax back into the mattress.

She murmurs something to herself that I can't quite understand as my kisses make their way up her body. When I reach her lips, I kiss her softly, but it's not enough. I bury my fingers in her hair, crashing my lips into hers again. The way I want this woman when I haven't even had her yet is an unfamiliar feeling. I pull back to gauge how she's feeling, brushing my thumb across her cheek.

"You tapped out yet?"

She's still, like she doesn't want to move away from where my thumb touches her skin, but after a moment she shakes her head, a grin taking over her face. "Not even close."

With that, she slides out from under me before I re-alize what she's doing and shoves on my shoulder until I'm on my back and under her. This girl doesn't waste any time. She twists the button of my jeans and yanks both them and my briefs down in one pull, my dick springing to attention. Her eyes immediately take me in with a glimmer of appreciation before they turn stormy, as if she's fighting between looking and touching. I kick my pants off the rest of the way as she decides.

She glances up at me, a question in her eyes, and I somehow know what she's asking. I nod toward the drawer of my nightstand, and she crawls across my bed to it, reaching in and pulling out a condom. She's back over to me, between my legs. Her face. Her mouth. Holy fuck. With no warning she wraps her lips around me, taking me in slowly. She pulls back just as slowly, her tongue dancing along my dick. Good lord, she could make me come right now. Thankfully, she has other plans. I hear the tear of the condom wrapper, and she pulls back, a wicked smile on her face, holding her gaze to mine as she rolls the condom on me. Fuck, that was hot. My teeth sink into my lip, and I reach for her hips and pull her toward me.

She hovers above me, using her hand to position me where she wants. She slides down until I fill her. It takes a lot more effort than I'd admit to keep my eyes from rolling back and coming way before I'm ready.

Pausing, she leans back enough to pull the lace–that's barely holding in her breasts–over her head. Fuck. I reach for her, and she falls forward, my hands meeting her in the middle, her breasts landing perfectly in my palms.

I play with her, nipples pinched between my fingers, as she rides me, rocking me in and out of her slowly. So slowly. Too slowly. I need more, now. My hands abandon their places, gripping her hips and pulling her closer to me, keeping us more connected. She tries to pull back, but I overpower her. "You're torturing me," I growl, and she smiles into a kiss, like she knows exactly what she's doing.

She's still straddling me just enough. My hand slides from her hip, around the back of her leg, until I'm close enough to finger her if my dick wasn't inside her. I rub my fingers against her clit and her head falls next to mine on my pillow, a moan escaping her. I drive into her from the bottom, hard, and fast, a much less torturous pace than before. Her moans in my ear tell me she doesn't mind. She was just being a tease.

I nudge my head against hers, hoping she'll get the hint I want to kiss her. Fuck, do I want to kiss her. I've never cared either way about kissing during sex, but I want to be as connected to her as possible. She follows my unspoken command, her mouth meeting mine. I swipe my tongue to open her lips. She lets me in and deepens our kiss. She kisses me hard for at least a minute, rocking her hips perfectly in sync with mine.

Then she stops. I can feel her tighten around me. She slows our kissing then pulls back, resting her forehead against mine. It's like she can't focus on anything else but coming undone. The way she says "don't stop" between pants is so fucking sexy it sends me over the edge, my own release pulsing through me as I continue to drive into her. I don't stop until I'm finished, and I'm positive she is too.

She's relaxed all the way into me now, her head back on the pillow and her hand holding the nape of my neck, her fingers gripped into my hair. She kisses the edge of my jaw a few times as her breathing slows, and I run my fingers up her back.

She pulls back, and I swear she's about to slide off me and into some sort of cuddle. That's something I don't do, haven't done since Emily. Instead, she gets off my bed and goes into the bathroom without saying a word. I hate how that makes me feel.

When she comes back out, her not so curly hair is tied back in a ponytail and she gives me a half smile as she picks her shorts off the floor. I'm already wearing my jeans. I could feel her walling herself off the second she slid off my bed. I may be a guy, but I'm not an idiot. I also know what happened was not just sex for either of us. I'm good at sex and reading women in bed. But that was a completely new level of being in tune with someone. I just have to figure out why she's acting like she's not on the same page.

"Come here." I'm sitting on the end of my bed when she hesitantly obeys me. When she's close enough, I pull her into me, between my legs. "You good?"

"Yup."

"Lexy."

"Troy." She says my name with sass and tries to pull away, but I hold firm to her, waiting for her to realize I want a better answer. "I'm good, Troy. Don't make this weird. It's just sex."

I'd be offended if I thought she was serious, but based on the war going on behind her eyes, I don't believe her for a second.

"Okay, I'll take you home."

"Thanks." She slips out of my grip and walks out to the living room.

I stand, grabbing a t-shirt out of my dresser drawer and pulling it over my head. Out of the corner of my eye, I catch her turn slightly, as if she's going to come back in here. She hesitates for a moment, but then starts toward the door as if she's thought better about whatever she was going to do.

When we get in my car, I push play on my Good Charlotte playlist and turn it to the volume I like when I'm alone. I have a feeling that's what she wants, especially when she curls the sleeves of her sweater into her fists and leans against the window the entire drive home. I can't help but steal glances at her the whole way and wonder why she's been so open about every thought she's had until now.

CHAPTER FIFTEEN
LEXY

With two minutes to spare before my shift starts, I walk into work. I had plenty of time to get ready after Troy dropped me off at home, but I stood in the damn shower for an hour, letting the water burn my skin. I severely misjudged my feelings, and I'm mad I got myself in this situation. I thought I could sleep with him, and it would just get him out of my system. It was just an attraction, a game, one I'd win like every other time I want something and get exactly what I expect.

Troy is exactly not what I expected. I mean, I knew he'd be good in bed. I could sense it. But even after Maci's play by play a few months ago, I was not prepared for that. It's not a secret I like sex. Regardless of the fact that it's rare for me to orgasm any way except on my own, I enjoy it. It's fun. I've slept with enough guys for some people to classify me as slutty, but that doesn't bother me. What fucking bothers me is Troy.

How he made me orgasm three times. Three. One of those times I was still fucking wearing clothes. How does that even happen?

Also, I let him go down on me, which is something I've never let anyone do. Ever. It has always seemed too intimate to me, too emotional, too uncomfortable with people I refuse to get close to. Sex is not about connection for me. It never has been, but that felt connected like he could read my damn mind.

The most irritating part of all is that I had the urge to snuggle him.

I don't even want to think about how he didn't force me to talk about it and just played music the whole drive home. It's like he knows me. But he doesn't. It's only been two days.

I turn on the lights above the bar and get to work in the place I feel most in control.

I lay the final $20 bill on my third stack of money, making exactly $300. Damn, I'm good. We used to have two bartenders on every shift, but then they realized they could get away with only paying me and run just as smoothly. Now, I work on my own during the week, and I make enough to afford an apartment in LA on my own which says a lot.

The only customers left are the three girls sitting on the edge of the stage. One of them has been crying for at least an hour, the other two consoling her, so I figured I'd let them stay until I had to lock the doors. I'm about to head over there when his voice comes from behind me.

"Hey."

What is he doing here? What part of "just sex" was I not clear about?

"What's up?" I say as I begrudgingly turn to face him.

"I was hoping we could talk. Considering I don't have your number, I thought this would be my best bet."

There's a reason he doesn't have it. Because then he'd text me. I'd text him back, and it would become a whole thing which is not going to happen.

"What do you want to talk about?"

"Earlier." He looks at me like he's annoyed I'm playing dumb.

"What about it?" I sass, shoving my tips into my cash envelope.

"So, you aren't afraid to have an opinion on everything else, but when it comes to this, you've got nothing?" There's a lack of judgment in his tone, and that's almost more annoying.

"There isn't a *this*." I wiggle my finger between the two of us. "You agreed it was just sex."

"Hmmm, that's not what I remember."

I recall our conversation over ice cream earlier. Dammit. I don't think he actually agreed. "Not the point. You knew where I stood."

"True. So, now you should know where I stand. I told you I was interested. I thought *maybe* it was just for sex. It's not."

"Thanks for the update." Ugh, I know I'm being a bitch, so I add, "I'm sorry that's not what I want."

He's looking at me like he can see right through me, and it makes me uneasy. Way too many feelings today that I prefer to avoid.

"Can you print me some receipt paper, please?" he asks, surprising me.

I walk to my register and feed a few inches through it before ripping the paper off and handing it to him along with my pen. I watch him scribble a phone number and slide it across the counter.

"In case you change your mind." He holds my gaze until I break it after what feels like a full minute later. The way he looks at me is like he's daring me to resist him, like he knows how hard it is for me.

"See ya, Lexy."

CHAPTER SIXTEEN
LEXY

The Uber I requested will be here in three minutes. Thank God. I need to get laid–by someone who is not Troy.

Sitting on the edge of my bed, I wrap the strap of my red heel around my ankle. I haven't been this trapped in my head in a long time. It's time to get the fuck out of it. I stand, tugging on the hem of my frayed jean shorts and adjusting my tucked in white tank top before looking at my full length wall mirror. Damn. I fluff my curls and twist my body, keeping my eyes locked on my reflection. Soul Cycle five days a week is seriously paying off.

Sliding my ID and credit card in my bra, I lock the door behind me as my phone vibrates in my back pocket with my ride's arrival.

Maci has been gone for a few months. Before she moved here, and prior to Mack living here, I was fine going out on my own; I don't let lack of company stop me from getting what I want. The past year I've grown accustomed to my sidekicks, but with Maci gone and Mack rarely in the mood, I'm back to being a party of one. Outside of them, I've never had friends I wanted to hang around consistently. I could call old acquaintances, but it's not worth the effort or the drama. I want easy.

Find a guy.

Hook up.

Get out.

A simple mission that doesn't require outside assistance–a well crafted game of which I'm a master.

Stepping out of the Uber, I sashay my way to the red velvet rope blocking the line of men from admittance to the club. The burly bouncer, who looks like he could John Wick you if necessary, unclips the gold hook to let me through.

"Lexy, it's been a while."

"Back on my bullshit, Damon," I quip.

His usual stoic expression breaks with a smirk. "I'll get you what you need." He waits for me to walk through the doorway and snaps the red rope in place. I know if I don't find someone suitable in the next few minutes, Damon will let a few of my type in soon.

The D is a cross between a bar and a club and a mix between classy and grungy. The actual bar is nice, but the floor and walls are trashed. It looks like they started to remodel and update then stopped halfway through the renovations. It's been stuck that way for a year. But the drinks are cheap, and its name aligns perfectly with the missions it helps me complete.

I'll talk crap about LA all day, but I can't deny it's perfect for some things. Tonight one of those things is a distraction from the only guy who has ever occupied my mind for more than five minutes because... fuck that nonesense. I really thought Maci hooking up with him in Vegas would be a deterrent. Apparently it was not. Troy has not only crossed my mind consistently since then, he hasn't left my brain at all over the past week. I'm usually more than content relying on my vibrator to take care of my needs, but this cursed blond has entered my fantasies without permission one too many times. Giving into the urge to make my fantasies a reality was supposed to get him out of my system. Instead, I'm shifting from the occasional daily thought to obsessing like a psycho.

Entering the edge of the dance floor, music assaults my ears. The DJ is mixing something new, and it's total trash if you ask me. Needing someone new in both my bed and my head, I ignore the sound thumping through my veins and scan the room until my eyes land on a well-built guy with his hip pressed against the bar. He's leaning into his elbow, finger floating in the air, asking for attention from the bartender.

Jackpot.

His perfectly styled light brown hair matches his perfectly styled clothes–dark jeans and a maroon button up with the sleeves pushed halfway up his forearms.

The denim is rough under my fingers as I graze the fabric at his hips to get his attention. "Excuse me." He turns, his eyes gliding up my body before landing on my face.

"Hello." He pulls his attention from his current task and shifts gears, flashing me a grin. "Can I help you?"

"You tell me. Can you get me a drink and a good time?" Over the years I've become exceptional at pinpointing exactly the kind of man who can get the job done–for one night only.

"That could be arranged." He steps closer, his hand finding my hip. I feel nothing from his touch except hope for waking up with a clear mind. "What are you drinking?"

"Tequila is good, thank you."

He motions to flag down the bartender before turning back to me. "So, do you live around here?"

"Born and raised," I say with more enthusiasm than I feel about the fact. "You?"

"Nah. Flagstaff. Here for the weekend."

I give myself an internal hi-five. Damn, I'm good at picking exactly the men I need.

The bartender slides two drinks in front of us, and I take a sip of mine while guy-whose-name-I-still-don't-know cashes out.

"Lexy, is that you?" I freeze. No. I spin on my heel slowly.

"Mother," I spit venomously, my eyes narrowing. What the fuck is she doing here?

"Hi, honey. It's so good to see you." She moves like she's going to hug me, but I step back, stumbling into my new date and catching his attention again.

She pauses her advance, and I'll at least give her credit for that. I haven't seen her since I moved out at 18. "What are you doing here?" My voice is flat.

"Same thing you're doing here by the looks of it." She smiles brightly like she's proud we are trolling for men together. "Seems I taught you well."

"You didn't teach me anything," I challenge. If there was more alcohol soaking into my stomach, I might have thrown it up at the thought of my mother and me being the same. We are not the same. She's here looking for love to consume her, destroy her. I'm chasing the elusive orgasm and anything that isn't love. But fuck if it doesn't make me feel all sorts of cringy seeing her at this bar like she's a cougar among the younger crowd on the dance floor. I might be looking back at a gorgeous, middle-aged woman with perfect blonde curls and fake lashes that make her matching blue eyes pop, but I refuse to be a younger reflection of her on the inside.

"So, how's my baby girl?" she asks sweetly, ignoring my hostility.

"We're not doing this, Mom."

"Mom?" Unnamed guy joins our conversation, confused.

"Not really," I tell him, spinning where I stand, his hands instinctively finding my waist. This is too fucking easy. Before he can question me, I add, "You down to get out of here?" I pinch the red straw to the side of my glass with my finger and chug what's left of it.

"Uhh, yeah." He tips his drink back then sets it on the bartop and lays out his hand in front of us. "Lead the way."

CHAPTER SEVENTEEN
LEXY

If I wasn't already convinced kissing Troy two weeks ago and hooking up with him last week were the worst mistakes I could have made, I am now. Sex has always been a way for me to, ironically, disconnect. I figure if getting physical is what typically forms bonds between a couple, my only option is to dissociate and prevent that from happening. It's a game, a good time. Get in, get out. That's it.

But not this time. This time, the Universe was like *Hey, hold my beer, and watch me kick your ass at this game you think you've mastered.* This time, I couldn't even try to focus on the orgasm I knew would never come. All I could think about was Troy. Hell, I almost did get off just thinking about him while I was with guy-whose-name-I've-already-forgotten. Levi, I think?

Maybe I just need a little more time to get him out of my system. If anything, my pull toward him is nothing more than the way he takes care of me in bed, in a way that no one else has even tried. Now that I've seen what a man is capable of, it's hard to want to choose my vibrator over that. The worst he can say is no. If he does, I'll be fine.

Me: *Can you come over tonight? I get off around one.*
Troy: *Hi, Lexy.*

Me: *How'd you know it was me?*
Troy: *You're the only person I've given my number to.*
Me: *Oh. So...*
Troy: *Does this mean you're willing to reconsider this possibly being more than sex?*
Me: *I already told you I'm not.*
Troy: *So, this is you booty calling me?*
Me: *What's the problem? You came when Lauren called.*

Okay, that was probably a little uncalled for. Why am I worked up about this?

Troy: *I didn't want to date Lauren. I had nothing to lose.*
Me: *Sex is all I can give you, Troy. Take it or leave it.*
Troy: *Sex isn't enough, Lexy. I'll see you around.*

What kind of guy turns down no attachment sex? Especially a guy who has literally been in a no attachment sex contract. Though, I guess it's good he's honest. I can't complain about him having the one quality I feel like everyone else in this town is missing.

I throw my phone on my bed anyway.

I'm fine. It's fine. Totally fucking fine.

CHAPTER EIGHTEEN
TROY

It's Friday, so I'm assuming she has to work tonight. I do too, but I have a couple more hours before my shift. I kicked myself all night for not taking her up on her offer. What the hell is wrong with me? Why wouldn't I take what I can get?

I ring her doorbell, and a few seconds later her feet are shuffling on the carpet as she walks toward the door. When she's on the other side, I feel her there. I know she's looking through the peephole and hesitating to unlock the chain because she sees me.

I hear her sigh as she finally opens the door. She swings it open but doesn't say anything. She stares at me for a moment then turns on her heel and walks away. I close the door behind me and follow her to her bedroom. She left her bedroom door cracked, so I take it as permission to enter. When I do, I see she's almost ready for work, checking herself out in her full length mirror that's leaning against the wall. I wasn't sure what I was going to do when I got here. I'd rather us be on the same page, but if that isn't possible, if all she wants is sex, then I'm going to make her dreams come true.

I move to the space behind her, stepping closer, until my chest is flush with her back. The smell of coconut from her shampoo invades the air around me as I gently brush her loose blonde curls over her shoulder, exposing her neck. She's watching me intently in the mirror, not leaning into my touch. She's not pulling away either, and I take it as the consent I need. I kiss her where her skin meets the plain black tank top she always wears to work.

One of my hands falls to her hip, my middle finger threading through the belt loop of her cutoff jean shorts and pull her into me. I slowly sweep my fingers along her neck, following the curve of her tank top until I reach the perfect spot between her breasts. I pause to kiss her shoulder before dragging my hand slowly down her stomach, never breaking contact with her body. When I get to the edge of her tank top, I slip my hand under, pushing up until my hand is flush against her skin, my pinky dipping below the top of her shorts.

"You want to be fucked, Lexy?" I whisper in her ear as my eyes meet hers in the mirror. "Then I'm going to fuck you every way I can." She holds my gaze for a moment, struggling to hide how much I affect her. I pinch the denim with my fingers, giving me just enough slack to pop the button undone. Tugging her zipper, I catch a glimpse of her lace thong in the mirror. Fuck. I love it when she wears red. I slide my hand slowly under both layers of the clothing separating us. My middle finger traces softly along her opening.

I can't read her at all. She keeps her eyes focused on the mirror, watching me. It's like she's determined not to give in to me and the satisfaction she can get from someone else instead of her vibrator. Maybe she really doesn't know what it can be like. She has me now, whether she's accepted it or not, and I want her to know what that means. I dip barely inside her and her breath catches, giving her away.

I spread her open with my fingers, before slipping further inside. She's so fucking responsive to my touch. Maybe this will be easier than I thought. "You're already wet. Have you been waiting for me, Lexy?" Her eyes shoot a dagger at me through the mirror, likely at my assumption that she wants me. I don't care because I'm not wrong.

I pull out of her slowly before sliding back in, hooking my finger to hit her G-spot. That does the trick because her head falls back against my chest, her eyes fluttering closed on a moan. My thumb finds her clit and massages slowly, earning me another gasp from her perfect lips. With that, her hand reaches up, gripping the back of my neck. Her breath gets heavy and a little ragged as I push in and pull out of her slowly, my thumb keeping pressure right where she needs it.

My other hand runs up her side, gliding along her skin until it catches on her bra, and I take a full handful of her breast. She bites into her lower lip, and I can tell she's close. I pull my finger out, slowly tracing her opening with her own wetness. My lips find her skin again, kissing up her throat as she presses her body into mine. I rub her in light, soft circles, only barely dipping into her. I want her to enjoy this as long as possible.

Her breath calms slightly, but I can feel her heart rate accelerate as I run my hand along her chest. My palm is flat against her now, and she attempts to press into me, her body begging me to be inside her again. I keep teasing her. I'm loving every second of watching her slowly fall apart.

All of a sudden her eyes fly open and meet mine in the mirror. "Troy. Stop teasing me, and make me come." Her words are said in a whisper but come out as a threat. "Now." With that final word, she tilts her hips, pressing into my hand as two of my fingers press into her, giving her what she wants. How could I not? I pulse in and out of her quickly, holding her to me as she tightens around my fingers, waves of contractions rolling through her. I can't take my eyes off the mirror, off her. Her head has fallen back against me, her breath strangled as she shatters. Watching her come undone by my touch is the sexiest fucking thing I've ever seen, and I'll do whatever it takes to experience it a thousand more times.

This is the moment I realize she's not the one fucked. I am.

I'm not sure I'll ever be able to deny her anything she desires from this point on. I'll pray to fucking God it's me she wants.

I slip my hand out of her shorts, zipping them up and fastening the button with my arms wrapped around her. When I'm finished, she turns into me, her hands softly pressing in my chest.

"I have to go to work," she whispers, like she feels guilty.

"I know. I'll be back tonight."

She contemplates her response. "I don't do sleepovers."

"No sleeping. Got it. I'll see you later." I resist the kiss I want to give her and leave.

LEXY

When I pull into my usual parking spot, it's dark, considering it's 2:30 a.m. Even so, the light above my first floor apartment door is bright enough I can tell it's Troy's car next to mine. I sigh, torn between sending him away and wanting him to come inside. He gets out of his car when he sees me open my door. When I get to my apartment, Troy is right behind me. I unlock the door, and he follows me inside. I guess I made my decision. I'm too exhausted to fight the pull to him.

"How was your night?" I ask as I flick on the kitchen light once we make it through the entryway and set my purse on the counter.

He tosses his car keys next to it. "Not bad. Nothing too crazy for a Friday night. What about yours?"

"I wasn't so lucky. Some girl showed up trashed, but I was distracted. I didn't realize it and served her when I shouldn't have. She threw up EVERYWHERE."

He steps closer, his hand sliding against my neck as he weaves his fingers through my hair. My body relaxes into his touch before I can stop myself. "It's not your fault. It's not your job to babysit 400 grown ass adults."

"I know, I just have a lot on my mind. And then of course Todd was there." His hand tenses at the douchebag's name.

"I hate that guy. Can't you kick him out?"

"He's the worst. My boss gives me a lot of flexibility, but he doesn't want me kicking anyone out unless it's absolutely necessary. He claims he doesn't want to get a bad rap. But I know it's because guys are more likely to buy drinks."

"He sounds like a douchebag too. I'm sorry." He's acting concerned and comforting, like a boyfriend. I think I like it. Which means I hate it.

"It's alright. You know how it goes. It evens out in the end, and it's usually worth the money."

He doesn't look convinced of my statement. "Do you want to talk about whatever else is on your mind?"

I only ever talk to Mack. And Maci. It would be weird to open up to anyone else, especially when said person is what I might need to talk about. I shake my head against my instinct to say yes.

"What do you want, then?" He says it gently, like he's willing to give me whatever I ask him for. The comfort of this moment and the softness in his voice gives me anxiety. What the hell is wrong with me?

I close the few inches of space between us and kiss him. My traitorous heart leaps at the contact. I ignore it. "That." I pull back, my fingers running down his forearm until they link with his and lead him to my room. I squeeze his hand. "Maybe these." I smile at him, and he returns the gesture. When I'm backed up against my bed, I run my thumb roughly across his mouth. "Definitely this." He bites playfully at my thumb before tossing me onto the bed.

By the time we are worn out, it's almost 4 a.m. I'm pretty sure I'll fall asleep the second I close my eyes, regardless of the fact that I'm still naked, twisted in my sheets. When I glance at Troy, it looks like he could do the same. I need to send him home. I've never let a guy stay over after sex, and there's no reason to change that now. He scoots closer to me, reaching for my hip, pulling me to my side so I'm facing him.

"Here's what I'm thinking."

I wait for him to continue, although I have a feeling I should cut him off now.

"You tell that voice in your head trying to convince you I should leave to fuck off."

In my entire life, Mack has been the only person who has been able to read me. Troy can do it better. I don't think I like that. He *has* to leave. I stare back at him.

"I slept with someone else a few days ago," I blurt.

He studies me, his brows furrowing. "Okay," he says slowly. "How was that?"

"What?" His response throws me.

"How was it?" he asks, as if he's genuinely curious. "Did he get you off?"

"That's none of your business," I say with attitude.

"Then why are you telling me?"

"Honesty is the best policy or whatever," I say as if it's obvious.

"Is that so? Then tell me," he demands before leaning in, his nose grazing the skin on my neck, sending a chill down my spine. "Did." He nips at the skin just below my ear. My instinct is to run my fingers up his side, but I keep them to myself. "You." A kiss lands on the sensitive skin at my throat, and the smallest moan escapes my lips without permission. "Get." His mouth meets mine for a long moment. "Off?" he finishes, still close enough his warm breath brushes my lips.

"I think you know the answer." I mumble as his lips press against my neck again. I don't know why my voice sounds like I'm embarrassed.

He pulls back so I can see his smirk. "No one can get you off like I can, huh? You know why that is, right?"

I shoot him a vexed glare. "You're going to give me some stupid answer about chemistry aren't you?"

"When two people have chemistry, it makes the sex better," he states, like it's the only possible reason our sex is *that* good.

"We don't have chemistry," I lie.

"You're trying to push me away. It's not going to work."

I glare at him before rolling on my back, his hold on my hip sliding to my stomach.

"Swear to me this is only about sex for you, and I'll leave right now."

Dead air hangs between us for a moment.

"Troy, don't make me say it." It comes out as a whisper.

He sits up, his eyes roaming my face, and I take the moment to read his. It's a cross between being hurt and contemplating if he believes me.

"Okay," he whispers, and despite being in opposition to the anti-relationship vibes I'm putting off, he kisses my forehead and tucks the covers in around me when he crawls out of them to leave.

CHAPTER NINETEEN
LEXY

Troy: *Whatcha doing?*

Me: *Just got to Mack's.*

Troy: *At 3 a.m.? What are you two getting into?*

I hate how you can never read intent behind words in texts. It's annoying. Not that I care what he thinks about my middle of the night habits. Was he hoping I'd be down to come over?

Me: *Picked up Chinese. Kind of our thing after the nights we work together.*

Troy: *I will say that's one thing I love about LA. You cannot get food in the middle of the night in Oregon.*

Me: *Sounds terrible.*

I'm half in this thing and half out of it, and I have no fucking clue what direction I want to go. I shouldn't be rude, though, and it's just texting. How much trouble can that get me into?

Me: *What are you doing?*

Troy: *Just got home.*

Me: *No wild Saturday night plans? No Lauren?*

Troy: *We had a drink after work. But that's it.*

Me: *Oh.*

Troy: *We called off our arrangement.*

Why do I feel relieved by that? And a lot of pressure I'm not sure I want.

Me: *Not on my account, I hope.*

I watch the three dots indicating he's typing appear and disappear three times before his text comes through.

Troy: *Lauren deserves more than sex with a guy wishing she was someone else.*

Me: *Troy.*

Troy: *I'm not expecting anything from you, Lexy. I'm just trying to not be a dick.*

Me: *Fine.*

Troy: *What's your fortune cookie say?*

Leaning toward the coffee table, I grab a cookie from the white plastic bag with "thank you" in giant red letters repeating on the front. I resume my criss-crossed position on the couch and crack it open even though I haven't finished my sweet and sour chicken.

Me: *"You didn't come this far to only come this far."*

Troy: *In bed.*

Me: *What?*

Troy: *That's what you're supposed to do. Add "in bed" to your fortune. It makes them better.*

Me: *You're such a guy.*

Troy: *True. But my statement is also true.*

Me: *If you say so.*

Troy: *Do you have any siblings?*

Me: *Random, but no. My mom only ruined me, thank God.*

Troy: *Sucks you didn't have anyone though.*

Me: *It's fine. I'm used to it.*

Troy: *Have you ever been outside Cali?*

Me: *I haven't even been outside of So Cal. Besides Vegas.*

Troy: *What's your favorite food?*

Me: *Is this about to turn into some 20 questions game where you try to get to know me like I'm your girlfriend?*

Troy: *Are you going to assume everything I say is because I want to date you?*

Me: *Yes.*

Me: *Am I wrong?*

Troy: *Friends get to know each other all the time. They are harmless questions.*

Me: *That's how it starts.*

Troy: *What exactly do you think is going to happen if I learn things about you?*

Me: *I don't know. You'll mash it with your stupid charm and trick me into wanting more than sex.*

Troy: *You're right. That sounds terrible.*

Me: *Can you see my eye roll from here?*

Troy: *Okay, how about this? You play with me. But we'll switch it up. We'll add "in bed" to each question. You agreed to just sex. So, we'll stick with that.*

Me: *Fine.*

Troy: *What's your favorite food... in bed?*

Me: *Gummy bears.*

Me: *Although, I'll give you a bonus answer and tell you that it's not just in bed. Gummy bears everywhere, all the time.*

Troy: *Noted. Provide a sugar rush as refuel between orgasms.*

I chuckle when Troy's text comes through. Mack glances up from his song notebook to look at me but doesn't say anything.

Me: *Now we are getting somewhere. What's your favorite thing to eat in bed?*

Troy: *You.*

Fuck.

Me.

My best friend stares at me, a range of emotions on his face–confusion, curiosity, amusement.

"You're smiling. At your phone. It's the middle of the night in Costa Rica, so I highly doubt it's Maci on the other end."

I cut off my smile, biting into my lip and saying nothing. He chuckles and focuses back on the song he's writing.

Me: *Morning person or night person?* I take another turn so I don't have to respond to his answer.

Troy: *All of the above. Plus the middle of the day. You?*

Of course he would say that.

Me: *Hmmm. Middle of the night? That in between where you're on the edge of being asleep where it feels like a dream, and you're a little more willing to do something you usually wouldn't.*

Troy: *Hmm. I like that answer.*

He seems surprised. To be honest, I am too.

Me: *Your turn.*

Troy: *Favorite color?*

Me: *What kind of answer are you looking for here? Sheets? Condoms? Underwear?*

Troy: *I'm looking for you to tell me you'll go buy red lingerie for every day of the week.*

Me: *Is that what does it for you? Haha*

Troy: *When it's on you, fuck yes.*

Me: *Noted.*

Troy: *What turns you on the most?*

Me: *I think you should figure out the answer to that one all on your own.*

Troy: *Challenge accepted.*

Troy: *At least help me out a little. Have you been having fun?*

Troy: *In bed.*

Troy: *With me.*

Me: *You know the answer to that.*

Troy: *Yeah, the sex is great, but you can tell me specifically what you like. If this is only going to be that, the least I can do is make sure it's worth your while.*

Me: *I don't know.*

Troy: *You're telling me the queen of honest, unfiltered opinions, once again has no opinion when it comes to me.*

Me: *I have an opinion.*

Troy: *Then what's the problem?*

What is the problem? This isn't even *that* personal of a question. I mean, in terms of sex maybe, but it's not like he hasn't seen me completely naked and had his mouth somewhere no one else has. Why does using my words seem so much more difficult than letting him use my body? Mack and Maci are the only ones who have trusted me with their personal thoughts, and one of them is in the room with me.

"Mack."

He snaps his head up from where he's sitting on the floor leaned against the couch by my feet. "What's up?"

"Why do you tell me all your secrets?"

He laughs. "Umm, is this a trick question?"

"No." I'm dead serious. "How do you choose who to trust?"

He shrugs. "You get me. You're always honest even if I don't want to hear it, but it's only because you care."

"It's the same with Maci?"

"Kind of. I trust you both, but I guess I tell her stuff because I want her to know who I am better than anyone and love me for that."

"Aren't you worried she'll learn something she doesn't like."

"You mean like how I used to do drugs and thought she'd be better off not knowing?" He looks dead in my eyes like that statement alone should prove his point. "What's going on? You aren't shy when it comes to your thoughts."

"Oh, yeah. It's just weird, I guess. Usually I don't care what the other person thinks."

"If they are someone you should keep around then nothing you tell them will scare them away."

When he realizes I don't have a response, he goes back to working on his song, and I pull up my text thread again.

Me: *No one has ever asked me that before.*

Troy: *I mean, you are easy to read.* He adds a wink emoji, thinking he's joking but not realizing the reality of that statement.

Me: *I think that's just you.*

Troy: *What do you mean?*

Me: *Kind of feels like you're in my head when we're in bed. Like you know what I want.*

Troy: *I feel the same, but about you.*

Me: *Is that normal?*

Troy: *Not to this extent. At least not from my experience. Must be the chemistry.*

Is that really the explanation? But also, Troy is the only guy I've been with more than once, and he has the perception skills of a bartender, so he probably just picked up on cues or something. That elevator kiss, orgasm, whatever the fuck you want to call it though, it's like he's been reading my mind since that moment. I ignore his incessant use of *that* word and give him credit where it's due.

Me: *Your tongue is magic.*

Troy: *Better than your vibrator?*

Me: *It's currently mad at me for being shoved into my nightstand, temporarily out of commission for underperformance.*

Troy: *It better get used to being there.*

Me: *Why do you like me?* I know it sounds a little self deprecating, but I'm genuinely curious. No one has ever taken the time to get to know me before in a dating sort of way, even if it's only in the bedroom. I notice the typing bubbles pop up and go away a couple times again.

Troy: *In bed or...*

Me: *Umm, either, I guess.*

He starts typing immediately. I don't know why I'm so nervous. I uncross my legs, one of my feet falling to the floor where my heel bounces anxiously as his text takes forever to appear on the screen in my hand.

Troy: *In bed... everything. How responsive you are to my touch. The sounds you make when I do something right. That you let me explore every inch of you and haven't stopped me yet. The way you taste.*

Once his text comes through, the typing bubble doesn't come back, so I consider my response for a moment.

Me: *I've never let anyone do that before.*

I imagine his face on the other side of his phone. I wonder if he's shocked by this information or thinks I'm crazy.

Troy: *That's another reason I like you–you let me throw rocks at your wall to see what's behind it.*

Why I'm allowing it I haven't quite figured out yet, but I don't want to stop him. When I finally set my phone down, Mack pushes his notebook to the side, directing his focus on me. "Are you going to tell me what that was about?"

"No."

He smirks at me before grabbing the remote and flicking on the TV.

CHAPTER TWENTY
LEXY

Troy: *(sends picture of motorcycle)*

Troy: *Freshly washed and ready for a ride.*

Me: *Is she here?!*

Troy: *Oh, I was talking about me.* He adds a wink emoji.

Me: *No. Troy. Just no.*

Troy: *Oh come on, humor me.*

Me: *Maybe if your bike was here.*

Troy: *That thing really does it for you, huh?*

Me: *I did picture fucking you on it. Have you done it? Is it tricky?*

Troy: *Oh yeah? I've never tried. But willing to test it out with you. Can't say the thought hasn't crossed my mind.*

Me: *Too bad it's not here then.*

Troy: *That decision will continue to bite me in the ass, won't it?*

Me: *Probably.*

Troy: *How can I make it up to you?*

Me: *You tell me.*

Troy: *I have some ideas. I'll show you. Tonight?*

Me: *I get off at two.*

It's 2:05 a.m. when I pull into my complex, which is pretty good considering I live five minutes from work, and we don't do last call until 1:45. I realized how on top of my side work I was all night. It usually doesn't take me long to finish up once we close, but it's like I was in a hurry tonight. Doesn't take a genius to figure out why, despite my constant denial. I don't know if I'm willing to let my growing feelings toward him overpower my insecurities about this. Apparently, sex is overpowering all of it right now. It's just so good.

Troy is already in the parking space next to mine, waiting for me. He gets out of his car when he sees me.

"I thought you didn't close until 2?" He works like 15 minutes from here.

"We don't. Lauren finished up for me. I didn't want you to have to wait on me."

This guy is so damn considerate. Is all dating like this, and I just had no idea? Or is it him? I'm stuck in my head as I slide my key into the lock. Before I can turn the knob, Troy's hands are on my waist, and he's twisting me until I'm pressed up against my front door. He closes the distance between us, surrounding me as much as possible. Our feet are alternating, so one of his legs is between mine, tangling us together. He's got an arm wrapped around my back, the only thing breaking my connection with the door. His other hand is buried in my hair, his grip tight on the back of my head pulling me into him. His lips are on mine before I can react. It all happens so fast. I'm nearly paralyzed by it. He deepens our kiss, and I feel it all the way to my fucking toes. I melt into him, my hands sliding under his shirt as I dig my fingers into his back. I have never been kissed like this. I don't even know what's happening. I'm not even sure I can breathe. Or think.

He's kissing me like he can't get enough, but then suddenly he's pulling back. Disappointment seeps from every part of my body that lost connection with his. "What was that?" I practically stutter over my words.

He smirks, leaning in until his forehead is pressed against mine. "Me trying to get you to forget about my bike. Is it working?"

"Hmm, maybe. You might need to keep trying." I'm surprised I can find any words at all.

He kisses me softly then takes my hand in one of his and opens my door with the other.

It's been three hours since we walked through my door. Three hours. Who knew that letting someone explore every inch of my body would take that long. I do now, and fuck, how will I ever go back to anything less than the worshiping that just took place? Troy took his sweet time, like there was no rush, like it wasn't the middle of the night and we weren't both exhausted. I've never been insecure about my body. I work hard for it. That's totally different than being comfortable with revealing every part of yourself to someone like this. The way he was looking at me, like I was the best view he's ever seen, any doubt I could have possibly had about him claiming my body instantly disappeared.

I roll off him after giving him the ride he joked about earlier. It was the least I could do. The lust in his eyes never faded once, and it was enough to keep me in the mood even after I got off four times. What is he trying to do? Set records or something? Fuck. How am I supposed to resist him?

I'm so exhausted I could fall asleep the second I close my eyes. Instead, I get up to at least brush my teeth first. Troy stands with me, reaching for his briefs and jeans on the floor.

"What are you doing?"

"Getting dressed." He looks at me confused. "So I can go home." He really will leave and respect my sex only boundaries. Damn.

"You can stay," I whisper, choosing to let go of some of my resistance.

He searches my face as if he's checking whether or not I'm serious. "Is this one of those 'it's the middle of the night so I'm more willing to make a decision I normally wouldn't' situations you mentioned?"

I bite into my lip as I stare back at him. Would I make this decision if it wasn't the middle of the night. Maybe not. I guess I'll find out in the morning.

When he realizes I'm not going to clarify, he adds, "If you let me stay, I'm going to read into it."

I don't want to lead him on, but I don't want him to leave either. "I know." I reach out for his forearm, steadying myself as I lean in to kiss him on the cheek before going to the bathroom.

When I come back, he's already under the covers, and I crawl in next to him. When our eyes lock, every part of his face tells me how excited he is about his victory, but he doesn't gloat. Instead, he kisses me on the forehead, and when I roll over, he pulls me into him.

I don't resist that either.

CHAPTER TWENTY-ONE
TROY

When I wake up in Lexy's bed, she's still asleep in nearly the same position she was when we went to bed. Her back is to me, but she's pressed against my chest, my arm around her. I worry if she wakes up being spooned by me like I'm her boyfriend, she'll fly out of bed and probably out of my life. I can't bring myself to pull away from her, though. I'll just spice it up a little–that seems to be the key so far.

I slowly graze my hand up her bare stomach until it reaches her breast. Fuck. The way she fits in my hand is like she was made for me. I kiss her neck, soft and slow at first, increasing the pressure from my hand and my lips.

I wasn't sure she was awake until her voice breaks through the silence.

"You're still here," she whispers, and I can't tell how she feels about it.

I nuzzle her neck and kiss her again before I respond. "Does it suck as much as you thought?"

She rolls over so she's facing me, and I let my hand fall to her waist. Hers fold under her head, her arms creating a small barrier between us.

"What's going on in that pretty head of yours?" I don't want to push her, but I can't figure out how to make this work if she doesn't tell me what she's thinking.

Her eyes search my face. "I don't hate it."

"Hate what?"

"You being here."

I try to hold back my grin. That's the closest I've gotten to her admitting she likes me. I lean in and kiss her softly, but it's nowhere close to what I need from her. I go back in for another, and it surprises me that she meets me halfway. Not only that, but she pulls her top hand out from under her head and lets it find its way to my waist as she deepens our kiss.

I'm the first to pull back. "Tell me you don't feel that." I whisper and catch her gaze. "This thing between us." So much for not saying or doing anything to freak her out.

She breaks eye contact, her gaze falling to the space on the bed between us.

My hand leaves her waist so I can bring my fingers to her chin, softly directing her gaze back to mine. "Why are you fighting it?"

She's silent for long enough I don't think she's going to tell me. As I'm about to tell her it's okay, she speaks. "I don't want to tell you. You're so good at not letting your mom or anyone else affect how you live your life."

That's not what I expected her to say. "That's not true. You just haven't been around me enough to see it yet. Tell me, please. I won't judge you."

She bites into her lip. I know this is a serious moment, but she's so fucking cute.

"Remember how I told you about my mom's boyfriend. The one who gave me my first CD?"

"Yeah."

"I don't remember his name. I don't remember any of their names. There were too many of them." She hesitates, like she's unsure if she should continue. I rub my thumb along her cheek, hoping to encourage her.

"My mom wasn't just a serial dater. She was so addicted to falling in love that whenever she had it, it was the only thing that mattered to her. And whenever she didn't, she acted like she'd die without her next hit."

I have a feeling where she's going with this. The specifics may be different, but our situations are comparable. "When you say the only thing that mattered to her…"

"I mean she loved them so much, there wasn't any left for me. Sometimes I'd go weeks without seeing her. My first memory of being left alone for too long is from when I was five. Luckily the bus stop was on the corner we lived on, and one of my teachers helped me get free lunches at school."

This is not something I wanted us to be able to bond over, but I haven't made the connection between this and why she's so afraid of giving in to me. I don't know what to say, but before I can come up with something, she smirks.

"At least I didn't have to eat pot brownies." That earns her a smile, even if it's her way of trying to escape this conversation.

I take a stab at what's bothering her. "You're worried you'll end up like her, once you know what it's like?"

She nods. She's showing me a vulnerability I suspect not many people have seen, so I give her time to gather her thoughts, threading my fingers into her hair in the meantime.

"What if I give it a chance and it distracts me from everything else that's important to me?" The genuine concern in her eyes makes me want to hold her, but I don't want to push it and risk her retreating.

"What is important to you?"

"I guess I don't have fancy dreams, or anything worth a lot..."

"It doesn't have to be material or grand for it to be important. The best things in life usually aren't."

"Then I guess... being able to rely on myself? My friendship with Mack. With Maci. And maybe part of it is... I'm still figuring out what I want in life. And I don't want someone to get in the way of that." I'm taken back by her openness.

"The right person wouldn't make you choose between them and your other priorities. Hell, the right person will share a lot of them and encourage you to discover anything that makes you happy."

"Okay, fine. Say I found the right person. What happens when they leave? What if I can't handle it? What if it breaks me and I turn into a useless human or worse, a useless mom–like mine did?"

"You're not your mom, Lexy. The fact that you're even thinking about this proves that. You've fended for yourself since you were at least five. I've watched you dominate a bar full of hundreds of people on your own. From what I've seen, you can take control of situations and conversations quicker than anyone I know."

"You haven't spent *that* much time with me."

"I know, but I want to. I want to learn so much about you that when you're worried you're not enough, you'll believe me when I say you are."

"So, what happens if I decide I like you, Troy? You don't even like California."

"Lexy, *you* don't even like California."

"Okay, fair. But I'm being serious. How can you even know you want to date me?"

"I don't know. My gut?"

"That doesn't sound trustworthy. Most people's gut can't even handle Mexican food," she says matter-of-factly as if the two are actually connected. I attempt to stifle a laugh. "It could just as easily not work out."

"Maybe it won't," her eyes widen at my words, "but maybe it will. How will we know if we don't try?"

"I don't like not having control."

"Look, I'm not going to lie to you. I have no idea if we will work. How can anyone know that at first? But I can tell you that I want to try, and I promise I won't let you be all consumed by us. I'll always be honest with you, and I'll never intentionally hurt you."

Her eyes shift across my face as she looks at me. "I do feel it..."

"Feel what?" I know what she means, but selfishly I want to hear her say it.

"Whatever this is between us."

"Oh yeah?" I grin and lean in to kiss her. I can feel her smile in our kiss before she pulls back.

"Mhmm. I felt it before you did."

She must see the question on my face.

"I kind of forced myself on Nolan, so I wouldn't think about you."

"You didn't." I laugh at her, reveling in this new information.

She giggles with amusement, and it's the best sound I've ever heard. Okay, maybe the second best. I'm about to get my favorite sound out of her. "You put a thought in my head that doesn't belong there. I think you need to make it up to me."

"Oh yeah? How do you expect me to do that?" she says as her hand disappears under the sheet.

We stayed in bed most of the day, outside of me answering the door to get food I ordered from the café up the street. You can bet I'm taking advantage of every second she wants to stay trapped in her room with me. I'm in the kitchen getting us a couple glasses of water. On my walk back to her room, I catch sight of a green Ducks hoodie draped over the back of the couch.

My alma mater.

I don't know why it hadn't occurred to me that she and Maci are *that* close, but seeing her things in a space they share hits me weirdly. It's like a dark, ominous cloud is forming, waiting to drench me if I handle the situation incorrectly, like I somehow did with Emily.

I hand Lexy a glass, and she thanks me before taking a sip and reaching her hand out for me. I don't want to ruin this day, but this will eat away at me if I don't tell her, so I might as well get it over with.

"Is that Maci's sweatshirt in the living room?"

She looks at me, confused, until she places it in her head. "Oh, yeah. All her stuff is still here while she's gone. It's like having a sister. I can steal her clothes." She smiles at the thought and tugs on my arm until I climb onto the bed with her. She's only in a plain black bra and black sleep shorts, and it's hard to not be distracted.

"Have you said anything to her yet, about me?" I attempt to keep my mind on track.

"Umm, no? In case you forgot, I wasn't telling *you* until five hours ago. Why..."

"I was thinking maybe we should say something to her."

"I mean, I'm sure it'll come up eventually." She shrugs.

"I know, but–"

"Troy, we both slept with each other's best friend. Let's call it even and not worry about it."

"It's not that. I'm trying to date you, and Maci is your best friend. I'd like to have a good relationship with her too. That isn't going to happen if ours starts as a secret."

"Whoa, let's not get ahead of ourselves. You're making this sound serious already."

"I'm sorry. I'm not trying to pressure you, but even if it's just sex, I would still feel better if she knew."

"I mean this in the nicest way, but Maci won't be jealous or anything. It's not like she wants to date you. You wouldn't be here if she did. Trust me, she's got bigger problems." She sighs, and I'm tempted to ask her what she means, but I stay on topic.

"Remember how you thought I didn't let my past affect me and my choices?"

"Umm, yeah..."

"Senior year of high school I was the quarterback of our football team." Lust fills her eyes, and I pride myself on how well I can read this girl already. "Don't get distracted. Yes, I will show you a picture. Yes, I still have my uniform at my parents' house."

"How did you..."

"Is that not what you were thinking?"

She rolls her eyes. "Just get to the point of this story." She moves to sit cross-legged in front of me and gives me her full attention.

"Of course I started dating the head cheerleader because that's all but a requirement of the job." I laugh, and she eyes me with curiosity as to where I'm going with this. "We were together for four years. Although, 'together' was apparently a loose term for her. The summer before my senior year of college, I found out she'd been sleeping with one of my best friends for two years."

Her mouth falls open. I can practically see the gears turning in her head. "That's why you ghosted Maci."

I nod. "Yeah, I took it really hard, and I still feel like a dick for how I treated Maci. I thought I was ready to date, and I wasn't. I didn't know how to handle it, and unfortunately Maci was the victim of that."

"I think she's forgiven you, Troy. You and your magic dick," she says, amused.

I keep my cringe to myself. "You don't think I used sex to make it up to her, do you?"

Her brows pinch together, and I let out a sigh of relief at realizing that thought didn't cross her mind. "Definitely did not think that."

"Okay, good. I swear that was not what it was about."

"I know." Her tone makes me confident she believes that.

"Anyway," I bring us back to the point, "things were shitty for a while. My buddy, Cooper, finally called me out on my crap. I could either decide to stop trusting people, or I could do my best to always be honest with them and hopefully attract the right people to my circle. It might not matter to Maci, but it's about more than that to me. I can't risk people's feelings based on my assumptions, and I don't want to withhold information when it's not necessary."

"I'm sorry she sucked so much. She sounds like a bitch."

"It's okay. It is what it is. I deserve more than that."

She takes a long moment before responding. "That's why you're pushing me to commit to more than sex."

I sigh, bringing my hands to her knees as she still sits cross-legged in front of me. "I'm not trying to push you. I'm sorry if it's coming across that way. I just think we click, and I like to be on the same page as other people."

"It's just really fast for me. This discussion alone is too much." She does look physically stressed. "I could probably count on one hand the number of times I've had conversations this serious. I don't think I've even had sex with the same person more than once. Besides you."

While that's a little concerning–but more in the sense that I'm sad for her she's never experienced the benefits of it–I'm choosing to read between the lines of her words. She's never let anyone else spend the night, and she's never slept with someone multiple times. Until now. Until me. "Well, thank you for opening up for me. Maybe you could do it again. Right now."

I reach for the edge of her sleep shorts and tug on them before it clicks that I've switched gears. Her smile returns. It tells me I just have to be patient. I can do that.

CHAPTER TWENTY-TWO
LEXY

"Hey, Lexy." His voice comes from above the bar, and I stand up from where I was crouched down sliding an extra tin of cut up limes into the fridge.

"Troy, hi. How did you get in here?" The place is completely empty, besides Mack and the rest of his band setting up on the stage. All the lights are still on, and we don't open for another half hour.

"I told security you forgot something, and I had to get it to you before your shift."

"What did I forget?" I can't think of anything.

He leans over the bar, his hand reaching for the back of my neck and pulling me closer once he latches on. His lips press against mine, and I feel it all the way to my toes. Again, I'm reminded I'm in way too fucking deep.

He pulls back. "That."

"How could I have forgotten?" I roll my eyes, making my way to the other side of the bar where I have lemons waiting to be cut and try to hide my smile.

"Also, I was wondering if you had plans tonight?"

"You tell me." There's hesitation behind my words because I haven't done what he asked. He asked me again to talk to Maci when he left yesterday afternoon.

"Did you talk to Maci?"

"It's been like a day, Troy, and she's in another country. I haven't had a chance yet. But I will. This really isn't a big deal. We don't even know if this is going to be a real thing between us. And Maci won't care either way besides wanting to know the fun details." I get his concern, but I still don't think it's something that needs to be remedied immediately.

"I don't think she will either, but you know that's not the point."

"Hey, Lex. It's Troy, right?" Mack's voice startles me when he joins us out of nowhere. Fucking fantastic. This will be a mess if I don't shut this conversation down.

"Yeah. Hey, man." Troy fist bumps Mack, who then moves to readjust his backward black hat.

"Troy, let's talk about this later."

"I don't get why this is a whole thing, Lexy. It's just a text message, and it's important to me." I'm about to attempt to send him away again, but he turns to Mack. "Mack, right?" He continues before Mack nods. "Tell me this. If you were interested in the best friend of someone you've hooked up with, the right thing to do would be to talk to them before pursuing a relationship." He says it as a statement, but waits for Mack to confirm.

"No one said anything about a relationship," I snap before crossing my arms over my chest and sighing in annoyance. Why am I so on edge about this?

What we are talking about hasn't clicked for Mack. Maybe we can avoid this, at least for now. "Yeah, I'd say so. Depends on the situation though, I guess."

I can't get a word in before Troy. "I'm very interested in this girl right here." He points at me with his thumb over his shoulder, and I know whatever comes out of his mouth next will open a can of worms he isn't expecting. I don't know how to stop this conversation, so I just watch the trainwreck unfold before my eyes.

"But *she* doesn't think it matters that the only reason we know each other is because I slept with her best friend. I don't want to start our relationship based on dishonesty, and omitting the truth is the same." He's starting to sound frustrated.

"Again, we are not in a relationship." I interject into their conversation.

I can practically see the gears turning in Mack's head, my comment and attempt at a conversation change being ignored by both of them. I rub my hands up my face before reaching out for Mack's forearm. His name is on my tongue, but his eerily calm voice overpowers mine. "How long ago did you sleep with her?"

Troy looks like he's trying to do math in his head. He hasn't realized the question is for Mack's benefit, rather than his. "I don't know, October. So, like three months ago."

His calculation isn't even out of his mouth before the words fly out of Mack's.

"You're fucking joking, right?" I swear his green eyes turn red as he focuses on me, his hands slamming on the bartop.

"Whoa, man. I know it's weird, but I'm trying to do the right thing here."

I cut in for damage control. "You two weren't together then, Mack. She can do whatever she wants." I feel bad saying that, but it is the truth. It's not like she cheated on him.

I focus on my friend, but I can see Troy piecing the story together out of the corner of my eye.

"Not because I didn't want to be," he growls at me. "Does she like him? Is that why you're afraid to tell her?!" He rips his hat off in frustration and runs his fingers through his hair, tugging on the strands.

"No. That's not it…"

"Tell me." His usually calm voice is all demand.

"She doesn't like him, Mack. I DO." It bursts out of me with frustration of my own. "And if I tell her then it's real, and I have to figure out how the fuck to have feelings for someone." I turn away for a moment to take a breath. When I spin back, I see I left Troy standing there a little stunned. Yeah, welcome to the club, bud. I'm as surprised about this situation as you are.

My eyes shift to Mack. I watch his anger dissolve into defeat as he mumbles under his breath. "Fuck." He meets Troy's gaze. His features soften a bit, although the clenched fists at his side makes me feel like he wants to punch something. "I'm sorry, man. You didn't do anything wrong." He speaks as if the words physically pain him to say, as if he *knows* they are true, but can't get himself to believe them. "I think it's cool that you want to be upfront." That part came out a little more genuine at least.

"I'm sorry too. I don't know what happened with you guys, but I promise there's nothing between Maci and me. She's just a friend. I really like Lexy. Even if she isn't having it yet."

"Keep trying." Mack grabs his shoulder and squeezes it like they are lifelong friends sharing a moment and talking about me as if I'm not still standing right here.

"Lexy." Troy shifts his attention to me.

"Can you leave please? I need to work, and I can't handle this right now." Before he responds, I head to the back to get some ice for the night and forget about everything else.

As soon as the last customer leaves, Mack slides into my bar area to help me finish closing. And to talk, I'm guessing. Although I could do without that part.

"Tell me about Troy."

"I swear Maci isn't into him, and he's not into her. He's not who you have to worry about." We both know that's Dean.

He walks over to where I'm facing away from him, wiping the bar down, and spins me toward him. "I know, Lex. Sorry I freaked out. I don't want to know about him for that reason. I want to know about him because of you. I've never seen you interested in someone like this."

"I don't want to talk about it."

"Kind of feel like you do. Your choices are Maci, or me, so who is it going to be?"

I sigh in resignation. "This is stupid."

He grins. "That you have a crush on someone? It's cute."

"Shut up. I don't need you to be my girl friend here. You want me to talk or what?" I snap.

"Okay, sorry." He takes the rag from my hand. "Why are you so stressed about this?"

"I don't know. It's weird. I've been attracted to him since we met. I thought maybe it was just a sex thing."

"And it's not?"

"The sex is great." I add another thought quickly before he gets in his head about that. "But in like a... because we are connected kind of way. It's gross."

"By gross you mean great?" He laughs, wiping off the counter in front of us as I glare at him. His demeanor changes, seriousness washing over him. "I'm failing to see the problem here."

"Everyone in my life makes relationships seem so complicated."

"And your sample size is what? Two people?" He smirks.

"Three." I shoot him another glare.

"You can't count Maci and me as separate for this." He laughs. I know he's hurting right now, so the fact that he's giving me his attention on this without letting his feelings interfere means a lot. I don't want to have this conversation, but I should probably figure this out.

"Fine. But still."

"So you'd rather be alone forever than try a relationship?"

"I'm not alone. I have you."

"Yeah, and I love you, but I don't want to have sex with you. No offense."

"Thank God for that." I laugh.

"What are you going to do when I settle down along with everyone else our age?"

I hadn't thought that far into my future. I never do. I collapse into my arms on the bar top with a groan.

"Look, Lex. Relationships can be hard. Life is *definitely* hard. At least when you find the right person it makes the hard things easier."

Dragging myself off the bar, I rest my chin on my palm and look at him. "How can they make it easier if they complicate things?"

"What do you like about Troy?"

I'm not sure where he's going with this. "Umm. The sex is good."

He frowns. "There must be more than that if it led to that conversation the three of us had earlier."

"Fine. He's not intimidated by me, and his flirtiness matches mine. It's fun. He's easy to talk to in a way that doesn't make me hate talking about stuff. He's spontaneous. He's a great tipper. You know how I feel about that," I say with a pointed look.

"I do." He laughs. "It's similar for me. There's so much to love about Maci, she makes it easy. She's easy to talk to. She's fun. She loves me back. She's proud of me for chasing my dreams. We like a lot of the same things. We have great sex."

"I'm failing to see your point."

"What do you not like about Troy?" he asks as he pulls the trash bag out of the can and knots it before setting it on the ground.

"Umm..." I try to think of something.

"I think you're worrying about things that haven't happened and might never. You're acting like he's already done something to prove your view on relationships right when he's only done the opposite from the sound of it."

"But it might not always be like that."

"True. But it also might. All those things you like about him, don't they make your life more enjoyable?"

"Yeah…"

"The things I love about Maci are the reason I want a future with her. My days are better with her because of all the little things I listed and more–things I found out over time because I took a risk on starting a relationship with her. Unfortunately the only way to know if someone is worth it is if you give them a chance."

"You're making this sound easy, like it's just a decision."

"That's all anything is. One decision after another. You end up in a good place when you lean into things that make you happy. It's not much more complicated than that, Lex. You deserve to be happy, and it can exist for you." His supportive energy falters for a second before it comes back. "Not that I've spent a lot of time around him, but Troy seems pretty great. And Maci obviously agrees to some extent too. Both of us have pretty good taste in people if you ask me." He grins. "You should probably talk to him. He must be making an effort because he believes you make his life better, and you're not making it easy on him. You need to decide if he makes your life better too."

"Ugh, I know. I didn't mean to disregard his feelings. I'm just scared of my own."

"We've all been there. What matters is what you do now that you've realized it."

"I should probably tell him I'm sorry, huh?"

He puts a hand on each of my shoulders and waits until I meet his eyes. "Actions speak louder than words, Lex. Don't make the same mistakes I did."

"I won't." I make a promise I hope I can keep.

CHAPTER TWENTY-THREE
LEXY

As I pull into the space in front of my apartment, my phone vibrates against the cup holder. I pick it up hoping to see Troy's name even though I know I won't. The notification brings a smile to my face nonetheless.

Maci: *Hey.*

I haven't talked to her recently because she's been busy traveling. There was a little tension in our conversation last night because I got defensive on Mack's behalf. Hearing Maci talk about being in Costa Rica with her ex, Dean, and her indecision about choosing between them made me feel like I needed to choose sides. But Maci means just as much to me as Mack does, and her happiness matters more than wanting my best friends to be together if that isn't what's right for them.

Me: *Hey! Isn't it late there?*

Maci: *Yeah. I was reading. Then I couldn't sleep. I'm sorry I abandoned our convo last night and that I have been bad about checking in in general. I haven't been great at focusing on anything outside of my bubble, and I've been worried you'll hate me or feel like I'm betraying Mack by staying in Costa Rica a little longer. I swear it was never my intention to get into this situation.*

I've been feeling a little guilty about our conversation last night too.

Me: *I know it wasn't. I get it. I'm sorry I was a little snippy about Mack and everything too. Things aren't always black and white.*

Maci: *I wish they were.*

Me: *You and me both.*

Maci: *What's going on? What did you want to tell me?*

I almost told her when we talked last night, but when she cut off our conversation it made it easy for me to chicken out. I regret that now. I should have just texted her this morning.

Me: *I ran into Troy a few weeks ago.*

Maci: *That's random! How is he?*

Me: *Good...*

Maci: *Is that what you wanted to tell me? Haha*

Me: *No.*

Ugh. Why is this such a big deal? It's not like I have to marry the guy if I admit to having feelings for him.

Me: *How would you feel if I told you I'm kind of into him?*

Maci: *WHAT!!!!!*

Damn. I really didn't think she'd be mad. It's fine. Easy out for me then.

Maci: *Lex, this is great! I honestly thought you two would be good together.*

Why do I feel so relieved? I stick my key back in the ignition. I was so afraid to get to this point, but now that I have, I just want to tell him. I hate that he's upset with me.

Me: *I knew you'd say that. I tried to tell Troy.*

I send my text then drive the ten minutes to Troy's already feeling relieved even though I haven't talked to him yet. I got off work early tonight. He probably won't be home for another fifteen minutes, so I turn my car off and pull my phone out of the cupholder.

Maci: *He thought I wouldn't?*

Me: *You know that heartbreak he mentioned in his letter? Apparently his best friend hooked up with his girlfriend.*

Maci: *Oooh ouch. That sucks. But that's sweet he cares about being upfront. Tell him it's not a big deal. If you're happy, I'm happy.*

Me: *He really is so sweet.*

Maci: *Umm, since when do you say things like that?*

Me: *Ugh, since now, apparently. I hate it.*

Maci: *You two are both so much fun. I'm so excited about this!!!*

I send a string of eyeroll emojis as I scan the garage for Troy's car just in case.

Me: *So, tell me about Costa Rica. What have you been doing? You know, besides Dean. Haha*

Maci: *I learned how to surf! I love it so much. We go almost every day. Have you ever been?*

Me: *Not my thing haha I prefer to stay on dry land.*

Maci: *Well, I'm going to change your mind. I don't want to talk about me, though. I want to hear about everything Troy.*

I miss my best friend. I know Mack is here, but it's just not the same. As anxious as I am about bringing up Troy, Maci is the first friend I've had to talk about guys with in a way I don't feel comfortable sharing with Mack. And she's never judged me for my sexcapades or fear of commitment.

Me: *So, Mack and I went out for New Year's Eve for karaoke. Yes, I sang in public. I'm having major growth over here while you're gone.*

Maci: *I'm so proud of you! I expect a second performance when I come home so I can see it for myself.*

I spend the next few minutes filling Maci in on the past few weeks, and it feels so good to finally get all of my thoughts out of my head. She's nothing but encouraging and understanding about my overwhelming range of emotions. As she's texting goodnight, headlights light up the aisle where I'm parked. Locking my car and stepping out, I take the few steps to the elevator.

I lock my phone and slide it in my back pocket as Troy's car quietly pulls into the space a few down from the elevator, and he shifts into park. Pulling the keys from the ignition, he looks up, freezing when he sees me waiting against the cement wall. He looks down, and I imagine him running his fingers along the edge of his key fob as he debates if he wants to see me.

After what feels like minutes have passed, he steps out of his car and makes his way to me. "Lexy." He stands a foot back, rolling down the sleeves of his black dress shirt. I watch shamelessly until his forearms are covered. Damn, this man is sexy, and he could be mine if I would pull my head out of my ass.

"Hey." It comes out as a whisper. Fuck, this is pathetic and not who I want to be right now. In general. With Troy.

He takes a step closer to me but then redirects toward the elevator for his next step like he had to remind himself not to let me off the hook. I'm thankful for it. I can't think straight when he's too close, and I need to make this right.

The elevator dings as the doors open, and he steps inside, using his eyes instead of his words to ask, *Are you coming?* I slip inside the metal box, the tension feeling nothing like the first time we were in here. I invade his personal space, and whatever is in his cologne–pepper and vanilla maybe–overpowers me in the best way as the doors close. His voice cuts through our silence. "I'm happy to see you, but I'm also a little not happy with you."

"I know." I chew on my bottom lip, not knowing what to say.

"I know this is all new and hard for you, but I don't think I'm asking for too much," he states as he reaches to press the button for the fifth floor.

"You're not." I reply quickly as the elevator jerks. The floor feels heavy under my feet, my apology flooding out as we move. "I'm sorry. I could give you all my excuses, but you already know them, and none of them are justified."

He cuts me off by reaching his hand out for mine. "Your reasons are understandable, but I think mine are too, so if you are interested in me, I need you to meet me halfway here. I'm willing to go slow and help you work through your insecurities, but I need you to accept I have my own I'm working on too. Can you do that?"

I nod. "I talked to Maci."

"You did?" His wide eyes and tone of voice display his shock.

I nod. "Yeah. Between Mack and her we practically have our own cheering squad." I force a laugh.

"Thank you. I appreciate it. But also. You could have warned me that Mack was Maci's ex. I felt like a total dick."

"Yeaaaah, that one was totally my bad. I'm sorry for that too," I say, looking at my hands. His finger catches under my chin, forcing me to look at him instead. "I'm not trying to fight with you," I add shyly.

"I know." His voice is soft and understanding as he slides his hand against my jaw until his fingers are buried in my hair. There's something about the way this man touches me that captivates me. I don't think I could pull away from him even if I wanted to.

But I don't want to.

I'm done running from what this could be. I'm done running from the man standing in front of me who somehow knows me better than I know myself.

Troy's eyes search mine, the crease between his brow deepening like he's trying to solve my fucked up puzzle. His thumb grazes over my cheek, and my breath catches in my throat.

The corner of his mouth twitches at the effect he has on me, and then his mouth is on mine.

The kiss is enough to pull a sound from my throat.

And then it turns into a whole lot more.

CHAPTER TWENTY-FOUR
TROY

"Tell me something," Lexy says, her breath warm on my chest where she lays.

I twist a blonde curl around my finger. "Like what?"

"I don't know. Something you haven't told me yet. Did you like being in a fraternity?"

"Loved it. It's like having a second family who has your back no matter what, and it lasts forever. That's how Nolan and I became friends. We got to talking at a bar one night and realized we were brothers. Did you have anything like that?"

"No. I played softball in high school. So, in theory, I could have. But the girls were all catty. It felt more like I was babysitting to keep them focused instead of forming a bond." She seems sad about the missed opportunity.

I'm not sure what pulls me to ask, but I do. "Do you want a family? Kids, I mean?"

She draws out her *Ummm* like she's using it to stall. "I don't know. No? I don't think. I don't know the first thing about being a mom. I wouldn't want to screw up a human."

"I think you turned out pretty great for being 'screwed up.'"

"Thanks," she whispers. "What about you?"

"For a while, I thought the same. But things are different now, especially since Mike and Melissa took me in."

"Yeah. Okay, tell me something else." I sense she needs a lighter subject when she shifts gears. "Tell me about your first kiss."

An amused chuckle escapes me. "Cooper's cousin. She came to stay with us one summer and told me I needed to know how to kiss before I got to high school."

"I bet you were a pro by the time school started, huh?" I can feel her smile against me.

"It didn't really matter. I'm not big on kissing." I pause. "Well, I wasn't," I amend.

She lifts her head just enough to catch my gaze as I look down at her. "You kiss me all the time," she states, resting her head back in its place on my chest.

My conversation with Lauren about the matter flashes through my mind. "You're different." I kiss the top of her head and feel her smile against my skin again.

"What's the worst date you've ever been on?" She shoots another question at me.

I immediately know my answer. "Easy. The first week I moved here I signed up for online dating to try and meet some people and find good places to go around here. I was on like... my fourth date of the week. She took me to a sex club."

Lexy sits, turning toward me in shock. "On a first date? She did not!"

"She sure did. I talked myself into giving it a try—I'm down to try *almost* anything once. When we got there, they gave us this thirty minute orientation. At the end, we had to choose colored wristbands to wear based on what body parts were acceptable to have foreign objects in." Lexy is so amused she's now folded over my chest choking on her laughter.

"Please tell me you stayed," she barely gets out.

Her giggling makes me smile despite the memory being so cringy. "I was going to, but the second wristband they asked about was for if we were okay having additional people join our party. The girl I was with reached for the band like *Sign me the fuck up*, and I said *Get me the fuck out of here*."

Lexy composed herself enough to reposition, facing me with her knees bent under her, leaned against my hip. Her finger softly traces my abs. "Not down for the threesome thing?"

"I don't share." I run my hand up her thigh, my thumb smoothing over the lace at her hip. "What about you?"

She rolls her eyes, and I'm not sure if it's at my question or her answer. "Almost. At one of the rich people parties where I did some girl's makeup. I was packing up all my things, and the girl who hired me came into the room. She started kissing me in the same moment her boyfriend entered the room and tried to join. It took me a few seconds to realize what was happening, but then I left. That was actually the last time I ever did makeup. The next morning, on my 18th birthday, I went to the Pub and got hired on the spot."

"Not a fan of sharing, either?" I ask.

"If you asked me then, I'd say that wasn't the problem. Sex has always been unemotional for me, so jealousy wouldn't have been a factor."

"And if I asked you now?"

She runs her hand across my stomach, gripping my hip and digging her fingers into my skin. "I'd say, 'Not a chance in hell.'"

"Oh yeah?" I say with a laugh, sitting in the process and flipping her on her back.

Her smile transforms into seduction as she says, "Yeah," and I don't use my mouth for talking after that.

CHAPTER TWENTY-FIVE
TROY

Lexy: *This motherfucker.*
  Me: *What did he do now?*
  Lexy: *I picked my phone up to let you know I'd be a little late, and this POS came out of nowhere, ripped it out of my hand and slammed it on the bar. My case's last leg is officially broken.*
  Me: *I can't stand that guy.*
  Lexy: *You and me both.*
  Lexy: *Tonight is crazy. I'll still be a while.*
  Me: *Okay, I'll see you when you're done.*

By the time I clock out, Lexy still hasn't responded. We're supposed to meet at her place when she gets off work, but I can't wait. The past few weeks since she talked to Maci and leaned into our not official relationship have been great, and I'm always anxious to see her. I was hoping she'd be starting her closing work by the time I showed up, but even with only fifteen minutes until last call, she's still slammed. You wouldn't know she's busy by the calm she brings to her chaos, but the fact that she hasn't noticed I walked in tells me otherwise. The past few times I've been here it's like she could sense me, immediately looking up when I walk through the door.

Her blonde ponytail swings over her shoulder as she reaches for Blue Curacao behind the register. I don't know why she doesn't keep that in the well since she uses it for her go-to drink when someone doesn't know what to order. Her system obviously works for her though, so who am I to judge? I'm just here to watch her work and love every second of it. Her sex appeal is off the charts with her jean shorts a little extra shredded in the front and a black Jack Daniel's shirt cut across the top to hang off one shoulder, revealing a glimpse of her bra strap. I feel lucky as hell knowing I get to rip that off her later.

"LEXY! HEY!" Fuck, I know that voice. Todd, the douchebag, screams to get her attention on the opposite side of the bar. I was hoping he'd be gone by now.

"What do you want?" I hear her snap, without taking her eyes off the drinks she's making.

"You mean besides you?"

My fist clenches at my side. I haven't felt this defensive in a long time, not that I need to be concerned. Lexy doesn't seem any more bothered by him than usual, but I really don't like this guy.

"It's last call, Todd. Tell me what you need, or get lost."

"Three shots of Malibu."

I catch her smirk from here even though it's dark. She thinks it's hilarious he won't drink anything with a bite. She looks up to make sure there are actually three people waiting on shots, knowing Todd is far too drunk to need that many. At least that's my assumption because I can tell how wasted he is from here.

She lines up three shot glasses before tipping the Malibu and running the stream of alcohol above them. Pushing them forward, Todd and two of his equally douchey looking friends each take a tiny glass before holding them up. "To rattlesnakes and condoms, two things I don't fuck with!" They cheers.

I choke back a laugh. I'm surprised I haven't heard that one before. Too bad it didn't come from someone else.

All three guys tip their shots back then slam them down on the bar. "Another!" Todd yells into the air even though he's talking to Lexy.

She turns around, her hand moving to the horizontal hatch within the bartop that can be lifted to let her out of the enclosed space.

"No."

"Come on, Lexy. Take one with me."

She ignores him, lifting the hatch enough to slide through before setting it back down again. She must need something from the back.

Todd steps in front of her, preventing her from getting past him. "Sugar, I promise I'll give you a tip this time. More than just the tip actually." He grabs her wrist. I shift off my seat but freeze as Lexy pulls away, releasing herself from his grip.

"Don't fucking touch me," Lexy growls. I can't see her face, but from here I can tell my girl can handle herself.

"Don't be such a bitch," Todd barks back. With his words, his hands are firm on her waist, yanking her to him. You've got to be fucking kidding me.

As I leap from my bar stool, I all but black out, barely catching the sight of his hands attempting to force their way under her shirt as he holds her to him. In the next moment, I'm on their side of the bar, and my hands are on him, my fist flying into his face with a crunch as I punch his nose. I'm only conscious of what I'm doing enough to make sure I don't hit Lexy in the process. I go to take another swing, but he's already on the ground, blood streaming through his fingers covering his face as he cries out in pain.

"What the fuck, man," he growls.

"She said not to touch her." I wait until he locks into my gaze before taking the step into Lexy, who stands there totally stunned.

"Hey." I close the distance between us, the palm of my hand resting against the side of her face, gently pulling her gaze from Todd on the floor, to me. "You okay?" I ask as soon as her eyes find mine.

Her arms are between us, and I feel her grab a fistful of my shirt as she leans into me and nods. She takes a deep breath. When she pulls back, a different emotion has washed over her. Anger, maybe. Justified. Wait, why does it seem directed at me?

"Get out of here before I get in trouble," she whisper-yells at me with a glare, giving me a soft shove before turning back to the bar.

"I'm not leaving you after that. I'll be right here." I take a seat on the empty bar stool, but she's already walking away, ignoring me. I watch as she takes off on autopilot, finishing last call and cashing out people's tabs.

I don't even know what the fuck happened to Todd, but by the time I turn around to check, he's gone. Thank fuck. I might have gone back for seconds if he was still within reach. I've never followed through on the primal need to punch someone in the face. Shit, my hand hurts. I shake it out, and Lexy catches it out of the corner of her eye. It looks like she's about to say something, but her attention is drawn to somewhere behind me when she hears her name.

"Fuck," she mutters, throwing the rag in her hand aggressively onto the bartop. She opens the folding hatch in the counter, letting it slam against the bar next to me. I watch her walk through a black door I didn't notice until now. It blends in seamlessly with the wall.

Five minutes later she returns, storming back into the bar with fire in her eyes–not the kind I like to see. She scoops some ice into a clean rag and twists the ends together, tying it closed with the elastic she tugs from her hair. She tosses the homemade ice pack from five feet away, and it lands perfectly in front of me, sliding across the bartop. I catch it before it falls into my lap.

"I need you to leave." There is restraint in her voice, like she wants to lash out but is holding back.

"What? Why?"

"Just go. Home. Or whatever. I don't know, but you need to leave. If you don't, security will escort you out."

What the fuck. I want to argue and figure out what the hell is happening, but it won't do any good right now. With Lexy's back turned to me as she does her closing work, I walk out the door, taking my ice pack with me. Fuck, that hurt.

LEXY

What a fucking night. I knew Todd crossing the line was bound to happen sooner or later, but I was too busy to see it coming tonight. My mind was so many other places it took me longer than it took Troy to punch him for me to understand what was happening. I didn't even realize Troy was there, which is weird because I usually notice him right away. Then he just had to go and punch Todd, like I can't handle myself, and ruin everything.

I dig my car key out of my front pocket and push the door open for the last time, leading me into the cold night air. The street lights glow in the alley where my car is parked and draw my attention to Troy leaning against the hood. "I thought I told you to go home," I snap when I'm close enough he can hear me.

"Yeah, you did, but I'm not going anywhere until you tell me what the hell that was about." He's angrier than I expected him to be, but that's his fault.

"You're not my boyfriend, Troy. It's not your job to protect me." If there were apartments nearby, the volume of my voice would definitely wake someone.

"So, I was just supposed to watch him put his hands on you?" Troy yells back, pushing off the hood of the car, bringing him closer to me.

I want to reach for him.

I almost say *no,* but the words that come out of my mouth have their own agenda. "Yeah, that's exactly what you were supposed to do." I try to move past him, but he holds his arm out to block my path. He drops it when I turn to face him, blood rushing to my face with my anger. "I got reamed for letting my 'boyfriend' come in here and cause a scene." I use air quotes so there's no misunderstanding. "Then I got fired. Did you even think about how this was going to affect me?"

"Excuse me? I caused a scene?" His hands ball into tight fists at his sides before he releases them, bringing his fingers to the bridge of his nose. He sighs out a rough breath. "How is this my fault?"

"Todd was drunk, and he doesn't know better. You do."

"Wait." His energy shifts as he reaches for my waist. "Did you just say you got fired?"

"Don't touch me." I'll cave the second he does.

He's hurt by the same words I also used with Todd, but he holds his hands up in surrender and takes a step back, no longer in the stream of light from the street lamp. "Seriously, Lexy. Did that dickbag fire you?"

"I just told you," I huff.

His anger redirects. "What the fuck is that bullshit? You're easily his best bartender."

"It doesn't fucking matter. Everyone is replaceable."

He stares at me, like he knows I'm not just talking about work. "You're not replaceable, Lexy. Let me talk to him. Please. I'll fix it."

"You can't fix this, Troy. I had a good thing going. I needed this job. This is the one area of my life I had control over, and you took it away from me."

"Fuck, Lexy, I'm sorry. I didn't mean to compromise your job. I wasn't thinking clearly, but I stand by my decision to defend you, and I won't apologize for that."

"You didn't even think about the consequences of your actions, did you?"

The mixed energy around him battles for dominance–half of it refusing to believe his actions were wrong and the other half panicked that he fucked this up. "No. I didn't. I'm having trouble compartmentalizing with you. You already mean too much to me."

"I hate this. I don't want to do it," I say, my frustration evident.

"Do what, exactly?" He waits for my response patiently, giving me time to collect myself, the way he always does, like he knows that's what I need.

"You don't fucking know me," I mumble under my breath.

"What?"

Irritated, I stare back without repeating myself.

"We'll find you another job. Hell, I can probably get you a job with me."

I scoff. "Yeah, like that's not the last fucking thing I want."

"This isn't just about the job, is it?"

Why does he just know things I'm not saying? I groan. "It's everything, Troy. You act like you're my boyfriend. My boss–ex boss–thinks you're my boyfriend. You're not my boyfriend, and this isn't your problem."

"Okay, okay. I'm sorry. I was mad and feeling a little protective of you. I know we aren't there yet."

"That doesn't even matter. What matters is I lost my job tonight because of you. You promised dating wouldn't negatively affect other parts of my life."

"You're still scared." He doesn't ask me.

"You think?" I roll my eyes. "I've been good at taking care of myself my entire life until you got here. Now it feels like I don't know what I'm doing. It's too overwhelming, and I don't want it."

"Look, Lexy." He steps toward me, his hands resting at the nape of my neck on either side before continuing. I pull back, but not enough for him to break his hold. "This relationship shit is hard for me too. I'm sorry I acted on impulse. My fight or flight is not always in check, but I didn't mean to hurt you."

"But you did. It doesn't even matter. I'm always going to get let down eventually, so what's the point?" I defend my anger even though it's coming from so many angles my arguments feel chaotic.

"I know you feel that way because it's shaped your life. You know I get it. I have a general anxiety around it some days still. I don't want to take that out on you, though. It's not the aftermath of what you did, and you shouldn't be punished for it. I shouldn't be either."

"Yeah, well." My thought stops there. I don't know what the fuck I think.

He takes a breath.

I look to the ground, focusing between us on the line that splits between the street light glow and the shadows. "I think we need to take some time apart."

"Don't do this." He's still gripping my neck, and his thumb forces my chin up until I'm looking at him again.

"What?" I feign ignorance, pulling away from his touch and refusing to admit to my actions. I know I'm driving him insane. I'm driving myself insane. Yet, I refuse to back down.

"Don't play dumb either. You're projecting feelings about your mom's choices onto me. I'm not her." He sighs when he catches my glare at his accusation.

I consider his words. They make too much sense and none at all. "I'm really mad at you."

"You're entitled to however you feel, but so am I. I know I took it too far with Todd tonight, but if you can't forgive me for caring about you, that's something you need to take into consideration when you decide what's next for us. I'm not a bad guy, Lexy. It took me a long time to believe that. Please don't make me feel like I am."

I stare back, unsure how to respond.

He resigns, and my traitorous heart sinks. "Maybe you're right. Maybe you need to take a few days and think about whether you're willing to trust me despite your anxiety about it. Every time we make progress, something knocks us backward. I want to be patient. I want to be with you, but you have to want this."

Nodding, I fidget with my key in my hand. "Bye, Troy," I whisper before meeting his gaze for a second then turning away to get in my car.

CHAPTER TWENTY-SIX
LEXY

The past few days have been torture–emotionally and physically. I know if I go back to Troy, I have to commit completely. I still haven't found a job–I haven't even looked. I know I can always fall back on the Pub, my first job, because the manager has asked me to come back more than once. I can afford to take a few weeks off, and I thought it would give me time to think about things, but all I've been doing is stressing out–and missing Troy.

I need stress relief.

The early morning sun streams through my window as I reach over from where I'm lying on my bed and pull on my nightstand drawer handle. I haven't opened this in a few weeks. The only thing I keep in here is an extra phone charger and my vibrator. Oh, and the few notes Troy has left me. Without looking, I feel around in the drawer for my hot pink toy. Instead, my hand lands on something I can't place. I sit.

Noticing the new note first, I pick it up. Written in Troy's slanted, barely legible handwriting on a piece of receipt paper it says, *Not a Valentine's Day gift.*

What day is it? I tap my phone screen to reveal today's date. Oh. I didn't even think about the holiday since I don't currently have a job. The upside is I don't have to work Valentine's Day which is a terrible day as a bartender. At the Pub, it was always cute couples that felt like they were using a Hallmark holiday as their reason to treat each other to a special night of each other's company. At Shot in the Dark, the day is filled with a combination of single sad people and predatory men trying to pick up entire Galentines' Day groups–or whatever the fuck they call themselves.

I've never actually dated anyone, let alone over a holiday. Was I supposed to do something? How did this even get here? Troy hasn't been over in almost a week.

I catch myself smiling as I add the note to my collection of receipts in the back of my drawer. I'm the least sentimental person I know, so I have no idea why I've kept these.

Under where the note was is a new phone case. I pull it out. It's red, of course, and when I flip it over, I see it has a metal loop on the back, the kind you slide your finger into so it's easier to hold your phone. It's also a bottle opener. Damn, that's kind of cool. I set it on my nightstand and open my text thread with Troy. The most recent text is from him four nights ago letting me know he was on his way to see me at work.

Me: *I found your gift.*

Troy: *Just now?*

Is he shocked it took me this long to resort to my vibrator?

Troy: *I thought you would have opened that drawer sooner. Unless...*

Me: *Unless what?*

Troy: *Nothing. Nevermind.*

Me: *Wait, did you think I was hooking up with other people this week?*

My heart sinks at the thought. I don't blame him for it, though. It'd be pretty on brand for me. I watch the typing bubbles for what feels like forever.

Troy: *I'm glad you found your case. I got it last week. Hopefully you don't already have a new one.*

Me: *I don't. Thank you. I couldn't have picked a better one myself. I love it.*

Me: *I didn't hook up with anyone else either.*

Troy: *Okay.*

I can feel his cold shoulder through the phone. The anxiety that has made itself right at home in my body bubbles to the surface. Knowing I need to do *something*, I log into my Soul Cycle account and sign up for the next available class.

TROY

Dropping the free weight from higher than I should, it hits the ground hard, rolling on its edge once before compressing into the mat. I give up on my workout. With my lack of *give a fuck*, it's wasted effort anyway. I haven't gotten much sleep the past four days. I can't help but wonder if Lexy hasn't been sleeping well either, considering her text came through at 7:30 this morning–far earlier than either of us ever wake.

I pick up the weight and place it back on the rack, so I'm not as big of a jackass as I currently feel like I am.

Confliction is what has been keeping me up at night. I'd punch Todd again in a heartbeat for putting his hands on the girl I. *No*. I shake my head, clearing the thought that I could possibly love Lexy already. I know her well enough to know I should have refrained from stepping in, regardless of how I felt about it.

I do what Cooper's parents, Melissa and Mike, have taught me about respect and what it takes to be in a healthy relationship, but I keep falling fucking short–first with Emily, now with Lexy. This time I really thought it was going to work, though. Lexy and I connect on a level I didn't realize was possible, and not just physically.

It was hard not to cave when she texted this morning. It's been a while since I've gone three days without seeing her, and I've hated it. I still want this to work, but I can't do it alone. I need her to want this too. A shot of relief rushed through me when she confirmed she hasn't slept with anyone else, but it wasn't enough to convince me she's willing to commit to us and not push back on any progress we make.

I slip my hoodie over my head, reaching for my phone and keys from the pocket of my gym shorts as I head for the door.

Sliding the key in the ignition, I twist it part way to only turn on the interior features and scroll through my contacts. My phone connects to the bluetooth as I hit *call,* and it rings on the other end. There's a soft click when she picks up. "Hello, Troy?" Her soothing voice comes through my car speakers.

"Hi, Mom."

"Hey, honey. Is everything okay?" Cooper's mom asks, knowing I never call anyone.

"Yeah... No." I admit, knowing she'll see right through me and there's no use in toning down my mood. She might not be my biological mom, but the way she knows me, she might as well be. "I met someone."

"You did?" Excitement fills her voice like she's already forgotten I've said things aren't okay. The running water in the background turns off like she's putting a pause on doing the dishes. "Like girlfriend kind of met someone?"

"Yeah. Well, that's why I'm calling." I take a breath. "Mom, I swear I tried to do right by her–Lexy. I've been trying to be better with her than I was with Emily, but it feels like it's pointless."

"Oh, sweetie." There's a whoosh of the sliding door opening, and I picture Mom sitting in the patio chair while she gives me whatever pep talk is coming. "First, I want to remind you that what happened with Emily was not your fault. You gave that girl everything you possibly could have at your age, and she didn't deserve you. It breaks my heart you're still blaming yourself for that."

I sigh, resting my hand on the steering wheel as I stay parked. "I thought I was over it, but Lexy pulling away has all those feelings coming back."

"What happened?" The chirping birds in the background send a ping of homesickness straight through me. A car at the end of the row I'm parked in honks, reminding me of the chaos of California and heightening the feeling.

I sigh. "I don't know. It was hard to win her over in the first place, but something just kept telling me I had to get to know her." I pause, not knowing what to say from here.

"And when you got to know her?"

"She's so great. You'd love her. She's sassy. She's such a badass bartender. And beautiful. We have so much in common–not just shallow shit like the same favorite bands, but also in ways I never want to relate to anyone–like childhood trauma and insecurities and all that."

"But..." she says softly, although I have a feeling she already knows.

"But she's letting her past hold her back from being happy, and I don't know what to do if she won't let me in." Fuck, I hate how pathetic I sound, but I don't know what else to do.

"Did I ever tell you the story of how Mike and I met?"

"Remind me." I humor her, reclining my seat and settling in for the story I've heard more times than I can count.

"It was the summer before our first year of college. We were both at the first Oregon Jamboree in 1992 with our friends and met standing next to each other waiting for Wynonna Judd to take the stage."

Mike and Melissa took us camping for the three day country concert every summer until we graduated, and each time they drank a little too much wine and retold their love story like we hadn't heard it the year before.

"We hit it off so well, we ended up ditching our friends," she continues. "But that was back in the day. We couldn't exactly exchange phone numbers, and he didn't have a landline in his dorm at U of O."

I chuckle at the flashback, trying to envision what it must have been like living in a world without cell phones. "And you went to Oregon State," I add.

"I sure did." Her smile is evident in her voice.

"So, what happened?" I indulge her with feigned curiosity.

"We decided to write it off as a good time and went our separate ways."

I keep quiet, waiting for the rest.

She chuckles on the other end of the line. "I lasted a day before I decided I *had* to see him again. I convinced my friends to road trip to Eugene every weekend to party, hoping I'd run into him. Then, Thanksgiving weekend I stayed in town for the Civil War rival game, praying he'd miraculously come to me."

"No fucking way."

"Way," she says as if she can still hardly believe it herself. "I ran into him in the soft pretzel line."

"Thank God for that." I don't even want to imagine the shit show my life could have turned out to be if Melissa and Mike had never found their way back to each other. "What does that have to do with Lexy, though?"

"Look, sweetie. Sometimes life blesses you with someone that fits you so perfectly you can hardly wrap your mind around how they exist. But that doesn't mean everything between you will be perfect. That's not possible–with anyone.

"I guess what I want to know is... say you think you found that person... how do you know if the not perfect shit is worth it?"

"Are you willing to do the work it'll take to see?"

"Yeah. I am. But she has to want to work too. I can't make her."

"Does she not want to?"

"I want to believe she does, but I don't know." My mind flashes back to when she left the other night. As well as I can usually read her, I have no idea how easy it was for her to walk away.

"There's a common expression about how successful relationships should be 100% on each side all the time. I've never believed that. Do you both have to be committed to working through the lows as much as celebrating the highs? Of course. It won't work otherwise. But there's also a difference between not being willing to work through it and needing help maneuvering through the struggle. Someone once told me the best thing I could do in any relationship is to meet people where they are based on *their* personal experience and the lessons they've learned. That doesn't always align with age or circumstances. There are so many factors. That's what makes a good team, Troy. You and Lexy might have a lot of your pasts in common which can be helpful on a level of understanding each other. But the differences in how you experienced those similar pasts are what brings different perspectives to the table, and that can be just as important. Sometimes it might be you that needs to step up and guide her down the path. At some point, she'll be able to do the same for you."

I'm hit with deja vu. I vaguely recall a similar pep talk directed at Cooper. It didn't hit the way it does now. If Lexy can commit to us in general, I can help her get through her insecurities. I had Cooper and our parents to help me work through my family shit. Hell, all my football friends, fraternity brothers and even Lauren played roles in pulling me from my toxic spirals with Emily too. Lexy hardly has that kind of team behind her. As long as she comes back, I know we can make this work.

I adjust my seat back upright and start my car all the way. "Thanks, Mom. I'll see you next week."

"Okay, sweetie. Can't wait. I love you."

"I love you too." I say the words easily, wondering if I'll ever get the chance to say them to the only other girl I imagine having a significant impact on my life.

LEXY

"Fuck," I mutter under my breath as my phone falls in what feels like slow motion to the concrete outside Soul Cycle as I reach for the door. *Please do not be broken.* I send out a silent prayer with a curse to myself for being so careless with my caseless phone. My stubborn ass refused to put my new case on this morning so I wouldn't be reminded of Troy during my ride–as if that would help.

Thank God my phone seems unharmed as I slide it in the pocket of my leggings before a second attempt at entering the building. Maybe I'd be less of a mess if I'd gotten any sleep at all last night. I've never had an issue sleeping until now. A groan leaves me as my head collapses on my arms on the receptionist's counter. Todd. Troy. My job. Everything is a mess.

"Are you alright, Lexy? You're here much later than normal." Hannah's voice is so soft it's barely loud enough to get my attention, but I lift my head to look at her through the fake eyelashes I never took off last night.

I groan again in response, feeling hungover even though I haven't had any alcohol.

"Jared is here today," Hannah adds in a hopeful tone.

"At least there's that. Thanks, Hannah," I force a smile as I take a towel from her and drag myself into the cycle room.

I find a bike in the back corner and adjust it before swinging a leg over the seat. I don't even bother taking my sweater off. I can't imagine I have enough energy to work up a sweat right now. *Why am I even here?* Jared runs through the side entrance and onto the stage, exploding with energy I typically try to absorb. Today, I want none of it. Every part of me feels like shit, and I have no idea what could possibly make me feel better.

"Who is ready to CLIMB today?!" Jared yells through his mic.

Not me. Considering my starting point is deep in a hole right now, it sounds like far too much work. I turn my dial all the way to the left, so there's no resistance. My feet spin out of control in jagged strokes without any pressure pushing back. I turn the resistance up just enough to maintain control.

"This course is going to be tough today, but you got this. First hill starts right out of the gate. Turn two full turns to the right and find your momentum. Chase the burn."

I leave my dial where it is and keep cruising with minimal effort.

His eyes scan the room then stop on me. "Lexy, what the hell are you doing?"

I mean-mug him while continuing my casual pedal strokes.

"Keep climbing this hill, everyone. Three minutes until the end of the song before recovery." He pulls his head-set mic off as he hops off his bike and heads toward me in the back row.

"What's happening right now?" He grips his fingers around my handlebars. "Where is Lexy?" he asks when I meet his gaze.

"I don't know."

"Why aren't you pushing through your ride like you usually do?"

"It's too hard," I mumble.

"What is? Because I know it sure as hell isn't this hill you've climbed a hundred times."

"Everything. I have no control over anything right now." As the words leave my mouth, my foot flies off the pedal where I never clicked my shoe in place. The pedal spins in a circle scraping against my shin as it passes by and breaks through the skin. Fuck.

Jared only glances down at my stopped bike for a moment before meeting my gaze again. "The things you're wanting control over... *do you* have control over them, but you're telling yourself you don't?"

I stare back blankly, not wanting to dig deep enough to find an answer I won't like.

He continues. "What would give you the confidence to feel like you can handle the things in your life that feel out of control?"

Troy. The answer pops into my head instantly, and my heart flutters as my anxiety spikes at the thought of him. I think partly I feel out of control because I don't have a vision for my life. I've always only focused on each day as it comes. I always have a back up plan, but it's for short term survival. Thinking beyond that has never seemed realistic or necessary.

The other night, though, when I was yelling at Troy for getting me fired, I also had this weird feeling that I wasn't actually worried at all. I know I can easily get another bartending job, but I think it was more than that. I think for some reason I trust Troy to ground me and to help me find my way if I get lost. He keeps showing up. No matter how many times I push him away or how often I frustrate him, he doesn't abandon me. I don't know if it's because he just understands or if he specifically understands me, but it feels like the latter–in a way I've never experienced before. Hell, I didn't even try to push my mom away, and she still left. Yet here Troy is, coming back like a yo-yo on a string every damn time, and I never stopped to consider the significance of what that tells me about him.

Even though Troy and I have never talked about our futures and what we want them to look like, for the first time I *want* to look past today, tomorrow or next week–with him, *because* of him.

"Seems like you know the answer?" Jared questions without pushing for me to say it aloud.

I nod.

"Are you ready to climb this hill now?"

I nod again. I'm tempted to go see Troy now–to apologize, to hope he hasn't given up on me yet–but he's probably getting ready for work. I'll go after class.

"Alright. Let's fucking go." With that he pushes off the handlebars of my bike and spins on his heel, heading back to the stage.

I clip my shoes into the pedals and increase the resistance.

I need to fix this. I want to fix this. I'm *ready* to fix this.

CHAPTER TWENTY-SEVEN
LEXY

There is absolutely no game plan in my head as I walk into 3rd Base. I'm not positive Troy is working tonight, but I slide into a seat at the bar anyway, not wanting to wait any longer to talk to him.

"Hey, Lexy?"

I glance up to see a beautiful strawberry-blonde, in a black bodycon dress, her spunky ponytail tied up with a red ribbon. Thank God I'm not the jealous type. Not like it'll matter if I can't get Troy to believe I'm sorry and that I can actually commit. "Hey, Lauren."

She smiles at my recognition of her. "Looking for Troy?"

"Yeaaah."

"I saw him in the back. I think there's a few minutes until his shift starts. Is everything okay?"

"Yeah, why?"

"You look kind of down for someone who has a boyfriend on Valentine's Day."

My heart stutters at the title, creating a panic that almost makes me leave. I've wondered how close she and Troy are outside of their arrangement. He must not tell her everything. I like that he hasn't shared my mess. She senses my hesitation, although she can't tell it has nothing to do with her. "It's okay, you don't have to talk to me. I get it. But for the record, I'm really happy for him. I'm glad he found you." I immediately like her vibe. Am I saying vibe now? Maci and Troy are rubbing off on me.

"Thanks... actually..."

She leans forward onto the white bar top separating us, propped up by her elbows. "Talk to me," she demands in her peppy but somehow encouraging tone, as if we are best friends sharing secrets.

"I kind of messed up."

"Well, I doubt it's unfixable, or I would have heard about it. What's going on?" She turns around to the tap behind her and pours a Mango Cart. When she sets it in front of me, I give her a look. She laughs. "Trust me, you have nothing to worry about considering how many Lexy fun facts I've been told already."

"I will give it to him, he pays attention better than any guy I've ever met. It's unfair really. I feel like I don't know anywhere close to what he knows about me."

"Well, if you're going to like someone, Troy is a good option. He's a great guy. I mean that platonically, of course." She looks guilty, like she might have upset me.

"I'm not worried." I chuckle. "Those aren't the trust issues I have."

"What is it then?"

"I'm not good at letting someone else take care of me. It's hard to rely on someone, ya know?"

"Because they might let you down?"

I nod as I take a sip of my beer. "He just wants a chance to prove he won't, and I couldn't even give him that."

"You know about Emily?"

I nod again, rubbing the condensation off my glass with my thumb as I wait for her to continue.

"Everyone has something they are insecure about. If you think about it, you both have the same insecurity."

"How do you figure?"

"He'll tell you his concerns are about being honest so everyone can be on the same page, but it's really just his attempt to avoid a betrayal of commitment. He's worried something will get in the way. Which is basically what you're saying."

"Huh. Yeah, I guess it is. Tell me how to make it up to him. You seem to know what you're talking about."

"I think you're probably giving me too much credit." She laughs. "Not to remind you, but I literally committed to a no-commitment relationship for the past three months. But in all seriousness, don't overthink it. Come up with something to show him you want to commit outside of the bedroom and that you are interested in creating memories with him. That's all a relationship is. Make it fun and spontaneous. He's into that."

"Thanks, Lauren."

"I got your back. Let me know if you need anything else." Smiling brightly, she gives me a wink before turning on her heel and walking to the other end of the bar.

As she does, Troy pushes through the swinging door leading into the room, stopping in front of the terminal to clock in. I watch Lauren say something to him, and he immediately glances up. We lock eyes, but I can't read him. I can't tell if it's okay that I'm here.

He makes his way over to me with an apprehension that tells me he's not confident about the reason I showed up.

"Hey, Lexy," he says cautiously as he looks at the sleeves of his black dress shirt, rolling them a few times each.

"Hey."

"What are you doing here?"

"Umm." Unwanted nerves fill my voice. "I wanted to see you."

"Oh yeah?" He meets my gaze then glances to my phone where I'm flipping the metal ring on the back of my new case open and closed. I catch a twinge of a smile before it disappears.

"Yeah. I thought about everything you said." I open my mouth to say more, but clamp it shut, unsure of where to go from here.

"Okay," he says, to fill the silence I've left.

"You punched him," I blurt. This is why I should have come up with a plan.

"I know?" Troy says–drawing out the words–when he realizes I'm not going to add to my thought.

Does he really not see the issue? I decide to make this part of the plan. "You're not a teenager, Troy, and I can handle myself."

He sighs. I'll happily accept that reaction over the anger I expected. "The point of being in a relationship is having someone in your corner so you don't have to fight alone, Lexy."

My heart races at the thought of a power shift like that. "I've never had that. It's weird. It's hard to give up that control."

"Are you here to end things between us or did you get off track with your point?" He leans on the bar top with his elbow, his fingers finding the bridge of his nose like they do when he's stressed. Irritation emanates off him as he locks eyes with me waiting for my answer.

"Either way, I still don't think you need to be punching people."

"Okay, no punching. Unless it's necessary," he says, folding his arms on the counter and leaning forward, his muscles straining against the fabric of his shirt.

"Okay." I accept the compromise even though I'm sure we have different definitions of *necessary*. "Can I be honest about something?" I ask before getting distracted by the forearms in front of me.

"Always." His face softens at my mention of his favorite quality.

I focus back on his face. "The titles stress me out... are they non-negotiable right now?"

His narrowed eyed stare burns through me. "You're acting like I broke up with you."

"No, I know. I'm sorry." The apology feels weird. I'm not used to having someone I care about stick around. "I know this is my fault."

"But to answer your question... no. Exclusivity, yes. But I don't need a title. I just need to feel like I'm not walking on eggshells with you. I can't be constantly afraid of freaking you out because I care about you."

"I can help with that," I say more confidently than anything else in this conversation. "No more freaking out. And I won't even let my vibrator touch me, so you don't have to worry about the exclusive thing." I hold my eyes to his so he knows I'm serious.

"Okay." The way he draws out the word makes me think he's still hesitant.

"I know words aren't enough, Troy. Just let me figure out how to prove them, okay?" I reach for him and he allows it, taking my hand in his. I can't help my sigh of relief. "I missed you," I say. The admission lifts a weight from my chest.

"I missed you more." He swipes his thumb softly across the back of my hand before releasing me. "Stay for a bit? Are you hungry?"

The bar is chaotic with the holiday crowd, but I sit at the corner trying to come up with a way to show Troy I want this next step. I'm not good at sentimental gestures, so I'm wracking my brain for something fun. By that I mean I'm googling date ideas–something I never thought I'd be doing–but adding extra search words like "unique" and "spontaneous." It's not until I add the key words "possibly illegal" that I come across a blog that gives me exactly what I'm looking for. This is perfect.

I wait until Troy catches my gaze from the other side of the bar. As soon as he does, he walks over to me. "Any chance you have a day off this weekend?"

"I usually have Tuesdays and Wednesdays off, but I can probably make something happen. What are you thinking?"

"Lauren!" She's pouring a beer from the tap directly in front of me.

"What's up?"

"Remember like an hour ago when you told me to ask if I need anything else?"

She laughs. "Am I going to regret that already?"

"Can you cover one of Troy's shifts this weekend, if you don't work? He'll owe you."

"Hey!" Troy interjects, but he doesn't seem bothered.

"Sure, I actually asked for Saturday off for something I'm not doing anymore."

"Thanks! I owe you one too!"

"I just want to hear about whatever you're planning." She gives a knowing look as she walks off with the beer, and Troy looks between us like he isn't quite sure what just happened.

"Okay. I have a date to plan! Check please!"

"Saturday is two days from now. How much time do you need?" He's teasing me, but there's curiosity in his tone.

"Who the hell knows. I've never even been on a date before." I shrug. "So, better safe than sorry."

He slides my check in front me, minus my appetizer and a couple of beers. I wait until he leaves to help another customer before I pull out enough cash for my bill, an extra twenty and my pen. Before I leave, I scribble on the bottom of my receipt.

Be ready at two. Wear a suit. Be prepared for a commitment.

Troy: *To be clear, I'm assuming you don't mean a swimsuit. Like a suit I'd wear to a wedding.*
   Me: *Exactly like that.*
   Troy: *See you on Saturday.*

CHAPTER TWENTY-EIGHT
TROY

This suit hasn't been worn since the last event my fraternity had before I graduated. It fits a little tighter now, but in all the right places. My hard work lately is paying off. Since I got to California, I picked up an exercise routine similar to the one I had when I played football in high school. My only consistent workout in college was keg stands.

My suit is dark gray, my dress shirt is perfectly white, and I'm not even annoyed with my solid black tie. I almost skipped it because they are not my thing, but if I'm going to do something, I might as well do it right. It's worth it because I look fucking fantastic. Satisfied, I strap on the watch my uncle gave me for my 21st birthday as there's a knock on my door. I have absolutely no idea what Lexy planned for us today, but I'm anxious to find out.

When I open the door, I see the girl standing in front of me, and my mouth instantly goes dry. My tongue swipes over my lip before I bite into it. Holy fuck. Lexy is wearing the red dress I recognize from her picture in Vegas, but it didn't do any sort of justice to this real life image. It's silky, the straps thin, the front is cut in a heart shape and the hem hits right above her knees. Her blonde hair is curled and falls over her shoulders, and her blue eyes are bright in contrast to the rest of her. She's looking at me through thick lashes, her skin fucking flawless, and red gloss on her lips that I desperately want to kiss.

"Fuck, Lexy." I drag my hand across my mouth.

She takes me in too, and I watch her eyes work her way down my body, seemingly happy with my appearance. "Yeah, you too." She takes a step, reaching for me. I take a step back, and she stops in her tracks, confused.

"If you touch me right now, we will not make it out of this room." I've gone longer without sex, but the way I crave Lexy makes not having her nearly unbearable.

"That's fine." She smirks and reaches for me again.

I grab her hands and spin her around slowly so she doesn't trip in her black heels. I'd rather her be in nothing but these heels as I fuck her on my bed, but instead, I wrap my arms around her, still gripping her hands, and pull her back into my chest. "God, you smell good." It's even more challenging to get my words out as I breathe in her coconut scent. "I want to know what you planned for us, but I'm hoping it ends with us coming back here so I can rip this dress off you." I kiss her skin, right above the red silky strap, as she nods.

I let her go. She steps away from me out the door, and it's now that I notice her dress scoops low in the back, showing off skin I want to run my hands over. Instead, I opt for smacking her ass and pull the door closed behind me as she looks over her shoulder with a look that nearly burns through me.

I spot Maci's car as soon as we get to the parking garage. She's letting Lexy borrow it while she's traveling the world. I slide into the passenger seat, second guessing pushing us out the door as Lexy leans over the center console to kiss me. I reach for the nape of her neck, holding her in place to extend the kiss longer than she intended. My dick twitching is the only thing that snaps me out of it.

Pulling back, I clear my throat and shift in my seat, attempting to get my hormones under control. "So, where are we going?"

She grins and puts the car in reverse. "To a wedding."

"Oh yeah. Whose wedding?" I didn't think she had any friends here.

"Don't know." Her smile grows. "Well, I know their names are Simon and Alana Woods."

It takes me a second. "Are we wedding crashing?" I'm amused as fuck and almost as excited for this as I am for getting back to my place after.

She nods her confirmation.

"So, what's our story?"

She glances over to take in my reaction to her plan, her smile bright when she sees we are on the same page. "Okay, here's what I'm thinking..."

LEXY

After about forty minutes, we arrive in Calabasas. I've been in this area before, back when I did makeup. There are a lot of rich people who live here, the kind of people who throw events so big they don't have time to greet every guest, let alone know who they are. It's perfect.

I turn down a winding road, following my GPS, but it seems like we are in the middle of nowhere. I'm worried I'm lost, but then I spot a massive black gate nestled among the trees. I pull up to it, harnessing my *fake it 'til I make it* confidence as I roll down the window. "Here for the Woods wedding." I shoot my best smile at the security guard.

"Welcome." He says it stone-faced and makes me wonder if he's paid well enough to stay emotionless or just really needs to get laid. "Follow this road to the valet." He points up the winding dirt road.

"Thanks." I leave the window rolled down, and I drive. We lucked out on the weather. It's about as nice as it gets at the end of January–66° and barely overcast. I might be a little cold, but after a few drinks and dances, I'll be fine. The trees lining the drive tower over the road, nearly blocking the sky between them, but streams of sunlight sparkle through.

Troy turned the music off when I got to the security gate and never turned it back on. I'm driving slow enough to glance at him. He's looking out the window like a kid seeing the magic of Christmas–not that I would personally know what that's like. I'm not sure if he can feel me watching him or if a thought slips out. Either way, it feels more like he's talking to himself when he says, "This reminds me of home. I miss the trees."

An indescribable feeling rushes over me along with a wave of emotions. I'm sad for him that he misses home. Sad for me that I don't have a home to miss. Worried that my time with him is limited because he might leave at some point. And freaked out because I've never had that thought about anyone before.

"It's pretty." My voice comes out soft, but it's enough to bring him back to reality.

"Like you." He smiles, reaching for my hand and bringing it to his lips. Part of me wants to ask him about Oregon again, but I don't want to ruin the moment. I pull up to the massive brick house, stopping under a huge driveway cover held up by white columns. I have been to some big houses, but they never cease to amaze me. When my wide eyes meet Troy's, I know he's thinking the same.

We both step out of the car, and I hand the valet my keys, along with a ten dollar bill. Troy meets me off to the side, offering his arm for me to loop mine through. I link us together and lean into him. Being here is obviously wrong, but being with him feels right. I'm tired of fighting it. I'm still freaking out a bit, but I'm as ready as I'll ever be to give this a chance.

"What's up?" He's walking in the direction the wedding signs point but looks over at me as if he can sense I'm thinking.

"Nothing, Mr. Bolton." I look up enough to grin at him mischievously. We agreed to use his last name, partially so we don't slip up, but also because after some thorough Facebook stalking and Googling, I found that Bolton is actually a distant family name. It's perfect. He kisses my temple before continuing down the path. Our skin may have touched in the smallest way, but I feel it everywhere. Between that and the way he smells like the perfect cross between sweet and spicy, it's overwhelming.

I take in my surroundings to avoid drowning in it. What the... This brick pathway is lined by extravagant white wooden bird cages filled with tropical birds. Rich people. I'll never understand them.

We make it through the ceremony, which was surprisingly shorter than I expected. As soon as the bride and groom, Simon and Alana–our third cousins–make it back down the aisle, everyone is escorted to a beautiful courtyard. Twinkle lights are strung between pillars and trees and a gazebo, attempting to contrast the night, now that the sun is starting to set. There's a ring of small, white, high-top cocktail tables around the edge of the yard, and as soon as Troy and I grab a beer at the open bar, we find an empty one.

"I've never been to a wedding before. At this rate, I was thinking my first one would be Mack and Maci's."

"Do you think they will get married? I didn't realize they got back together."

"They haven't yet. She was in Costa Rica with this Dean guy." I take a sip of my beer before continuing with my thought, but Troy interjects, his glass freezing in midair on its way to his mouth.

"Uhhh, what?"

It's weird he cares about this. "What?"

"She's with Dean Porter?" He's not thrilled or upset about this news, just intrigued.

"I don't know his last name. Why?"

"He's a buddy of mine."

"Small world. Kind of. So, he's a good guy?"

"He is. I don't know what happened between them, though. Can't imagine he'd let her go if he could help it. I only saw them together once, but he was very protective of her."

"I would be too if I were him and you were hitting on my girlfriend." I don't have to lean up too far to kiss him since I'm wearing heels. He smiles into our kiss, his hand finding the bare skin on my back where my dress dips.

"Hey, I wasn't flirting at all."

"Troy, you're always flirting." I laugh. "But for real, while she's stuck deciding between the two of them, I need you to pretend to be Team Mack with me, okay? That's your job as my–" The word boyfriend flashes through my mind, but I push it away. "–wedding date."

The way he's looking at me, I know he caught my near slip up and is debating on whether or not to call me out on it. When he's made up his mind, he says, "You'll look amazing in a suit as best man."

"Thank you." I lean into his chest as he wraps his arm around me, taking a sip from his beer with his free hand. I'm about to ask if he's ever been to a wedding when a couple around our age walks up to us.

"Hi!" the woman says in a peppy voice. Unlike Lauren's, hers is obnoxious. "I'm Bri, and this is my husband Will. We are cousins of the groom. What about you two?" I'll never understand people's need to talk to random strangers like this. At least our story lines up with the bride's side. Just have to see if it holds up. The way Troy and I can play any conversation at work every day, I'm not worried. Plus, we are mostly sticking to our true story and memorized random things about the bride and groom's family.

"Hey, I'm Troy." He sets his beer on the table before reaching across it to shake Will's hand. "This is my fiancée, Lexy."

Damn, why does that word sound different rolling off his tongue than it did mine when I proposed the idea? I pull away from Troy so I can shake their hands.

"Oooh, you two are engaged? Congrats! Let me see your ring!" Bri squeals.

"It just happened. It's getting sized." Troy's quick thinking cuts in.

"How did you ever part with it?" Bri catches my gaze. "Tell me what it looks like!"

"Yeah, babe, tell her." I can hear the grin in Troy's voice without looking over at him. His fingers run along my lower back, leaving me wanting more of his touch.

I lean into the table, my chin propped up by my palm, searching my mind for an idea since it never occurred to me someone would ask. "It's a diamond band, with a teardrop halo. The big gem in the middle is a ruby, though." Dang, I'm not big on jewelry, but I'd wear this.

"Your ring is red?" She sounds judgmental as fuck.

I nod before looking at Troy to flash him a smile. "That way I'm always wearing red for him."

Based on the heat in his eyes, you'd think that was the sexiest thing ever said. He smirks, his gaze holding mine. "That's right." He leans in closer and whispers, "You're so good to me," before kissing the skin below my ear.

"You give me everything I need. It's the least I can do." The words are part of the game, but I try to show him through a kiss that I truly mean them.

"You can totally tell you two just got engaged. It's so cute how in love you are." Bri bursts the bubble we were in. Not even the high pitch whine of her voice can overpower the intensity of what she said. My smile falters at the mention of the L word. It's something I've never felt before and definitely don't feel right now. "So, how did it happen?!" God, this girl is incessant.

My mind is blank.

"First, I took her for a ride on my motorcycle..." Troy starts, but is abruptly cut off by Will, who apparently wants to join the conversation now.

"You have a bike? What kind?" He's eager to talk about it, but Bri rolls her eyes as if this is a topic she shuts down frequently.

"A zx-10."

"Dude, that's sweet. How long have you had it?" The guy is clearly jealous.

"I'm surprised that someone in Alana's family rides a motorcycle. They don't seem like the type." Bri's words come out snarky, void of all the excitement she had a moment ago.

"They do actually. Her great uncle, my grandpa, taught me how to ride." Troy answers confidently, as if it was true. It could have been. The guy in reference was part of a motorcycle gang in the 70s. You can discover a lot on the internet.

She stares back at Troy as if she's offended by his answer. He chuckles.

"Well, tell me the rest of your story." She demands it, and I notice her ring finger wrapped around her wine glass is bare. Love makes people crazy.

"Nah, I think I'd rather keep that memory for ourselves," Troy smirks at her before leaning in to kiss me. How is a pretend conversation making me... I don't know. I want to kiss him. I want to rip his clothes off. I want to keep him.

Bri drinks the last half of her glass in one gulp before turning to the man who is clearly not her husband. "Will, I need another drink, let's go."

As soon as she's out of ear shot, I look back at Troy, shaking my head.

"Rich people." The words leave both of our mouths at the same time, and we burst into laughter.

"We work well together, Lex."

"Yeah, maybe we do." I sigh. "Oh, I LOVE this song," I squeal when "Yeah," by Usher, comes on, shocked at the quality of music on this reception playlist. Middle school wasn't exactly full of happy memories, but how can you not feel nostalgic with it? I down the last few sips of my beer before locking my fingers around Troy's wrist. "Dance with me."

"Do I have a choice?"

"Nope. You have to do what I want now if you want to do what you want later." I pull myself into him.

"That's not fair, you want to do what I want later too." I catch him grin as he buries his hands into my curls before kissing me the way that he does, hard and soft at the same time. How does he do that? Why do I love it so much? "Okay, let's go." He leads me onto the nearly full dance floor.

For how fancy this wedding seems, I'm surprised these rich people are dancing like unchaperoned high schoolers. Even though the temperature is cold, I'm on fire, surrounded by all these people, grinding into Troy, his hands running down my sides. My body moves in sync with his. It's still strange to me how in tune we seem to be most of the time. I'm having fun, but I wish we were back in his condo, alone, instead of surrounded by strangers. I can't believe no one even attempted to call us out or question us.

Three minutes later the song ends, and I hear the soft chords of a guitar, of a slow song. I twist toward Troy, about to ask him if he's ready to go home.

"Mm-mm. No." He shakes his head, knowing I was attempting an escape. His hands find my waist, and he pulls me to him. "I love *this* song."

I listen for the words to start. "Kiss Me Slowly," by Parachute, but an acoustic version. I love this song too. I've never slow danced with someone before, but I loop my arms around Troy's neck and lean into his chest anyway.

"Based on how you were whining, I would have thought you were a terrible dancer," I whisper in his ear.

"I can't tell you all my secrets at once." His laugh vibrates against me. "What would be the fun in that?"

"Tell me something else I don't know about you."

"What do you want to know?"

"Have you thought about going back to Oregon?"

He holds me tighter against him and kisses my hair. "I'm not going anywhere."

I pull back just enough that I can see him. "Except to take me home now, right?

"Yeah, except for that." He smiles before leading me out of the wedding, back to the car, and into his bed.

CHAPTER TWENTY-NINE
TROY

Lexy is sleeping on her back next to me when I wake. Her hair is draped across the pillow, her wedding curls almost completely gone after a night of more sex than sleep. She's wearing my old Fall Out Boy concert tee, my black sheets pooled around her waist. Fuck, I love this girl–not that I'll tell her that anytime soon. I know it's quick; it came out of nowhere. I realized it yesterday when we were fucking around at the wedding, pretending. It felt like it all could have been real.

I have to tell her I'm leaving next week. I haven't been sure how to bring it up, especially since she seemed a little insecure about Oregon yesterday for some reason. I want to invite her. I know she said she won't freak out anymore, but she's barely been out of California, and she hasn't even committed to being my girlfriend yet.

"Stop watching me sleep." Her eyes open lazily, and she smiles at me.

I lean up on my forearm, my other hand falling to her waist before I kiss her. "I love having you here when I wake up."

She makes a whining sound to let me know she'd rather me use my mouth for kissing her instead of talking. I give in but don't take as much as I want. I need to get this over with. I kiss her once more, my hand running over her stomach under my t-shirt. "Thank you for yesterday."

"You're welcome. I had so much fun." She looks genuinely happy and hopefully stays that way.

"So, next weekend..."

"Oooh you want to find another wedding to crash?!" She's so excited at the idea, I would go every weekend if she wanted.

"Actually, I'm not going to be here."

"Where are you going to be?"

"Oregon."

Worry fills her expression at my answer. "Oh. Okay."

"I'll only be gone a week." She visibly exhales relief.

"Oh, that's fun. And you'll get to ride your bike!" Thank God she's totally fine with this. I don't know why I was worried.

"Yup. I would have invited you, but I made plans with Cooper before we started... hanging out."

She hesitates, her brows scrunching together, as if she didn't consider inviting her was even an option. "That's okay. This actually works well because it's Mack's last weekend here. I would have ditched you anyway."

"Wait, what? Where's he going?"

"He's moving home–to Oregon." She sighs. "I guess that's the place everyone wants to be, huh?"

My brain goes to a fucked up place–one that considers Mack going to Oregon as potential leverage for maybe moving home one day too. Fuck, that fake fiancé shit at the wedding really got in my head. It's like I switched to the relationship fast track and can't help wanting Lexy to jump her slow moving train and join me. We should probably get to the boyfriend stage first. "How do you feel about him moving?"

She sits up and shrugs.

"I bet that's hard, especially with Maci gone." I prompt her to share her feelings.

She concedes easier than I expected. "Yeah. It is. It feels like the people I care about are abandoning me. I know it's not the same as my mom, but it sucks even more since I actually like them."

"I get that." I pause. "Is that part of the reason you don't like to get close to anyone?" I can't keep myself from asking.

She stares back, like she's debating what level of honesty to give. Her eyes fall to the mattress between us before she says, "Yeah. It is." She breathes out like admitting it is a weight off her chest and shifts to a lighter tone. "But I know he'll be happier there. I might just need you to distract me more often." She grins as she moves to straddle me, reminding me she never put underwear on last night. My hands automatically move to her thighs. She tugs on the elastic band of my sweats, but then her smile fades again. "Just a vacation? You're not going to remember how much you love it there and not want to come back, right?"

I can only make a promise on half of that, and I don't want to lie to her. "I already can't wait to come back to you."

She leans down to kiss me, and I don't want to leave her in the first place.

CHAPTER THIRTY
LEXY

My alarm wakes me, ringing as my phone simultaneously vibrates violently against my nightstand. I crawl over Troy to grab it. As soon as I hit *stop*, his hands are on my hips, rubbing over the red lace of my underwear. Besides those, the only thing I'm wearing is his Fall Out Boy t-shirt which I've stolen and claimed as my own. He pushes up on my hips, causing me to lose my balance enough for my hands to fall to the headboard behind him.

"Troy, we gotta get ready so I can take you to the airport."

He shakes his head, but he's not looking at my face. "Come here." He moves his hands to grip my knees where they hold me up on the mattress near his waist. He tugs on them until I'm aligned with his face. This is exactly why I set my alarm for 30 minutes before we needed to get ready. This guy can never get enough. I'd be lying if I said I wasn't more than willing to be on the receiving end of his need.

His hands hook under my legs and grab my ass, pulling me toward him. "Hold onto the headboard," he demands before his tongue drags across the lace between my legs, the sensation from the mixed textures causes me to moan. I mutter a curse as I grip the wood.

He kisses me on that sensitive spot of my skin at the edge of my underwear then evens it out by pressing his lips into the other side. I can't help but squirm in anticipation.

He hooks his fingers in the top of the lace and tugs gently as he kisses my inner thigh. "Off," he commands, and I do as he asks. I climb out of them, flinging them off once they are down to an ankle, and resume my previous position. Moving his hands to my inner thighs, he grips them, pushing them apart to give him better access. He rubs his thumb across my wetness, opening me up for him ever so slightly, and without hesitation he sucks my clit into his mouth.

"Fuuuuck."

I feel him smile against me the moment before he takes a long, slow lick. He snakes his tongue inside me. I push onto it reflexively, needing more, and his groan vibrates through me. One of his hands runs up my thigh before gripping my hip, his thumb brushing along my sensitive skin.

His tongue swirls around, curving into me before pulling out. I whine at the loss of contact until two of his fingers are deep inside me. He pulls them out only to thrust them back in as he continues to lick at me. My head falls forward against the headboard. "Oh my god."

"I'm going to make you come so hard, you won't want any other mouth to own you the way mine does," he pulls back just enough to say, fucking me with his fingers as he does. Then he's back to sucking, licking, flicking his tongue against me, and I can hardly hold myself up. I grip the headboard harder, my head still pressed into it, as I slip closer to him. His fingers slide out, his tongue replacing them as it laps inside me. Holy fuck. I can hardly breathe.

He presses my thighs apart, his fingers rubbing against my skin. He takes one more slow drag across me with his tongue before dipping in deep, and it sends me over the edge. I squeeze my eyes tight as I come, a wave of heat and tingles flushing through my legs, my stomach fluttering, as he pulls my orgasm from me. It's almost too much, and I try to pull away, but Troy holds me in place, licking me slowly until I'm shaking too much to hold on anymore.

I push off the headboard, awkwardly tumbling backward until my back is on the bed, lying in the opposite direction of Troy. In the next second he's spun around, and he's kissing up my stomach until he's hovering over me.

"God, Troy. How am I supposed to let you leave after that?" I manage even though my breath is still ragged.

"Just the feeling I was going for. Don't want you to forget me while I'm gone."

"I definitely won't forget you. But maybe you should fuck me too, to be sure."

"Ask and you shall receive." He grins, before grabbing a condom from my nightstand. Yanking off his sweats, he doesn't waste time pushing into me.

CHAPTER THIRTY-ONE
TROY

"How the fuck are you?" Cooper says as soon as I slide onto the passenger seat of his black 4Runner.

"Happy to be breathing fresh air." I chuckle.

"All that smog isn't doing it for you?"

"Yeah, not quite."

"So, just come home, man."

"I might have considered it a few weeks ago."

He glances over at me with a shit-eating grin as he pulls away from the airport. "Finally listened to me and decided to give another girl a chance."

"Something like that." I pull my phone out to text Lexy and let her know I made it here.

"Who is she?"

"Do you remember Maci?"

He looks confused trying to place her. "Umm, Dean's ex-girlfriend?"

"Yeah."

"Yeah. Is that who you're seeing? Wait, in California?"

I laugh. "No. Although she did move there. It's her best friend, Lexy."

"Lexy, sounds hot."

"You have no idea. I almost missed my flight this morning." I would have if she hadn't refused a second round so I could make it to the airport. "She's my Sophie."

Maybe I shouldn't have mentioned that name. Cooper grips the steering wheel tighter and takes a breath. "In that case, get the fuck out while you still can."

I laugh. "Nah, I'm winning her over on the relationship front." I reach to shake his shoulder. "Like you will Sophie."

He doesn't seem convinced.

Five minutes later, we pull up to Mom's house.

Without knocking, we enter through the front door as if it hasn't been over four years since we lived here. This place will always be my home. We walk straight through the living room into the kitchen, and Melissa turns around from her place in front of the oven when she hears us.

"My boys! Hi." She skips right past Cooper to give me a hug. She feels like comfort and safety, something I'll never take for granted.

"Oh yeah, your real kid is chopped liver over here," Cooper jokes.

"Well, maybe if you came around more than just when Troy visits," she sasses him back, and he ignores her.

It smells so fucking good in here. I glance around them to see the casserole dish on the stove. Melissa follows my gaze. "Made your favorite. Mac and cheese."

Hell yes. She makes the best mac and cheese with a Ritz cracker crumble on top. It's not just delicious, it was also the first home cooked meal I ever had. At ten, I didn't realize you could even eat mac and cheese any other way than out of a box.

"Thanks, Mom." I turn to Cooper. "Can I have your keys? I forgot my phone in the car."

"Damn, you really like this girl, don't you?" he jokes, tossing me his key fob.

Melissa's attention is caught by those words, a smile lighting her face as if she knows things are better than the last time we talked about Lexy. She turns around without saying anything, grabbing the casserole dish with pot holders to carry it to the table.

As I hit unlock on the key fob, I catch movement out of the corner of my eye. I turn and see Sophie pacing back and forth in the space between her driveway and ours. I watch for a moment before she glances up and catches me. If it was solely based on looks, I'd say my best friend has good taste. Sophie has always been cute. She has soft waves in her dirty-blonde hair and big brown eyes. She's almost always in a sundress, even when it's cold. Like now, she's wearing a light yellow dress with flowers all over it. She looks innocent, but she's far from it. She's a heartbreaker, at least when it comes to Cooper. She's got it in her head they shouldn't be together even though they're clearly in love.

"Troy... hey. What are you doing here?"

"Just visiting."

"That's fun," she says flatly.

"Yeah. What are you doing... here?"

"Umm, I still live here with my parents." Sophie's family has lived next door to Cooper's their entire lives.

"I mean out here, pacing like you have bad news to deliver or something."

"I saw Coop's car. Was thinking about saying hi."

"We're about to have dinner. Do you want to join us?" Cooper might kill me for asking, but Melissa loves Sophie. She's been rooting for them to get together since they were kids. She doesn't know everything that's gone down, though. Hell, even I don't know what their issue currently is. Last I knew, Sophie refused to date him, and I actually thought Cooper was seeing someone else, but apparently I can't keep up.

"Oh, I don't know." Her fingers pick at the hem of her dress.

"Come on. You won't figure your shit out by staying away from each other." Call me a sucker, but now that I have Lexy, I'm back on team relationship, and regardless of their problems, anyone with two eyes can see Cooper and Sophie are end game.

"Yeah, okay."

She waits while I grab my phone out of the car and then follows me inside.

"Look who I found." I walk past the table, grabbing an extra plate and bringing it to the empty place next to Melissa, leaving the seat next to Cooper open.

Sophie sits down hesitantly, off to the side of her seat like she's worried about invading Cooper's personal space.

"Sophie, sweetie, it's so nice to see you." Melissa smiles sweetly at her, counterbalancing Cooper's flat stare. I definitely know I'm missing an update now.

"You too, Mrs. Montgomery." She gives an uneasy smile.

I reach for the spoon in the mac and cheese, ignoring the tension I've created. I'm not worried. Cooper looks like he wants to fuck her more than run away from her anyway.

Melissa speaks again. "Troy, stop making me wait. Tell me more about your girl."

Cooper dropped me off at Jameson's on his way to our house since Sophie is with him, and my being there isn't going to help any problem solving. Although they probably do need a mediator considering how stubborn they both are. When I walk through the glass door, the bar is exactly how it was a year ago. It's dark and kind of dingy but feels worn and comfortable. The brown leather booths line the wall connected to the front door and a long wooden bar stretches across the back of the room. It's the orange and dusty red lighting that contributes most to the 70s vibe. Regardless of my uncle's best friend being the owner, it's always been my favorite bar. If I was running the place, this carpet would have to go, though. It's some weird brown and green design and ugly as fuck. How carpet ended up as flooring in a college bar in the first place is beyond me.

I slide onto the black leather stool, and the bartender turns around to greet me.

"Troy! Hey! You're not who I expected to see today."

"Hey, Jess. It's good to see you." She's a few years older than me and has been the head bartender here for as long as I can remember. "Just in town for the week. How ya been?"

"Troy." I spin on my stool to see Tony right as his hand lands on my shoulder. I know he's the owner, but still, this kind of thing never happens in LA. I love when someone knows you everywhere you go. He seems much less surprised to see me than Jess did. "I was hoping I'd run into you."

Tony is my uncle's best friend. They grew up together and are still close even though my uncle moved to California decades ago. They own our family cabin in Sunriver together. I'd probably be as shitty as my real father if it weren't for the two of them and Cooper's dad serving as real male role models.

"Hey, Uncle Tony."

"James said you'd be here this week. I wanted to talk to you about something."

"Oh yeah?" I catch a beer being set down in front of me out of my peripheral and turn to thank Jess before giving my attention back to Tony. "What's up?"

"Your degree is in business, right?"

What a random question. "Yeah."

"How are you liking California?"

"It's alright. Different from here, that's for sure. Are those two things supposed to be connected?" I laugh before taking a sip of my beer, having trouble following his train of thought.

"Surprisingly. As you might know, my daughter's husband is stationed in Alabama. They moved down there a few months ago, and she recently found out she's pregnant with our first grandbaby."

"Congrats, that's exciting!"

"Yeah, Diane is thrilled. She's also decided we should move down there to help. We don't want to miss out on anything important, and there's nothing keeping us here anymore. Nothing except this bar."

I'm still not sure where he's going with this.

"I was talking to James about my options, and he thought maybe you'd be interested."

"Interested in..."

"Buying this place and taking it off my hands."

"What, really?" There are so many conflicting thoughts in my head.

"Yeah, I'd love for it to stay in the family, if possible. I know you'd take good care of it."

"Wow, thank you." I pause to decide on my next words. "This is a lot to think about. I'd have to talk to my girl. And find a way to come up with the money. But I think it's something I'd be interested in. Can I get back to you?"

"Absolutely. I'm not in a rush to sell, and we won't leave for a few more months anyway. I just wanted to mention it since you're here."

"Thanks, Tony. I appreciate your faith in me to follow in your footsteps. I'll let you know when I've made a decision, so we can discuss it."

I stand from my stool to give him a hug before he wanders off into the back of the bar. What the fuck just happened? My immediate reaction was to say yes, but the thought of leaving Lexy kept the word in my mouth. This would be a big move, and we aren't in a place for me to suggest something like this and think she'd be open to following me.

I lean into the bar on my forearms after pushing up the sleeves of my black sweater. Where the fuck do I even begin to wrap my mind around this?

"Hey, Troy." I hit the break on my thoughts and look to my left where I find Marcus standing. It's been a while since I've seen him. His dark brown hair is tied back into a small bun, his facial hair thick in a way every man would envy. He's always been the complete opposite of me, evident by his tight gray jeans and his black v-neck.

"Marcus, hey. Long time."

"Yeah. So, I'm going to cut to the chase. I didn't mean to eavesdrop, but I heard about the offer Tony made you." It wouldn't have occurred to me that Marcus knows Tony, but I do know he and Dean frequent this bar too, so it makes sense that he would.

"Oh yeah?" I'm used to being able to read people, so it's weird that I haven't seen the direction of any of my conversations tonight.

"I'd like to offer up a partnership. If you're interested."

"I mean, I'm definitely considering it, but I don't have the funding. And I can't imagine a bank loaning a 22 year old whatever amount I'd need to buy this place. That's my first issue."

"Yeah, I could take care of that."

Who the hell has that kind of money? Especially at our age. "You have enough money to buy a bar? How?"

"Let's just say I'm willing and capable of discussing the investment in this bar and you."

"Wow, okay. Are you thinking more along the lines of running this place together or being a silent partner?"

"I'd be interested in helping out with operations."

"Fuck." I shake my head, I'm getting way too far ahead of myself. "I don't know about this."

"What's your second issue?"

"A girl." I correct myself. "Not *a* girl, *the* girl." How I already know that is beyond me, but I'm certain.

"Ahhh. That I can't help with. How about this? Let's get all the numbers from Tony, you talk things over with your girl, and we can go from there?"

"Yeah, that sounds good," I tell him even though I have zero idea how to bring this up to Lexy, or if I even should.

"Great. Hey, Jess." Marcus catches her attention as she walks past us, ordering us each a glass of bourbon.

CHAPTER THIRTY-TWO
LEXY

"Are you packed?" I ask Mack, my feet dangling, as we sit on the cement block wall that separates the boardwalk from the beach.

"Yup. I ended up selling almost everything. I want new stuff anyway. Everything reminds me of Maci."

"Are you trying to get over her?" I deflate at the thought but try not to show it.

He laughs like it's a dumb question. "You and I both know that's not happening. I'm just trying not to think about it. I have to make choices I'll be happy with regardless of what she decides. If we do get back together, I'd rather get new things and make new memories anyway."

"Makes sense. Do you already have a place to live?"

"Not yet. I'm staying with my sister and her fiancé. They are letting me crash with them until the school year and my new job start."

"What are you going to do until then?"

"I still have a few more shows to play on the road, so I'll be gone part of the time. I'm also going to help remodel Avery and Miller's house."

"Then once you're finished touring, you'll get your own place?"

"That's the plan."

"Tell me about your new job. Are you excited?"

"I am. My music teacher from middle school ran into Avery a few weeks ago. He got funding to create an after school program for kids who can't afford extracurriculars or just need a more positive environment."

"Mack, that's perfect for you."

"Yeah, I hope music can impact their lives the way it did mine, ya know? I don't know where I'd be without it."

"You're going to be so great for them. They are lucky to have you."

"Thanks, Lex." He wraps his arm around my shoulder, pulling me into a side hug.

"I'll miss you." I sigh with the admission.

"I was thinking maybe you could come visit in April. It will be Where We Are's final show. We are playing at the first place we got paid to play. Should be a good time."

"Yes! I'm down." My phone vibrates in my pocket, and I reach for it, falling away from Mack's hug.

"You finally got a new phone case." Mack has been harassing me about getting a new one for months.

I can't help my smile. "It was a Valentine's Day gift from Troy."

"What! Gifts? This sounds a little like a relationship to me. Who are you, and what did you do with Lexy?!" he jokes.

"I know. It's weird, huh?"

"Nah, I like it. Where is he? I thought maybe he'd be tagging along today." The three of us came out here a couple weeks ago. It wasn't weird at all; the guys got along well.

"He's actually in Oregon."

"You didn't want to go with him?"

"He already had it planned before we started... whatever we are doing. Plus, I wasn't going to miss out on my last weekend with you."

"You two have been spending a lot of time together. Is he surviving without you?"

"He texts me all day. It's ridiculous." I chuckle, shaking my head before somberness takes over. "But I think he'd rather live in Oregon," I admit. "He hasn't outright said it, but it's the impression I get."

"How do you feel about that?"

"I'm not sure. I'd be upset if he left. I think I'd lose him. It's different from how I feel with you." The thought terrifies me. I tried to deny how strong my feelings are for Troy when Bri accused us of being in love at the wedding, but every day since, I keep thinking maybe I'm getting closer to her being right. I wonder if I'll know, *how* I'll know.

"What if he asked you to go with him?" He seems almost hopeful at the idea.

"I don't think I'm against it, but I have never been before. I might hate it. He wants to make things official, but it's been less than two months. Moving to another state with someone I just met? Sounds crazy."

"You're talking to the wrong person about that. I talked my girlfriend into moving in with me after only spending like ten days together in person."

"True. I'll cross that bridge if and when we get to it. It's not something I'm ready to worry over."

"Well, either way, I hope you can come in April. If Troy can't come with you, you're more than welcome to stay at my sister's with me. She wants to meet you."

"Whatever happens, I'll be there."

CHAPTER THIRTY-THREE
LEXY

Troy is waiting outside my apartment, leaning against the front door, when I get home. He got back from Oregon today, and I've missed him more than I would have wanted to admit in the past. I think I'm ready to own up to my feelings and take another step forward. I keep recalling my run in with my mom a few weeks ago. The realization that maybe I was more on track to end up like her than I thought hit me hard. I'm still scared of being part of an all-consuming love, but I also think I have better judgment than my mom. I know I do. Plus, my relationship with Troy feels significantly different than any of my mom's relationships.

Anxious to be near him, I quickly lock my car, slamming the door shut behind me. A moment later, I'm standing in front of him, the word "hi" barely out of my mouth before his hands frame my face and his lips are on mine. I can't help but smile into the kiss as I cling to his waist and tug myself to him. Breaking our kiss just enough to speak, he mutters, "I missed you."

"I missed you too," I say, pulling away to unlock my front door. I want to make up for our week apart and relax into the comfort of him, but I also need a shower.

I started a job at another bar and music venue a few days ago, knowing places would be hiring right before spring break season. It's less stressful than Shot in the Dark, but I always feel the need to wash off work even if I'm not running my ass off. Troy closes and locks my door behind him and I kiss him again before taking a quick body shower. I throw on my black sleep shorts and tank top as Troy grabs a pair of gray sweats from his suitcase. He said he only had enough time before work to swing by and pick up his car after Nolan picked him up from the airport. I'm going to suggest he leaves a pair of pajamas here. Just the thought of mentioning him leaving something at my place gives me an urge to run, but I try to ignore it and allow the undeniable excitement I also feel by it take over.

I brush my teeth then head out to the living room where Troy sits on the couch waiting for me. I assume my go-to position, straddling him, my arms looping around his neck and sigh as I take a second to shamelessly let my eyes roam his shirtless body. He's quiet, letting me do what I want while rubbing his hands against my freshly lotioned skin, up my thighs and under the edge of my shorts.

His attention is pulled from me, and curiosity flashes in his features as he looks to the space behind me. His hand moves to my back, bracing me as he leans forward so he can grab something from the coffee table.

He pulls the postcard between us with one hand, the other finding its place back on my thigh.

"Oh yeah, that's for you," I say.

"For me?" He examines the front. It's a picture of the Eiffel Tower with the word *Paris* written in cursive across the bottom. He flips it over, resting it where our bodies connect as he reads.

Troy, Thanks for the idea to show up at the airport and take the first flight out. It landed me in Paris, and I absolutely love it here. Like I love your girl. Take care of her for me. I'm so happy for you both. Maci There's a hand drawn heart in front of her name.

I wonder if he realizes he's smiling at Maci's words. "Told you she doesn't mind."

"I love that she just hopped on a plane." His gaze shifts from the postcard to my eyes.

"I'm surprised she did." I laugh. "I usually have to talk her into going to the bar up the street."

"Well, good for her. This isn't weird, right?" He holds up the postcard, but I know that's not really what he means.

"I have no insecurities about it, if that's what you mean. It's totally weird, though. What are the chances of us even meeting?" I shake my head. It's an absurd thought.

"Someone has to be the one in a million." He holds his stare.

It's hard for me not to be uncomfortable when he's affectionate like this. It's easier for me to skip straight to the part where neither of us have clothes on, but I want to talk about our relationship. I want to be comfortable with this. I'm tired of being afraid.

"Can I ask you something?"

"Always." He gently flings the postcard back on the coffee table the way he does with his drink coasters at work, freeing up both of his hands to touch me again.

"Does it bother you when I flirt with guys at work?"

"Depends." He pauses, seeming caught off guard by my question. "Is what you do with Todd your definition of flirting?" His chuckle vibrates through him.

"Ha ha. You know it's not." God, I'm thankful I never have to see him again. Best part of getting fired. "I was thinking about it when I was cashing out tonight. I usually get a few numbers a night. I guess I didn't really think about it until today."

"Do you use the numbers?" He's not judging me, he's just asking.

"Once." His brows scrunch together, preparing to get worked up, until he realizes I'm talking about him. "It would be a lie to say it's not intentional, though–the flirting I mean."

He reaches up and brushes a curl away from my face before burying his hand in my hair. "I mean, I get at least a handful of numbers each week. I don't use them, but I work for them. Well, for the tips that come with them. So, if you doing it is wrong then I guess it's wrong for me too."

"It's always felt like part of the job, like if I'm going to be there, I might as well make the most of it. But then..."

He pulls me into him with his grip on my neck to kiss me softly like he can't hold back from having his lips on mine as he waits for me to finish my thought. "Then what?"

"Some guy tonight asked if I had a boyfriend."

His hand untangles from my hair and falls to my hip, his expression untelling. "What did you tell him?"

"Yes." My gaze drops from his eyes to where our hips connect. I'm uncomfortable with this conversation, but eased slightly because it's Troy.

"Oh yeah?" He's surprised. "Do you say that often so guys back off?"

"I've never said it before."

"What are you saying, Lexy?"

"Umm." I chew on my bottom lip. "I want to be with you. Officially."

He cracks a smile and bites into his lip like it'll help him hold back from whatever he really wants to say in response. It's fucking sexy. "Oh yeah?"

I nod, holding his gaze with more confidence now. I am confident about this. It's just a big step.

His hands grip my hips a little tighter. "Okay."

It's so cute how excited he gets when I give into him a little more, but he always refrains from showing it. He thinks he does anyway.

"Just this once you can have it." The words come out with a half sigh and a half laugh.

"Have what?"

"Your 'I told you so' moment. Or some 'fuck, finally' you want to curse under your breath." I can't help but smile.

He shakes his head. "I don't need anything but you." His hand caresses the nape of my neck, the other one sliding under the bottom edge of my tank top. I love the way he feels against my skin.

For the first time in my life, the thought of needing someone doesn't completely freak me out.

His arm wraps all the way around my back, holding me tight to him. In one smooth movement, he flips us so I'm lying flat against the couch and he's straddling me now. Damn, he's sexy. I sit enough to grip his neck and pull him down into a kiss that I feel all the way to my toes, like I always do.

"I guess we better consummate this relationship," Troy whispers against my lips.

"Yeah, there it is. You couldn't help yourself." I can't help but laugh.

"I never can around you." He doesn't give me a chance to respond. He slides his fingers under my tank top, pulling it along as he drags his hands up my body. He tugs it over my head before leaning back to look at me. It made me nervous at first, the way he takes his time, like I won't notice. Now it's like some kind of foreplay I'm obsessed with. I watch as his eyes roam over me, like he can't decide what part of me he wants the most. It turns me all the way on.

His fingers loop around the top of my shorts, and I lift my hips to help him tug them off. He pulls a condom out of the pocket of his sweats before kicking them off. I want to pull him in to kiss me again, but I hold back. As much as Troy loves spontaneity, and he's always down to try anything in or out of bed, he also has this routine with me. Who am I to mess that up?

With his legs on either side of me, he leans back and rubs his thumbs against the apex of my thighs with a groan. "You're fucking sexy. And mine," he mutters more to himself than to me, I think.

When he's finished undressing me, and hitting every part of my body with his eyes, he scoots back on the couch enough to give him the access he needs. He runs his hands up my legs, stopping at my inner thighs before pushing them apart. There's never any teasing or warning. It's like he's used up all his patience by this point and can't stand to drag out the torture for me without torturing himself more.

The flat of his tongue presses against me and fuck, that's all it takes to make me melt into the couch. Thank God I stopped resisting this man. His tongue dips inside me with slow strokes as his hands run over my hips and up my stomach at the same pace. Fuck that feels good. I'm always torn between wanting this and needing more. Tonight, I'm opting for him because he's not close enough to me. I tug on his hair, and he stops what he's doing to look up at me.

I'd tell him what I want, but he already knows. He grabs the condom from the couch next to us, tearing the packet open with his teeth, never taking his eyes off me. He shifts my hips so I'm angled on the couch. Staying between my legs, he slides one of his feet to the floor and his other knee finds stability on the couch. Once he's aligned, he presses into me as I wrap my legs around him, pulling him deeper. We never need to warm up or go slowly. I'm turned on and wet enough from the way he fucks me with his eyes first.

He grips my hips as he thrusts into me, going as deep as he can with each one. "Fuck, Lexy, you feel so good," he mumbles as a moan escapes me. One of his hands leaves my hips so his thumb can rub across my clit, and I almost come undone at that touch alone. My arms fly over my eyes as I bite into my lip. How can he feel this fucking good?

He slows his movements, and I peek up at him through my crossed arms. His eyes catch on my bedroom door before he looks down at me again. "Did you use your vibrator while I was gone?"

As he thrusts into me again, my breath catches, the word "No" coming out like a whisper as I shake my head under my arms.

He feels too good to keep my eyes open, but I feel him shift forward, his lips brushing against my ear. "Why not?"

My heart pounds, but all I can do is arch my back, desperate to feel him deeper.

He curses at my movement then repeats himself. "Why not, Lexy?" Troy says in my ear again, and I let out a moan.

He thrust into me harder. On a ragged breath, I force out, "Because." Fuck, I love how fast and hard he fucks me.

Suddenly, his movement comes to a halt.

I pull my arms from where they cover my eyes to find him looking at me expectantly. "Why are you stopping?" I whine in frustration.

"Tell me I'm better than your vibrator."

"You feel better than everything," I say, thrusting my hips up in hopes of resuming his rhythm again.

He groans at my response, picking up his pace. "Good. I want you disappointed by anything that isn't me."

Pressure builds in every part of my body as he pounds into me. It hurts so fucking good. The few seconds I stay stuck at the edge feel like forever before I fall over it, a wave of ecstasy flooding through me. I feel my orgasm everywhere, a thin layer of tingles under my skin as I contract around Troy. His rough movements tell me my undoing was also his. He continues to thrust into me, until I relax into the couch, my arms moving from across my eyes to run my fingers into my now sweaty hair. "God, I never get tired of you." I lock my eyes with his on a sigh, and I can see how happy my words make him.

Troy falls forward, propping himself up on his forearms that frame my face, without pulling out of me. He leans in to kiss me, and the contact sends another wave of pleasure through me. He grins at a delayed twitch from my orgasm before kissing me again, like he didn't get enough. I'm not sure I'll ever get enough.

CHAPTER THIRTY-FOUR
TROY

My cousin has been in town instead of away on business, so since I got back from Oregon, I've spent every night at Lexy's. Even though my place is less than ten minutes from hers, I haven't been home in two weeks. Selfishly, it's just easier. I prefer being wherever it's most likely for her to wear the least amount of clothing.

Living with a girl is nothing like I thought it would be, not that I would know considering I've never lived with one before. Even though Emily and I were together for four years, I went from the Montgomery's house to the fraternity house to renting a house with Cooper. Thank God I didn't sign a lease with Emily. That would have been a nightmare, but being around Lexy all the time is a dream.

I know it's only been a couple weeks, but she's never in my way, and I never seem to be in hers. Our schedules are almost identical, so we've spent a lot of time together and haven't had any issues. I guess I expected something to come up. I haven't mentioned the idea of buying the bar back home, and I'm not convinced I will. I'm worried about ruining the good thing we have going.

I just walked into my place after work. My cousin left for a business trip a few days ago, so I needed to come back to fulfill my plant watering and mail retrieving duties. Lexy should be here soon. I washed my clothes once at Lexy's–and left a few things there–but I stayed long enough I ran out of clean laundry again. Dumping everything from my suitcase I brought to Oregon, I pull out the clothes to toss them in the washer.

The front door clicks open as I'm measuring out the detergent. "I'm in here!" I yell, knowing it's Lexy. She told me she was on her way, and I left it unlocked for her. By the time I'm finished throwing my clothes in and starting the machine, Lexy hasn't come to find me like I expected. I wander out to find her.

When I get to the living room and see the back of her blonde ponytail, I make my way to her. Fuck, her ass looks good peeking out of her shorts as she leans against the kitchen breakfast bar.

"Heeeey." My excited tone drags into hesitation when I glance from the look on her face to the papers in her hand. Fuck, I forgot I left those on the counter.

"What is this?" She looks more confused than any-thing.

"Can we sit?" I don't want to have this conversation standing in the kitchen.

She nods and lets me lead her to the couch. When I sit, I'm surprised when she straddles me, setting the stack of papers next to us. My hands fall to the waist of her jean shorts, sliding barely under the bottom of her tank top until they meet skin. She leans forward to press her lips against mine before pulling back.

"Okay, I'm ready to listen now," she says, as if her kiss was the first item of business she needed to check off.

My heart races both from being so close to her and being afraid this talk will change that. I take a breath. As long as she isn't mad I didn't tell her right away, it'll be fine because if she doesn't want to move then we won't. Easy as that.

"You know my Uncle James." I know she knows who I'm referring to, so I phrase it as a statement. She nods anyway.

"He grew up in Oregon, so he's known his best friend Tony basically his whole life. They own that family cabin together–the one I told you about." She nods again, slowly. "Well, Tony also owns a bar. One of the main ones the college kids go to. But he's selling it, and he asked me if I wanted to buy it."

I watch a range of emotions flicker across her face like a *Wheel of Fortune* wheel before she lands on one–it's a look I haven't experienced yet.

She pulls away, my hands reluctantly loosening their hold on her as she slides off me and onto the couch, her legs curling under her.

Fuck.

"I thought you'd tell me everything." Her statement is caught somewhere between being directed at me and a realization muttered to herself.

I turn toward her, reaching for her hand, but she pushes mine away. She scoots back on the couch until she's leaned against the opposite arm rest and pulls her knees to her body.

"Lexy. I'm sorry–"

"You're leaving me."

"What?" I ask in a panic. "No!"

She ignores my response and continues talking quietly to herself. "Maci left. Mack left. Now you're leaving."

Her devastation breaks me. I move to her side of the couch, refusing to let her push me away again.

"Lexy." Her gaze is stuck on her knees. I lift her chin with my hand, and she hesitantly lets me guide her dulled blue eyes to me as she stares blankly. I shift to grip her neck, my thumb firmly locked on the side of her face to keep her focus on me. I need her to hear me.

"I'm *not* leaving you."

Her eyes narrow as she studies my face as if she's trying to determine the answer to her question before she asks. "Then why didn't you tell me?"

"I'm sorry I didn't tell you. After what happened with Todd, I'm trying to be conscious of how my actions affect you. I don't want to be selfish with you." I pause. "Except with your body," I add, chuckling, in an attempt to lighten the mood. The corner of her mouth twitches up before resuming its downward position. "This is a big decision, and I want to include you in it. I just wasn't sure how to bring it up."

Her face softens like my words are getting through to her. "Do you want to buy it?"

I sigh, letting my thumb skate across her cheek. "I don't know. I haven't really thought much about what I want to do yet. I love bartending. It would also be nice to use my business degree and have something that's mine. But it's in Oregon, which is a problem."

She's silent for a moment. "Why is that a problem?" Is she asking me a trick question?

"Because we don't live in Oregon..."

"Do you wish we did?"

Why am I nervous? I've gotten so good at reading her, but I really can't tell how she feels about this. "Uhhh."

"You can tell me. Honesty is your thing, Troy. It's the reason I trust you. I know I'm not the most comfortable in serious conversations, but I'd rather have them with you than you be worried about talking to me."

"Yeah? Okay. I don't know. As far as location, I like Oregon more. Part of me thinks it would be great. But these past two months have been great too."

"This is such a big opportunity for you."

"What are you saying?"

"If you did want to move to Oregon, would you want me to come with you?"

I don't hesitate. "Yes. I wouldn't want to go if you weren't with me, but I can't ask you to do that."

"How long do you have to decide?" she asks before chewing on her bottom lip, vulnerability filling her eyes.

"I have a couple months, but Lexy–"

She cuts me off. "I'm not promising anything. I don't want to be like my mom—blindly following some guy. And I've never been to Oregon. I might hate it."

She hesitates, and I take the opportunity to interject. "I would never ask you to make any sort of move in your life you aren't comfortable with or don't truly want."

Her eyes flicker across my face as if she's searching for the truth in my words. "I told Mack I would be at his final show in April. Maybe we could go together and check it out?" Once she finishes, it looks like she's holding her breath waiting for my response. It's so fucking cute.

"I love that idea." I stick with that instead of confessing that I love her. "Thank you for this, Lexy."

She grins, but then it fades. "I don't want to say something ridiculous like 'I don't care where we are as long as

I have you' because that's... well, ridiculous. We basically just met. But I can admit I kind of like you, Troy, and I want to see where things go with us before a big decision is made that takes an opportunity away from us."

"You kind of like me, huh?" I stand, reaching for her hand and finally pulling her out of her fetal position on the couch. I wrap my arms tightly around her waist, pulling her into me.

"Shut up, and do some of the other things I like." She smirks right as my lips land on hers, and in one smooth jump, her legs wrap around me tightly before I carry her to my bed.

CHAPTER THIRTY-FIVE
TROY

Lexy: *Let's have a contest.*

   Me: What does the winner get?

   Lexy: *You don't even want to know what the competition is first?*

   Me: *Nope. If the prize is worth it, it doesn't matter what I have to do.*

   Lexy: *I'm going to use that against you some day.*

   Me: *Can't wait. What am I going to win?*

   Lexy: *If you win, we'll try that thing you've been wanting to try.*

   Me: *And if you win?*

   Lexy: *I get to drive your motorcycle.*

   Me: *You think I'd let you?*

   Lexy: *As long as I fuck you on it after.*

   Me: *Sounds like I can't lose either way.*

   Lexy: *And whoever loses has to pay for our flights home from Oregon.*

   Me: *Hey, you can't add stuff.*

   Lexy: *I can do whatever I want.*

   Me: *Okay, deal. What's the bet?*

   Lexy: *Whoever gets the most numbers tonight wins.*

   Me: *A bachelor party just walked in, didn't it?*

   Lexy: *Two of them. But you already made a deal.*

   Me: *It's on.*

Lexy: *May the best flirt win.*

"Alright, what's your count?" I slide onto the bar stool at the bar where Lexy works now as she punches an order into her computer. She spins around and grins.

"I don't know! My shift isn't over yet." She looks back at the clock on her register. "We don't close for another hour."

"Uh uh. I'm finished, so you're cut off." I already know there's no way she beat me, even if I gave her the extra time. My girlfriend is hot as fuck, and on a normal day I'd always bet on her, but it happened to be ladies' night at work. We offered a free appetizer for every two specialty drinks. I've *never* seen so many single women in one place.

"Okay, hold on." She pulls a stack of credit card slips from her cash bag behind the register and sorts through them. "I have eight." She's smirking at me like she thinks there's no way I got more.

The most I've ever gotten was four, but that was before I was in a competition with my girlfriend on ladies' night with the prize being that thing I've been wanting to try and said girlfriend keeps rejecting. I was shocked when I ended the night with 12. But fuck, she looks so proud of herself, and I'm honestly shocked she didn't get more. The ratio of guys to girls here is strongly in her favor.

"I really thought I had you tonight." I rub my thumb against my lip in an attempt to hide my smile.

"Really? How many did you get?"

"Seven." Her eyes light up at my answer, and it's absolutely worth my white lie. "Guess I better get us some flights and pray you don't crash my bike."

She squeals with excitement. Like actually squeals and does some little dance as she heads to the other side of the bar to help a customer. Fuck, she's cute. I can't wait to see her on my bike. I can't wait to fuck her on my bike. Yeah, I definitely won.

CHAPTER THIRTY-SIX
LEXY

Me: *I'm here.*

I text Troy as soon as I pull up to his condo complex. It's only another minute until he comes out, tosses his bag in the back and slides into the passenger seat of Maci's car. Whether she chooses Dean or Mack, she's not coming back to California and asked if I could bring her car with me. "Hey, Lex." He smiles and leans over the center console to kiss me. I can't help but smile into it. "Are you excited?"

"Are you nervous?" I counter.

He looks at me confused. "About?"

"This is my first real road trip. That's a lot of pressure on you to make it epic."

"If you have nothing to compare it to, how will you know if it's not?" He smirks.

I shove on his shoulder playfully. "Hey!"

"Don't worry. It'll be epic." He gives me a knowing look that makes me feel like I'm not in on a secret.

"Okay, so I'm thinking we will drive until we feel like stopping today? Then get a hotel and go the rest of the way tomorrow?" We already discussed this plan, but I confirm anyway.

His mumble of acknowledgement makes me feel like he's uninterested in the plan. Maybe he's distracted by the Spotify playlist he's making.

We make it almost five hours before we have to stop for gas and go to the bathroom, ironically in a town called Los Baños. When we come out of the gas station, Troy stops me in front of the car. "May I drive?"

"Yeah, sure." I toss him the keys and slide into the passenger seat.

When we get back on the road, my phone, that's sitting in the mount on the dash, reroutes. "Did you get on the wrong freeway?"

"Depends what you think is right." The corner of his mouth quirks.

"Where are we going, Troy?" I ask him as we pass by a sign that says we have 120 miles to San Francisco. I didn't think we would drive through there.

"You'll see." He grins.

An hour later, we enter Mountain View, a town I've never heard of, and pull into a hotel parking lot. I'm even more confused. "Why are we here? We haven't driven very far today."

"I know, but this is where we are staying tonight. We can have a long drive tomorrow." He takes the keys out of the ignition and gets out, grabbing our bags from the back seat. "Come on, Lex!"

I'm pretty sure he's not going to tell me what we are actually doing, so I just go with it.

He gets us checked in, and we find our room. As soon as we walk in, he tosses our bags on the king bed with a fluffy white comforter, setting our room key on the dresser. My hands find his hips, sliding under his shirt and around his back so I can pull him to me. He drapes his arms over my shoulders. "Hi."

"Hi." He chuckles, pulling his hands to cradle my face as he kisses me. I still feel his kisses all the way to my toes. Every time. I'm getting used to this, to him. As much as it scared me at first, it gets easier every day. It's almost a familiar feeling now. I break our kiss. The only thing I want more than it is to know what the hell is going on.

"Tell me what we are doing here."

He looks at his watch. "Soon. Go get ready. I'll tell you when you're finished."

"I'm ready now!" I'm not. If we are going somewhere, I'd rather curl my hair, and put on some makeup. I'm surprised I've reached the point where I'm so comfortable around a guy without that. I didn't even think twice when I got ready this morning. My hair is in a messy bun. I've got on jean shorts and my red hoodie.

"You look perfect. You are perfect." He kisses me again, this time burying his hands in my hair and taking more than a simple kiss. He finally pulls back. "But if you do want to do your girly things, we gotta leave in like 20 minutes so we can get some dinner first."

"Fiiiiiine." I grab my bag and pretend stomp to the bathroom. His chuckle echoes through the air behind me.

Fifteen minutes later I exit the bathroom, hair curled and makeup done. "Can I wear this or do I need to change?"

"Okay, don't be mad, but I went through your closet the other day."

"Okay…" He pulls his hands from behind his back. "You brought my most worn out t-shirt?" I ask, as he holds out the Good Charlotte concert shirt I found at Goodwill when I was in high school. I take it from him.

"We can get you a new one when we get there." He smiles and pulls out two tickets, fanning them in front of my face.

"What?" I can't register what's happening. "We're going to see Good Charlotte?" He must be kidding me. "Like… in person?"

"Unless you don't want to go…" His smile turns when he sees the tears in my eyes. They just appeared all of a sudden. What the fuck. I don't think I've ever cried in my life. "Wait, what's wrong? I thought you'd be excited." He looks genuinely concerned.

I take a breath, tipping my head back, willing my tears not to fall. These things better not come out of my eyes. When I'm certain my voice won't crack, I respond. "I'm excited." I smile up at him before pulling my hoodie over my head and sliding on my t-shirt. When I meet his gaze again, he's still worried.

"Baby." His voice is gentle. He's never used that term outside of sex. It makes me melt a little. Who am I turning into? "Tell me what you're thinking."

"Nothing. It's not a big deal. It's dumb."

He stares at me, expectantly.

"It's just that no one has ever done something this nice for me. I got overwhelmed for a second." I turn away from him to go put on my gray Converse that are sitting by the door.

He reaches out and stops me with his fingers wrapping around my wrist, waiting for me to turn to him. "Lexy. Can I say something?"

I nod.

"These past few months with you have been great. I haven't been this happy in… I don't know, maybe my entire life. I'm not telling you so you put pressure on yourself or our relationship or anything. I know this trip is mostly about seeing Mack, but it still means a lot that you invited me and that you're going to let me show you around my hometown. I wanted to do something so you know how much I appreciate you. I also want you to get used to it. This will not be the last nice thing I do for you." He grips my chin, tilting my face until my gaze meets his and runs his thumb against my cheek.

"Thank you," I say, meaning it more than the inflection of my voice might imply. I hold his stare for a moment then bend down to slip on my shoes. By the time I stand, it's registered what he did for me and that I actually get to see my favorite band live. "Troy!" I startle him from where he's digging in his bag. "I'm so excited!" I practically scream my words as I tackle him onto the bed.

"There's my girl," he whispers into my ear and holds me tightly to him.

CHAPTER THIRTY-SEVEN
TROY

It's only 7:30 a.m., but we have another nine and a half hours to drive, and I told Cooper's mom we would try to be there in time for dinner. She's excited to meet Lexy. I can't wait to introduce her to everyone. I know they will love her as much as I do.

As I checked out, Lexy headed to the car. By the time I get there, she's already curled up against the window falling asleep, the morning sun softly streaming across her face. I gently set my box of breakfast down and quietly pull out my phone to snap a picture, immediately setting it as my new screensaver. When I pull up to the light at the freeway entrance, I take a good, long look at her. She's changed back into her jean shorts, and she's wearing her new Good Charlotte t-shirt from the concert last night. Her blonde curls have mostly fallen from sleeping on them–not that we did much of that. By the time we got back to our room and had sex, it was almost 3 a.m.

"What?" Apparently she's not asleep yet.

"Nothing." I smile at her. She's so fucking cute. And mine. These ten days will be great. We've both been so busy with work and spring break crowds that we've hardly spent time together. Plus, I get to show her around my home for a change. Not that it's my home anymore.

She's looking at me like she's trying to read my thoughts when the light turns green.

"I got you breakfast while I was checking out." I pull one hand from the steering wheel to hand her the to-go box full of bagels and fruit that I had resting on the center console. "And." I reach into the pocket of my hoodie. "Got you these out of the vending machine." She glances down at the pack of gummy bears in my hand. She smiles as she rips them open, not even bothering with the fruit on her lap.

"Thank you," she says as she digs out an orange and a white bear and eats them together. It's her favorite combo. She searches through the bag for another moment, and I see the red and yellow out of the corner of my eye–my favorites. She holds them in front of my mouth until I lean forward to bite them from her fingers.

"Thanks." I smile at her quickly, and catch a weird expression wash over her face. I bring my eyes back to the road while I question her. "Why are you looking at me like that?"

"I love you," she blurts. Before I even have time to process, she turns her gaze to the road and adds, "But don't say it back right now or anything. I don't want it to be a big deal, okay?" She mumbles "okay" again under her breath as if she's trying to convince herself it's not a big deal. But I know it's a big fucking deal for her. It's a big deal to me too. Fuck, I love her so much. I'll wait to tell her, though. Instead, I smile and reach my hand over, letting it land between her thighs. She goes right back to picking out the gummy bears she wants next, like nothing happened.

CHAPTER THIRTY-EIGHT
LEXY

We pull into the driveway of the cutest two story house I've ever seen. The white trim pops as the sage green paint attempts to blend in with the huge trees on either side of the house. There's literally a white picket fence that encloses a perfectly manicured yard. I've never lived in anything other than an apartment. Outside of a few celebrity homes, I've never actually spent time in a real house. I feel dumb, but it's a lot to absorb.

"You ready, baby?" Troy notices I haven't made a move to open my door.

"There's going to be a real family in there. Like, with a family dinner and people who don't hate each other." Part of why this decision is terrifying is because of how different my life will be compared to everything I've ever known. Yes, I'd have Troy, Mack and Maci–I know that makes this seem like a no brainer, but what if something happens? I'd be stuck in an unfamiliar place, surrounded by a lifestyle I'm not accustomed to.

He reaches over and threads his fingers through mine, no sign of judgement on his face even though I'm acting like the most normal thing in the world is foreign as fuck. It is for me, though.

"I felt the same way when Cooper invited me over for dinner the first time. I was nine, I think. Our meal came out of a casserole dish instead of a TV dinner tray, and I was so confused."

Scanning my memory, I realize that at 24 years old, I'm not sure I've ever had a dinner from a casserole dish. Tingles of anxiety flood my body. "I'm nervous."

"I'll be with you the whole time." He kisses my temple and untangles our hands. "Let's go."

I nod, pulling the handle on the door so it swings open.

The front door opens before we reach it.

"Troy, you made it!" The woman wraps her arms around him, and he immediately does the same.

"Hi, Mom." I can hear the smile in his voice as he pulls back. The woman standing in front of us looks like a mom from my imagination. She's wearing light washed blue jeans, a navy-blue blouse with slightly ruffled short sleeves and matching navy flats. Her light brown hair curls toward her face right above her shoulders. She's beautiful, and her joy in seeing Troy makes me smile.

He takes a step back, so I'm now between them. "This is Lexy. Lexy, Melissa."

She wraps her arms around me and pulls me to her like I mean as much to her as her own kid does. It's weird. And wonderful. She smells like vanilla, and I linger in her hug even though this is such a strange moment for me. "It's so nice to finally meet you," she whispers in my ear before holding my shoulders at arms length to get a better look at me.

"Yeah, you too. I've heard so much about you."

Dinner flies by with just the three of us. Cooper's dad had to work late, but we'll be back to spend a day with them. I'm excited to meet Cooper since Troy knows both of my best friends. It's already fun seeing him in his element and with his people. Oregon isn't his home anymore, but he feels different here than I've seen him in California–in a good way. It reminds me of the feeling I get when I close up the bar and the last customer leaves–like I can finally relax and not have to worry about anything else.

Melissa is sweet. I imagine she's the kind of mom anyone would love to have, although I would have been happy having one around in general. Everything we talked about at dinner was pretty surface level. I'm not sure if Troy said anything to her, worried I'll feel pressure to move here, but I appreciate it either way for now. I can't help but picture having some sort of relationship with her, since she's so important to Troy, especially if we did move here. It might be nice, but I don't want to get my hopes up.

As we rinse our dishes in the sink after the most delicious mac and cheese I've ever eaten, the sound of the front door swinging open tells me the action was dramatic even though I can't see it.

"I'm here!" The voice, belonging to who I'm assuming is Cooper, echoes through the hallway as it reaches us. It's only another second before he appears in front of us, his light brown hair barely long enough to be mussed on top, and light facial hair that looks good on him even though it's not my preference. His eyes are as bright blue as my own, and that's about all the look I get of him before he wraps me in a bear hug, lifting me off my feet before placing me back on the ground. "Finally," he exhales like he's been waiting for this longer than the four months Troy and I have been together. Something tells me he's not talking about us meeting. Troy hasn't said much about Emily, but based on what I do know, it sounds like he wasn't the most fun to be around for a while. I'm selfishly more than okay with being part of the reason he's happier now.

"I guess you're Cooper." I laugh.

"The one and only." He grins as he and Troy do a ridiculous secret handshake then makes his way to Melissa to kiss her on the cheek. "Sorry I'm late. My client would not stop talking."

"Sure, blame them," I sass. I don't know what it is about this home that makes me feel free to be myself.

Cooper shoots me a playful look before turning to Troy. "What did you tell this girl about me?"

"Bro, everyone who knows anything about you knows you don't shut up."

Cooper shrugs before walking to the living room. "What game are we playing?"

Game? Are they one of those families that actually plays board games together? Is that a thing that happens in real life? I thought it was only on TV. My question is answered when Troy squats down in front of the coffee table chest. He opens it, giving me a perfect view of stacks and stacks of games. He rummages through them for a few seconds before pulling one out.

"Don't worry, it's easy, and we can be on the same team," Troy tells me as he pulls me onto the couch next to him, sensing my hesitation. I don't think I've ever played a board game.

"That's not fair. I bet you two can practically read each other's minds," Cooper whines, taking his seat on the floor on the other side of the coffee table. I wonder what kind of game this is.

"I gave you life, kid. Don't underestimate my ability to read your mind," Melissa teases her son.

"Okay, so we agree to go with what we both think I'll say?" She nods at his scheming.

Troy turns to me. "It's called Think 'N Sync. Super simple. Each of these cards has a topic. The opposing team reads a fill in the blank prompt and counts down from three. On one, the other team has to say their answer at the same time. If they say the same thing, they get a point. Make sense?"

"Yeah, so I say whatever I think you're going to say?"

"Yup. Watch, they can go first." Troy draws a card out of the box. "Okay, the topic is music. A classic rock band... 3. 2. 1."

"U2." Both Cooper and Melissa say simultaneously.

Everyone grins, and Troy turns to me. "'Beautiful Day' is Mom's favorite song. It's on her house cleaning mix between every other track." He laughs, clearly recalling a memory before he turns back to Cooper on the floor and Melissa in the lounge chair next to him. "Okay, male country singers... 3. 2. 1."

"Mitchell Tenpenny!" Cooper yells at the same time Melissa says, "Russell Dickerson!"

"Moooooom. You're supposed to pick what I'm going to pick," Cooper whines playfully like he's in middle school and not a grown-ass adult.

"You played his album in the car the last two times we went out for lunch." She laughs.

"That was like three weeks ago, Mom. Keep up."

She rolls her eyes at him, and he returns the gesture while Troy laughs at them both.

"Well, I've never heard of either of them."

Cooper addresses me. "You'll learn. Half of this town listens to country."

"Tell me I'm not in LA without telling me I'm not in LA." I laugh. Some people listen to country, and I know of a few bars near my apartment that cater to it, but I don't know any songs myself.

I get confirmation Troy has been hesitant about specifically bringing up anything related to moving here by the look in his eyes when it comes up. I appreciate him not wanting to pressure me, but I also want to love it here. I've felt like I'm outgrowing California for a while. He doesn't contribute to the conversation but looks down at the card for the next line.

After two more turns for Cooper and Melissa, it's our turn. I'm nervous, mainly because I have a feeling it'll either make me believe Troy and I are as in sync as we think, or our short four months of dating will prove otherwise.

Cooper draws a card. "Ready?" He looks at me and waits for my nod. "Topic is sports gear. A sport where cleats are worn... 3. 2. 1."

"Football," Troy and I say at the same time. Easy. I'm about to voice my next thought when Troy cuts me off, reading my mind again. "Mom, do you still have my jersey somewhere?" He shoots me a wink.

I feel my face heat at the possibility of someone catching on to the fact that I only want to see it on him so I can take it off him. Troy takes notice and grins as Melissa says, "Yes, of course. It's still in the closet where you left it," without questioning.

"Okay, next!" Cooper pulls our attention back to the game. "A company that makes athletic shoes... 3. 2. 1."

"Nike," Troy says as I draw a blank.

"I only wear converse and cycle shoes." I laugh, feeling like I should have been able to come up with something, but no one makes me feel dumb.

"Nike was founded here. Originally called Blue Rib-bon Sports, though." Cooper shares this fun fact. "It's basically a requirement to be the go-to for anyone who plays football here, which is something we are also obsessed with."

That part I knew. Troy somehow convinces his bar to play the Oregon Ducks game every single week, even if a California school is playing. If that doesn't tell you how charming the man is, I'm not sure what will.

"Okay, a form of protection besides a helmet... 3. 2. 1."

I know we are on the same page when I see a smirk on Troy's face the split second before the word "condom" comes out of both our mouths at the same time.

Cooper laughs hard as he falls back onto the floor dramatically.

Melissa is quick to jump in. "So young you still think sex is a sport." She laughs then adds, "Well at least I know you listen to the things I taught you." She directs her statement at Troy, more amused than anything. I'd be caught up in how ideal their relationship seems, but I can't stop thinking about how strange it is to feel so in sync with someone.

I'm only thrown off more when we play a few more rounds and Troy and I have the same responses almost every single time. How on earth we are so in tune with each other, I have no idea. After an hour of back and forth, Troy excuses us, and after saying goodbye to Melissa, Cooper follows behind us.

By the time we get back to Cooper's house, it's almost 11 p.m. For being someone who usually goes to bed at two or three in the morning, I am exhausted. We hardly slept at all last night after the concert, and we drove thirteen hours in two days. Troy grabs our bags and walks us to the guest room, which doesn't feel like a guest room at all.

The closet door is open, and I see a couple of what I'm assuming are Troy's hoodies hanging there with a few pairs of sweats folded on the shelf above them. The black bedding matches everything on his bed in California, the same blackout shade hangs in the window. If I didn't know where he actually lived, I'd swear this was his room. "Creature of habit?" I question after I finish my inventory of his room.

"I know what I like." He grins and takes a step toward me to close the distance between us. Reaching his hands for my waist, he pulls me into him before pressing his lips into mine. "I am surprised it's exactly how I left it. I told Cooper to rent it."

I pull back slightly. "It kind of seems like you never left." I'm more curious than judgmental. He looks nervous at my statement, though, so I add, "It's okay. You don't have to tiptoe around the idea of moving here or you loving Oregon. This isn't only my decision, and it should be based on whether this is what's best for you too. If it's what's best for you, I want to love it here. So, stop holding back."

"How'd I get so lucky to find you?" he mumbles against my lips before giving me another soft kiss.

"Ummm, you wouldn't leave me alone. I had no choice but to give in." I smile into another kiss, but I feel his happiness falter. I pull back. "What is it?"

He shakes his head. He rarely keeps his thoughts to himself. I run my hands up his back, under his shirt and wait. He takes a deep breath. "I was so fucked up after Emily. She wrecked my world." I can see in his eyes how hard it is for him to recall that time of his life. "A few months ago, I decided I was ready to start dating, but I wasn't convinced I could be happy in a relationship again. But somehow I found you." He presses his forehead to mine before lowering his voice. "Whatever we decide about Oregon, what's most important to me is that we do it together. Some of the people who were supposed to be on my team didn't take it seriously. But you care about what I might need, you tell me that you love me and it feels like you mean it. You healed what I thought would always be broken, Lexy. I can't thank you enough for that."

I pull myself into him, feeling his heartbeat where my head rests on his chest. "You've done the same for me," I whisper.

CHAPTER THIRTY-NINE
LEXY

When I wake, I roll over and find the other side of the bed cold. Troy and Cooper are going for a ride this morning while I hang out with Mack and meet Avery. He promised it would be my turn when we both got back this afternoon. He must have left a while ago for his spot to be cold. I turn back over to grab my phone off the nightstand and check the time, noticing a blue sticky note on it.

Can't wait to show you around later. I love you.

My breath catches at reading the last three words. It's not that I thought Troy didn't feel the same way, but seeing it in writing makes it much more real. Reading this note not only confirms what I'm feeling but that Troy knows me—he knew I would need a minute to process. I told him to wait because I was overwhelmed enough when I blurted it out. I suddenly had an undeniable urge to tell him. At the time, I was worried I would panic if he said it back right away. But now, all I feel is the need to hear those words spoken aloud. He's been so patient and understanding with me, but my patience is suddenly gone.

I pick up my phone, finding his name at the top of my favorites. He answers on the second ring.

"Good morning, baby." I can hear his smile through the phone.

"I'm surprised you answered. I thought you'd be on the road."

"We stopped for coffee. Is everything okay?" He sounds more hesitant now. He has to know I saw his note since it was stuck to my phone.

"Mhmm." I can hear the smile in my own voice.

He chuckles on the other end. "Lexy."

"Yeah?"

"I love you."

The breath I was holding rushes out of me. "I love you too, T." The nickname slips out unexpectantly. I've never used a pet name for anyone before so this feels like a good compromise.

"Good. Now go have fun with Mack. I'll see you in a few hours."

I walk into Troy's bedroom to find him sitting on the edge of the bed. He's looking down at his phone but glances up when he hears the door open, a smile instantly lighting up his face. God, I love him so much it's overwhelming. I didn't imagine I'd ever feel like this about someone, especially after such a short time.

I make my way to him, bringing a knee to either side of him on the bed. He tosses his phone aside and scoots back enough to give me room to straddle him. His hands fall to my hips, his fingers running along my skin under my red hoodie. "How's your day been?" he whispers against my lips before he kisses me.

"Good, but about to get better now that I get to drive your bike." I grin into another kiss, looping my arms around his neck.

"You know I've never let anyone but Cooper drive it." He says it like it's a miracle he's letting me.

"Only because I won our bet," I laugh, "but no taking it back."

There's a shimmer in his eyes as he smirks.

"What?"

"Nothing." He shakes his head, running his hands up my side as he kisses my neck.

I pull back. "Tell me," I demand.

A grin lights up his face. "I lied to you. I'd say I'm sorry, but I'm not."

I'm confused for a moment, my brows pinching together as I trail my fingers along either side of his neck. "Are you telling me *you* actually won our bet?"

He shrugs. "As long as I have you, I'm always winning."

I playfully push against him until he falls back on the bed. "There's no way you would have let me win with that bet on the table."

"I love you, Lexy. I would have let you drive my bike no matter what. I'd let you do anything you want," he says with adoration in his eyes as he looks up at me.

My heart flips. Like it actually feels like it somersaulted inside my chest. What a weird experience this entire journey has been. "I love you, T."

"A nickname, the L word, your stack of notes I found hiding in your drawer. Are you getting soft on me, baby?"

"It's your fault," I tease. "You made me this way."

"I love you this way." Gripping my thighs, he pulls himself back to me and kisses me softly before adding, "But I loved you before too." He reaches up to bury his fingers in my hair, his other hand still running across the skin on my side. "Really though, you're not freaked out?"

I shake my head slowly. "It's different, but I like it. Way better than I thought it would be." I grin. "Now, I want my bike ride and my tour. Let's see if you can make me love this town too. Then maybe later I'll make sure you win."

He rakes his teeth across his lower lip, heat apparent in his eyes as his fingers dig into my hip like he wants to skip to the end of the plans right now.

I laugh and move to slide off his lap. "I said later."

Shaking his head as if to clear his thoughts, he stands too, following my lead. "Anywhere specific you want to go?"

"Hmmm, I was thinking maybe you could give me a tour of the college?" He nods. "And… oh! To your favorite spot, the one you took Maci? Definitely food, somewhere we don't have in California."

"Let's do it," he says as he motions to the door. "We'll go to school first while it's still light out. I'll drive there. Once we get to the overlook around sunset, I'll let you drive up that road. It's straighter, and there won't be any people or traffic."

"And then we can do something else illegal once we get there?" I wiggle my eyebrows at him, a smirk on my face as I reach for his hand.

He chuckles. "We can do whatever you want," he says as he brings our conjoined hands to his mouth for a kiss.

TROY

"Wow," Lexy whispers after climbing off my bike and taking off her helmet. She spins in a slow circle, taking in the entrance to campus. I parked on the only driveable road that goes through it and runs under an archway made of trees from each side weaving together in the middle. I can't help but smile at her amazement, refusing to take my eyes off her. "I can't believe you went to school here," she says loud enough that I know it's intended for me to hear.

"Yeah, I love it. Come on." I take her hand and pull her out of the street, toward a path that will lead us to my favorite building. "That's the math building." I nod at the building to our left.

She instantly stops walking to look up at it, jerking me back a little. "Where you met Maci." She smiles as she says it. After Emily, I promised myself I'd never get into a situation involving best friends–that I'd avoid any sort of fucked up love triangle. I'm so fucking glad I went with my gut on this because while there are similarities, there are also no betrayals, backstabbing or lying like before. Knowing this could have potentially ended up entirely different is wild to me. Instead, the past worked out in a way that's best for everyone. I guess that makes me thankful for how my relationship with Emily ended. I hadn't really thought of that until now, but I wouldn't be here with Lexy if it had played out any other way, and this is absolutely where I want to be.

"What?" Her voice breaks through my thoughts.

I smile and continue tugging her down the path. "Nothing. I just love you."

She grins back at me. "You're going to say that a lot now, huh?"

"I have to make up for every time the past two months I held back when I wanted to tell you."

She tugs on my arm until I stop again then pulls herself to me for a kiss. I keep falling deeper for this girl. Even though I'll be happy wherever we decide to live, I would rather be here, if she likes it. I reluctantly pull away from her to point to the building in front of us. "This is my favorite one." It's cement gray and kind of looks like a mental hospital out of the 1800s. I'm pretty sure that's around when it was built. It's surrounded by mossy trees. "No idea why, it's just old and cool. Oh, and it was originally named after Oregon's first federal judge who didn't believe state schools were of use to anyone. It's funny how ironic that is."

"Okay, that part is weird." Lexy laughs. "I think it's cool too." She leans into me as she looks at the building. "I love that the old places here are full of character. Everything old in LA feels dirty and sketchy. Did you have any classes there?"

"Nah. Most of mine were in that building." I point in the direction we came from, behind the math building. "That's the business complex."

She walks toward it. "What made you choose business? Did you know what you wanted to do with it?"

"Not really, to be honest. Coop's dad started his own real estate company. Not that I had much to compare to, but I always thought it was cool how he could work around his life for the most part. He was always at our football games, graduation, or anything else that was important to his kids, me included. And once his company grew, he would pick up the slack when he could to make sure his employees had the same luxury. I'm attracted to that level of freedom and flexibility, I guess." I shrug. "But bartending has kind of given me that, so I haven't been in a hurry to find something else."

"Do you think you'd have that kind of freedom owning the bar?" She seems genuinely curious.

"Maybe not at first. Actually, definitely not at first. It would be a lot of work to get the hang of it. But I think it would help not starting from scratch. Tony already has it established, it's in the perfect location, it's profitable. That would all help. I know he's rarely at the bar now and spends a lot of time with his family. Growing up, they always came on vacations with us to his and Uncle James' cabin. So, I'd say at least eventually I'd have that. Plus, I'd be completely in control, unlike now where I'm at the mercy of my manager. I've just been lucky to have a good one."

Lexy looks up, taking in the massive five story ground to roof glass windows of the business complex. When her gaze comes back to me, I lead her to the wooden bench near the entrance. "What about you? Did you ever consider going to cosmetology school? Or something else?"

"It was a good gig for a teenager, but I don't want to do makeup as my job."

"How did you get into that anyway?"

"Kind of by accident. I loved watching my mom get ready for her dates. It was the only time she," Lexy uses air quotes, "spent with me. I hated when she left but always thought it was so cool how she could create all these different looks. Sometimes, when she was in a phase where she was happy and in love, she'd do my makeup or let me play on my own while she got ready. From there, I read tips in magazines and taught myself."

"How'd you get a job so young?"

"Right place, right time kind of thing. I had taken the bus to the beach one day and didn't want to use the public bathrooms, so I snuck into a fancy restaurant to use theirs. Some woman was crying about getting her heart broken, and when her tears finally stopped and she tried to fix her makeup she was shaking too badly. I offered to help. Turned out she was a trust fund kid and had a bunch of rich friends. They started hiring me for parties and events."

"Only in California." I laugh. It's fucking wild there, especially compared to Oregon. "So, why did you stop?"

She turns toward me, folding her legs criss-crossed on the bench. "I think I started getting bitter and resentful. My mom was gone for weeks at a time by this point, and it felt like I had nothing, and these people had everything. Then I got a job at the Pub and learned quickly that even the rich people have problems. I also learned how much I loved bartending."

"You're really good at it. Is that what you want to do still?"

"For now. I think my mom was always in such a rush to find something that would last forever, and it never worked out because she didn't take the time to figure out what she really needed and what made her happy. Right now bartending is work I don't mind. I think if there's something else I'd enjoy more, I'll know when I come across it. Kind of like when I met you, I think. You just know when you're ready for something new or different or whatever."

Ever since she's said "I love you," she's been more comfortable with her feelings, and I fucking love it. I have no doubt when it comes to her. It's such a relief.

I pull my bike up in the side street that leads to Skinner Butte. I flip my kickstand out but leave it running as I swing my leg over, hopping off so Lexy can slide forward. "You ready, baby?"

She pulls off her helmet so she can focus on what I'm showing her. Her gaze meets mine, a fire in her eyes, a smile on her face that's void of any fear. She's sexy as fuck straddling my black seat in her cut off jean shorts, her toes barely touching the ground on either side. I should have told her to put jeans on, but selfishly her ass just looks too good in these. She watches intently as I give her a quick tutorial on everything she needs to know and point out the path. The sun is starting to set, but she's not going to drive it far, and it's a one way road up the hill to the overlook. When she's confident and ready, I swing my leg back over, this time finding my place behind her.

Lexy puts her helmet back on, flipping down the visor before reaching for the handlebars. I slide my hands around her, resting them lightly on top of hers. A slight tip of her head toward me lets me know she's ready. I kick up the stand and help her roll the throttle back. The bike jerks but smooths out as we move forward, following the straight road that leads to the path. Feeling confident she's got this, I pull my hands off hers, letting them settle loosely into the center pocket of her red hoodie. Halfway up, I know she wants to go faster, but this road winds too much to allow for that.

We make it to the top, and she slows until she's near enough to the curb to hit the break. She flips the kickstand out, and I reach around to pull the key out of the ignition.

"So, was it everything you dreamed?" I laugh as she takes off her helmet.

"If we move here, I'm getting a license." The look on her face makes me think that might be my biggest selling point. It terrifies me how much she loves it.

"We'll see," I say, grabbing her hand and tugging her toward the overlook. One of the main reasons I didn't bring my bike to Cali is because I actually don't think they are safe, and the older I get, the more I'm actively aware of how dangerous they are.

"Hey! You can't tell me what to do," she sasses.

This is not a battle that needs to be fought at this moment. "Okay, baby. Let's talk about it later." I lean in to kiss her before she can respond.

She pulls back, seemingly satisfied with my statement, turns and leans against the metal railing. I box her in, an arm on either side of her as her eyes roam over the view. Below us is the road we just drove up, blocked off from the rest of the town by a layer of tall, green trees. We are up high enough that you can see a lot of the main town past them. On the far left is a nearly perfect overhead view of Autzen Stadium, where the Ducks play, and the rest of the buildings that lie in front of us are mostly downtown businesses, restaurants and bars–including Jameson's. The sun is setting to the right. It's my favorite time to come here.

"It's such an incredible view," Lexy says.

"You know what else is an incredible view?"

"Hmm?" she questions, still taking it all in.

I lean forward until I'm close enough to whisper in her ear. "You bent over my bike."

She twists immediately into me, her bright blue eyes lighting up with a smile. "Lead the way, T."

We get back on my bike, and I drive over the curb of the path to the overlook onto the dirt hiking trail that leads into the trees. When we get to the top of the trail, I confirm no one is hanging out and park my bike. I swing my leg over, giving Lexy room to do the same.

Lexy sets her helmet down and stands back up to look at me. "Come here," I demand, a little more forceful than usual. I never really considered messing around on my bike until Lexy mentioned it. But seeing my favorite girl in my favorite place... fuck. This is a fantasy I didn't know I had, but now I *need* it to happen. When she's close enough to reach, I grab her hips and pull her into the space between me and the side of my bike.

She eyes me like she's daring me to take control of the situation, and it's sexy as hell the way she lets me take whatever I want from her. I crash my mouth into hers, her lips parting on contact, allowing my tongue to tangle with hers. It's a desperate and forceful kiss so fucking satisfying it makes me wonder why kissing was never my thing before Lexy. My fingers find their way to the button of her shorts, popping them open and tugging down the zipper without my mouth ever leaving hers.

My fingers slide under the lace to find her already wet, and she presses against me, urging me inside her. I slide two fingers in easily, her moan into our kiss vibrating through me. As my fingers work inside her, her breathing picks up enough that she breaks our kiss. Her head falls to my shoulder, her hands gripping my biceps as if she needs to keep herself from falling over. Seeing her so turned on by me is the sexiest thing I've ever seen. It turns me on so much that I need more. Right now.

I pull my fingers away from her and spin her around so quickly she doesn't even have time for her usual whimper at the loss of contact. I grip the top of her shorts on either side and shimmy them down her legs, and she steps out of them. I slide the condom I grabbed on our way out the door from my wallet before I undo my own jeans, sliding them down enough to give me access. I tug her body into mine until she can feel how hard I am against her ass. Brushing her wind blown blonde hair off her shoulder, I kiss her neck before whispering into her ear, "Bend over for me, baby."

She does as I ask, her hands gripping the seat of my bike as she spreads her legs for me without being told. The orange and pink glow of the sunset streams through the trees, casting just enough light on her. I bite into my fist, while taking her in and simultaneously trying to calm myself because the way she looks there's no way I'm going to last long.

Lexy senses my hesitation. "T, don't make me wait for you," she snaps playfully.

I pull the thin strip of lace separating us to the side and align with her entrance. I run my hands up her back under her red hoodie before settling them on her hips and gripping her tightly before I thrust inside of her.

I continue to slam into her, with equal force on my pull on her hips so she doesn't lose her balance.

"Fuck, Troy," she mumbles between breaths, her fingers white from her grip on the seats. With each thrust, I bury myself deeper inside her. She feels so fucking good.

"God, you're perfect." My words come out as rough as my breathing. I want her to feel as good as I do right now. I test her steadiness by removing my grip with one of my hands. When I note her core is strong enough to keep her stable, I reach one hand around, rubbing her clit in fast circles.

The moan she lets out with the extra connection is my undoing. I feel her tighten around me in waves as my own orgasm explodes through me. My entire body is overcome equally with pleasure and weakness after holding us steady and experiencing one of the most intense feelings I've ever had.

I run my hands up her back slowly, feeling her heart beating fast against my fingertips as she relaxes into the seat.

I tug on her sweatshirt lightly as I pull out of her and spin her around as she stands. Pulling her to me, I cross my arms around her neck, and she returns the motion by wrapping her arms around my waist. I breathe in the smell of her coconut shampoo. "I love you," I whisper into her ear.

"So much," she murmurs back.

CHAPTER FORTY
LEXY

Troy's arm feels heavy draped over my waist, but I lift it slowly. Slipping out of bed, I gently release his arm to the mattress in my place in an attempt not to wake him. We came back to Melissa's house last night so I could meet her husband, Mike. It was two in the morning before we were all too exhausted to keep talking, so we stayed the night here.

I make my way downstairs. After filling a glass of water from the fridge, I check out the backyard through the floor-to-ceiling sliding glass door off to the side of the kitchen. It's only fenced in on the left side. The back is lined with trees, and there's no divider between the neighbor's yard. I try to imagine what it would be like to not only have a loving family but have a second family living next door.

"Good morning, Lexy." Melissa's sweet voice fills the quiet morning air. "Coffee?"

"Yes, please." I make my way back to the kitchen to help her. Once we both have steaming mugs–mine maroon with a high school football logo–she leads us to the patio chairs outside. It's a little chilly, even in a pair of Troy's old pajama pants, but I don't mind. It's so peaceful, and the smog free air is refreshing to breathe.

As we sit, a woman perched on an identical outdoor furniture set next door waves. We both return the gesture. "Have you met the Porters yet?"

"Not yet. You guys must be close?"

"They are like a second family, have been for over twenty years now."

"Like you are for Troy."

"No. Troy *is* our family."

"He's lucky to have you. You raised great kids."

"Thank you, sweetie, but I think you make more of a difference than anyone now."

"I don't know about that."

"I do. I love Troy as much as I love my biological kids, but I'm just so happy he's finally found his person who can love him in all the ways he deserves."

My hands are wrapped around my coffee mug in an attempt to warm me, and I run my thumb slowly along the top edge as I stare into the hot liquid. This is such a rare conversation for me, but I don't want to be uncomfortable with it; I want to be able to talk about it. I want it to be normal. I want to be part of a family like this too.

"Can I ask you something?"

"Of course. I'm an open book."

"Taking Troy in must have been a big decision. I mean, you had to completely rearrange your life. It was so selfless. How did you know you were making the right choice for you? For your family?"

"As a mom, I couldn't imagine a little boy growing up without a loving family. It was a no brainer. To be honest, Mike and I hardly thought about it before deciding."

"I wish I had that. A loving family I mean." I feel safe opening up to her. It's clear why Troy thrived despite such a rough first decade of his life.

"Troy is one of the greatest joys in my life even though some wouldn't consider him family. Your family can be whoever you choose, Lexy. I'm so sorry you didn't have one growing up, but you can change that now."

"I want Troy to be my family."

"Well, if that's the case then you're stuck with us too." She smiles before taking a sip of her coffee, and I do the same. "I know you have a big decision to make once you leave here. I know you'll make the right one for you. My advice is to not overthink it. No matter what has happened in your past, you always have the ability to change your future. Unfortunately, there's no guide book on what choices you should make, but your gut will usually lead you down the right path. I know it did for us, with Troy."

"He is pretty great," I say, my smile even more telling than my words.

"He feels the same about you. I could tell the second he started talking about you that you were different." I don't know how to reply, so I take another sip of my coffee, and she continues. "Troy is so special, despite the obstacles he's endured. He always comes out on top."

I nod in agreement.

"The fact that both of you beat the odds and are together makes you stronger than you know. I'd be willing to bet you two can handle anything. But I want you to know you're always welcome here if you need help with anything. You're important to Troy, so you're important to us."

"Thanks, Mrs. Montgomery. That means a lot."

"Melissa."

I smile as the door slides open, revealing my sleepy boyfriend with... a bowl of ice cream? It's impossible to hold back my grin. He glances up from his spoonful of mint chip with a smile that says he's just as happy to see me. I take him in again before glancing back to the yard, and I'm swept into a vision of our kids running around, playing with Grandma Melissa and Grandpa Mike. Of Troy sneaking them inside for ice cream when he thinks I'm not paying attention.

I think I *want* to be a mom.

This is the first time I've ever felt that way. It never seemed like a possibility before since I didn't have a healthy example. Now it's like I'm immersed in a world conducive to raising a family, and it hits me how much I want that. With Troy.

"Morning, boyfriend." I smile up at him–suddenly not afraid of anything when it comes to him–and reach my coffee out for him to share.

CHAPTER FORTY-ONE
TROY

I don't really know any of Mack's band's songs. I've only heard them a few times at Shot in the Dark when Lexy worked there, and when she played a couple of their albums on our drive up here. They don't play the type of music I prefer, but they are talented. His final show is on Sunday night, but they picked up a second gig tonight. "This song is good," I say loud enough for Lexy to hear, leaning into her as we stand at a small, round high top table in the corner of the bar.

Her eyes are glossed over with sadness when they meet mine. "This is the one he wrote for Maci."

"Wow. He must really love her." I can tell by both the lyrics and the way he's singing.

"Yeah, he does."

"Do you know what she plans to do?"

"I don't. Guess we will all find out soon enough."

"Are you excited to see her? Two more days."

She smiles so big I can't help but do the same. "Yes. I miss her." She pauses, laughing to herself. "Look at me, I've got a boyfriend I love, friends I miss. Who even am I anymore?" Her voice is laced with humor, but I have a feeling she loves every part of this change.

"If we lived here, you'd get to see both her and Mack more." I'm a little hopeful, but I'm still hesitant. We haven't talked directly about how she feels about Oregon, at least not in regards to us moving here. We've enjoyed our week, but that doesn't necessarily mean anything.

Before she has a chance to respond, Cooper joins us. He carefully sets down the three beers he has pressed together in his hands.

Lexy thanks Coop as she picks up her glass, examining it before she takes a sip. "Is there any business in this town that doesn't rep the football team in some way?" She's noting the University of Oregon logo on her glass.

Cooper and I both chuckle. "I'd be surprised if there was," he says. "Everyone has school spirit here and will always come together for football."

I add, "You haven't even been in a grocery store yet. Totally decked out in green and yellow and Duck decorations. It's nothing like the melting pot of So Cal."

"I like how different it is. No one is loyal to anyone but themselves in LA. People seem less... only out for themselves here, from what I've noticed."

I start to speak, but Cooper cuts me off. "I'm just saying, you guys can stay with me as long as you want to if you decide to make the move."

"Thanks, man." My best friend makes this move sound simple. I wonder if Lexy gets that impression too.

"Incoming," Cooper mutters under his breath, but it doesn't register until Emily is in front of us. Her blonde bangs have grown out and are swooped to the side. She's painted on more makeup than she used to wear. I wouldn't recognize her if I hadn't completely memorized her at one point. It's not that she's not pretty, she just doesn't ignite a fire in every fucking part of me the way Lexy does. My first instinct is to take Lexy, walk away and avoid whatever drama is about to ensue, but there's no time for that either.

"Hey, Troy." Her words sound like poison coming out of her mouth, remembering the death that took place after the last time my name rolled off her tongue. "Can we talk?"

"I don't think that's necessary," I state. My hand finds Lexy's lower back out of comfort? Self preservation? To keep my fist from balling at the fucking nerve of the girl in front of me? Likely, all of the above.

The touch gets Lexy's attention, and I realize she wasn't even aware of what was happening until now. I've let go of what Emily did–I'm thankful for it even. I've been happier with Lexy in these past four months than I ever was with Emily in four years.

"Please, Troy," she begs, and I feel Lexy tense under my fingers. I run my thumb across the skin below her crop top–whether to reassure me or her, I'm not sure. My pulse accelerates from how much I want to get out of the conversation unscathed, but knowing how our relationship ended, I can't imagine anything less than a narcissistic encounter with a selfish goal. "I want to apologize. I miss you, Troy. You were my best friend." She brushes her fingers against my hand holding my beer, letting them linger. I stare in unfounded shock at where our skin has touched for the first time in over a year.

I pull back, my beer threatening to slosh over the edge of my cup. I can't believe she's doing this shit in front of Lexy when we are clearly together.

I'm about to tell her to leave when Lexy's calm voice cuts in. "Hey, I'm Lexy," she says brightly, reaching her hand out expectantly. Emily looks at it then cautiously takes the hand in front of her, like it may be a trap. The second she does, I watch Lexy's grip tighten around Emily as she locks her eyes confidently onto my ex. "Whatever sob story you want to tell yourself to feel better, do that if you need. But you don't get to stand here and apologize to make yourself feel better. You and I both know your time to do that has expired. And you lost the privilege of your friendship the second you decided fucking someone else was more important. Your loss is the best thing that ever happened to him. Don't you dare try to take that back just to clear your conscience."

Emily's wide eyed stare flits from Lexy to me, and I vaguely hear Cooper chuckling off to the side. I shrug. "What she said." It's not my job to come to her rescue anymore.

"It was so not nice to meet you, though. Have a great night." Lexy releases her hand and twists into me. She presses up on her toes as she wraps her arms around my neck and locks her lips with mine. I deepen the kiss, only vaguely cognizant of Emily storming off in a huff before forgetting anything else in the room exists. When she finally pulls away, she looks a little guilty.

"Sorry, that was petty. I don't know what came over me." She bites into her lip nervously.

I brush a stray curl from her face and tuck it back with my hand buried in her hair. "That was your equivalent of punching Todd." I laugh. "It was fucking hot."

"Tony!" I call as he's sliding the key into the lock of Jameson's. I'm glad we caught him. I wasn't sure we would since it's a few minutes after closing.

"Troy, hi!" He retracts the key and turns to Lexy. "This must be the girlfriend?"

"Lexy." She smiles, reaching her hand for his.

"I was hoping to show her around the place, if it's not a problem."

"Not at all." He holds his key out to me. "Gail is waiting on me, though. Can you lock up when you're finished?"

"Yeah, of course. Thanks, Uncle Tony."

"Thank you," he says, and I know even considering this deal means a lot to him.

We say goodbye, and I reach for the door handle, pulling it open for Lexy then stepping next to her in an attempt to read her face as she takes in the room. She struggles to see in the dark, so I head behind the bar and flip the switch. The burnt orange light illuminates the alcohol bottles behind the bar, and a glow comes from under each dusty red cover hanging above the booths that line the wall.

She silently makes a loop around the main room, walking behind the bar and past where I stand at the end of it. Her face and lack of words leave me wondering what could possibly be running through her mind, but I don't want to push her. I follow her to the billiards room. I'm not sure where the light switch is, so it remains dark, the reddish glow from the main bar barely lighting it.

After scanning the room as much as she can, she turns toward me and leans against one of the pool tables. I step to her, my hands immediately tugging on the ends of the flannel wrapped around her waist. Melissa was getting rid of some clothes the other day, and Lexy asked for a couple of the flannels so she could "fit in" around town. I don't know what that even means, but she looks cute as fuck with it tied over her black t-shirt dress with her Converse.

"So, what do you think?" I ask, apprehensively.

"I can't think about anything with you this close to me," she whispers seductively. I take a step back, pretending not to catch her drift. Her glare shoots through the shadows. "No."

"No, what?" I tease, taking another step away from her.

She growls at me, actually growls, and it takes everything in me not to pounce on her. "You can't fuck me from over there."

My pulse races at the dirty words coming from her pretty mouth. Of course the one fucking time I don't have a condom with me I have a chance to fuck my bartender in a bar.

I take the two steps back to her in one stride, lifting her by the waist in a smooth movement so she's sitting on the edge of the pool table.

"Hi." She smiles, pleased with my new reaction to her. She reaches for my jeans and bites into her lip with mischief in her eyes when she finds me hard already. I lean to kiss her. "Fuck me, Troy," she whispers against my lips.

"My little rebel." I laugh. "You're hot when you demand what you want," I add as I slide my hands up her thighs, catching on her dress and taking it with them. When I reach where I expect to find lace, there isn't any. My eyes shoot to hers, and she smirks. On a groan, I shove her dress up above her ass so she's bare in front of me. "Spread your legs for me, baby."

She obliges, now following my command and opening for me, her feet dangling barely off the ground.

I drop to my knees.

Running my hands up her thighs, I kiss the inside of her knee, and goosebumps cover her skin from the contact. "I love the effect I have on you," I breathe against her skin as my kisses make their way up her thigh.

I thread my arms under her legs and grip her ass, tugging her forward until she's close enough to the edge to give me full access. Her hands are behind her on the orange felt, holding her steady as she looks at me like she knows I'm about to rock her world.

I kiss her hip, teasing her, and she whines in anticipation. Her impatience today is such a fucking turn on, I can't resist. I press her legs open wider with my shoulders as I move closer and drag my tongue across her center, sending another wave of chills through her. I twirl my tongue slowly against her clit, savoring being intimate with her this way, knowing I'm the only one who has ever tasted her. Her fingers weave into my hair at the base of my neck, soft at first. Then they take hold, forcing me closer, asking for more without words. I stiffen my tongue, driving it deep inside, fucking her with it as she cries out.

I slide one hand out from under her, my other holding her ass, pulling her toward my face as I suck on her clit and drive two of my fingers inside her. The sexiest moan comes from above me as I curl my fingers and she falls over the edge, her legs shaking around me. As her walls pulse around my fingers, I slow my thrusts–how she likes it when she comes this way–and run my tongue over her softly as she trembles with her orgasm.

I stand as she slides off the edge of the pool table and into my arms. "God, I love when you come undone for me," I tell her as I tug the hem of her dress back down.

"I love you," she whispers, still breathless, before she kisses me.

CHAPTER FORTY-TWO
TROY

"Come here," I say to Lexy as soon as we are through the door at Jameson's where we are meeting Mack. When she steps closer, I wrap my arm around her and pull her into me. She smiles into our kiss. I love how comfortable she's gotten around me in public and how comfortable she seems to be in Oregon. I can imagine our life here, an extension of how amazing this past week has been. That doesn't mean she sees it as any more than a good vacation. If taking over this bar is not in alignment with my life right now, I'm okay with that. I can find another job. I have a job. I can't find another Lexy. But I'm still hoping she's leaning in this direction.

"Whatcha thinking about?" She looks up at me, her bright blue eyes standing out in the otherwise dark bar.

"You." I bury my fingers into her hair and lean in until my lips reach her ear. "And how much I want to fuck you on top of this bar." I feel her smile against me, her hands that were pressed into my chest move to loop around my neck and pull me closer.

"The pool table the other night wasn't enough?" she whispers back.

I shake my head against her. "It's never enough."

"Well, if you owned this bar, we could probably make that happen." Fuck, if those words didn't go straight to my dick for more than one reason. I avoid overthinking it.

"You want to go home?"

"I wish. But I told Mack I'd hang around. I'm only going to see him once more before we leave, and we don't know when we will be back, ya know?" Her statement contradicts the one she made a moment ago, and the hope I didn't realize I was holding onto fades.

"Yeah, I know. Speaking of." Mack walks up to us. "Hey, man," I direct the greeting at Mack as Lexy pulls away from me to aggressively wrap her arms around him. He stumbles backward, unprepared for her tackle.

"Lexy, I'm only going to be a short plane ride away. It's not like you're never going to see me again. And we still have another day." He reads her mind. I've come to like Mack. I wouldn't say we are friends or anything, but we've ended up alone a handful of times while Lexy is in the bathroom or off doing something, and I don't mind his company. He's also important to the girl I love, and I appreciate him, knowing he cares about her too. I wouldn't be surprised if he's given her a push toward me more than once these past few months. We might not be where we are without him.

She pulls away from him and leans back into my chest. "I know. It just won't be the same."

"Oh fuck," I mumble under my breath. It wasn't intentional, but it was loud enough Lexy hears it and looks up at me, confused. Before I can say anything, Dean is in front of us.

"Hey, man. It's been a long time."

"Sure has." I reluctantly let go of Lexy to bro hug him. I don't know all the details of what's going on between him and Maci and Mack and Maci, but I remember the possessiveness Dean showed toward me for just talking to Maci once. Considering his reaction toward someone who has been his friend and neighbor half his life, I should probably be ready for possible punches to be thrown between him and a stranger.

I clear my throat to prepare me for God knows what. "This is my girlfriend, Lexy." I catch her smile out of the corner of my eye. It's the first time I've introduced her as my girlfriend to anyone, and I love that she's happy about it. I choose to hold onto that.

I laugh to myself. I'm not trying to think about the time I slept with my girlfriend's best friend, but it's kind of unavoidable at this moment, standing here with two dudes who have done the same. Thank God I'm not in either one of their positions.

"And this is Mack."

Mack reaches his hand out. I feel like a teenage girl watching a high school drama.

"Hey, nice to meet you. I'm Dean." He says it right as their hands connect. In the same moment, they both realize exactly who the other one is.

It takes Lexy a second longer for it to register. Then her eyes go wide. Mack pulls his hand away, and his fists clench at his side. Dean's do the same. Their eyes are on each other as if they are assessing the competition. I've seen that look on Dean after playing football with him for four years. To their credit, they both keep it together.

"I'm going to get a drink, do you want anything?" Mack looks at Lexy when he asks. As far as I know, Mack doesn't drink, but Lexy gives him the out.

"No," she says hesitantly, "but I'll join you in a second."

Mack walks off–out the front door instead.

Dean takes a breath and shifts his gaze to Lexy. "It's nice to finally meet you, Lexy. I've heard a lot about you."

"Yeah, you too." I can tell she's uncomfortable. Her eyes shift toward the direction Mack went like she feels guilty for even talking to Dean.

"So… you and Troy. Does that mean Maci is finally going to get her wish and you'll move here?"

She looks at me, letting herself be distracted from the situation. "We'll see." She smiles softly, but not at Dean. She's still looking at me. I kiss the top of her head and pull her into me. God, I love this girl.

"I'm going to check on Mack." She whispers it even though we both know Dean can hear her. "I'm sorry, Dean. It really was good to finally meet you."

She kisses me on the lips before she leaves. It's not a short kiss either. It's one that says she doesn't want to leave. Fuck, it does all sorts of things to me. Ever since I told her I loved her it's like the last little bit of doubt she had was washed away. I fucking love it. "I'll come find you guys. I love you." I catch a small cringe from Dean, but I have a feeling it has nothing to do with Lexy or me.

Lexy tries to cut off her smile but isn't successful. "I love you too." With that, she walks off to find Mack.

"Shit. That was more uncomfortable than the time you made me wear that damn loincloth on Halloween for losing that bet." Dean laughs, but it's uneasy.

"Yeah, sorry, man. I didn't see any way out of that one." I squeeze his shoulder. I might be a fan of Mack, but Dean and I have been friends for too long to not be there for him. He's never done anything to make me question our friendship, and that shit is important to me.

"She's coming home in two days."

"Yeah, I know."

"Level with me, do I have a shot?"

"I think you'd know better than I would. The few times it's come up, it hasn't been a productive conversation. Mack is Lexy's best friend. Of course she's going to want them to end up together, so she's biased, but that doesn't necessarily mean anything. She also really wants Maci to be happy."

Dean looks devastated, the same look I saw in the mirror after I found out about Emily kind of broken. I can empathize.

"Does she know that you love her?"

He shakes his head no but says yes. I'm confused.

"She knows, but I haven't told her. Not directly, any-way. I screwed up." That's what that cringe was about.

"Well you should tell her. If she's the right girl for you it's going to work out."

"Yeah. I'm just worried that maybe I'm not the right guy for her." He runs his hands through his hair. "He fits her life better, ya know? With Avery and Lexy."

"And I could be going into business with Marcus," I counter. "We're all connected here, Dean. None of it matters because we aren't the ones in the relationship. He could be the logical choice, doesn't mean he's the right one."

He changes the subject. "I'm happy for you, by the way. You deserve this, especially after all the shit with Emily."

"Thanks, man. Now let's get you a beer."

CHAPTER FORTY-THREE
LEXY

I find Mack–not at the bar, thank God. He's sitting on the curb outside with his arms propped up on his knees, one hand grabbing his other arm, where his baseball shirt sleeve cuts off. He's staring into the dark street.

When I sit next to him, I'm so close our thighs touch, but he doesn't look over. Somehow I can feel his pain radiating off him, and I hurt for him. I may not love him the way I love Troy, but Mack is my person, and I hate that he's suffering. I also feel a little guilty that he's the one who convinced me to give this love stuff a try, and he's the one struggling with it.

He finally looks at me. He hasn't been crying, but his eyes are red. Defeat is written all over his face.

"*That* is my competition."

"It's not a game, Mack."

"Isn't it, though?" His voice sounds beaten. "Someone will win, and someone will lose. Did you see him?"

"I did..."

"Yeah, then you can't tell me he's not attractive. He was genuinely excited to meet you and totally torn up. I know what that looks like. The guy is invested."

"This isn't you, Mack. You're a good guy. You're patient. You're caring. You're talented. You have your life together. Don't even give me that crap about Dean being good-looking. I've been watching girls throw themselves at you every damn week for years."

"Does it even matter though?"

"As much as you think it matters on his end." I squeeze his forearm, wishing I could take some of his hurt away.

"I just want to see her, hold her. It kills me he was the last one to be with her."

"I know. She's going to be here soon, and you'll be with her all weekend."

He stares back at me as if he's wondering how much that matters.

"You know I'm team Mack, 100%. Whoever she chooses, you'll always have me."

"I know. Thanks, Lex." He bumps my shoulder with his. "So, does that mean you're considering moving here?" He cracks a smile, and it's only half forced.

"That would be crazy, right?"

"Nah. Crazy would be not doing something you want to just because you think it seems crazy. I really think you'd love it here."

"I do love it here. It feels like home. I've never felt that way before."

"I don't know if that has anything to do with Oregon. Might just be Troy." He reaches his arm around my shoulder and pulls me to him. "I'm so happy for you, Lexy. I couldn't have picked a better guy for you. No matter what happens with Maci and me, everything that has already happened led to you two finding each other, and I'm thankful that something good has come from it."

"Hey." Troy's voice comes from behind us, and I look up at him. Damn, I love him. The feeling washes over me the second our eyes meet. Maybe it *is* just him, but I really love it here too.

Mack stands, and I do the same. "I'm going to head home."

"Will you be okay? Do you want me to come with you?"

"No, I'm good. You two go back inside. Actually, make Troy buy you some dumplings from that cart over there." He points up the street. "If anything will sell you on Oregon, it's those things." He's trying to lighten the mood, but there is so much sadness in his voice I can't help but hug him.

"Let me know when you make it home," I whisper.

"I will. See you later," he says as he pulls back, fist bumping Troy before turning to walk away.

Troy's hands immediately come to my waist, pulling me into him as if he didn't just have his hands all over me ten minutes ago. "How is he?"

"About how you'd expect. Can't say I'd want to be in his shoes."

"Yeah, either of them. Love sucks sometimes."

"Not with you."

He grins at my words, his fingers threading through my hair as he kisses me right there in the middle of the sidewalk as if no one else is around. It's hard and soft, everything I need and not enough all at once. This moment tells me exactly what I need to know.

I pull back. "Buy me some dumplings?"

"Hell yes. Mack is right. These things will sway you hard," he jokes.

"Hmm, guess we'll see about that."

He moves to drape his arm around my shoulder, guiding me to the food cart up the block.

He orders and pays, and the guy hands over two paper food trays. Troy takes them both, and I take the receipt from the cart owner. Troy walks back to where I was sitting on the curb with Mack.

"I'll be right there. I'm going to grab napkins."

"Okay," he says over his shoulder.

"Hey, can I borrow your pen, please?" I ask the dumpling guy, and he hands it over. I scribble on the receipt before giving it back and joining Troy.

I sit down, and he hands over one of the trays. "You will love these." He grins, picking one up and taking a bite.

I take a breath. I'm sure, but I'm still nervous as fuck. "Yeah, I think I'll change my life with this purchase."

He swallows his bite. "They are good, but that's a lot of power to give to food, baby. You haven't even tried them yet." He laughs.

"I don't have to. I already know."

He looks at me confused, and I hold out the receipt. He sets down his food and takes it from me.

He reads the words I wrote up the length of the paper.

Move to Oregon with me?

He stares at it like he has to read it a few times to comprehend. Then his blue eyes meet mine. I bite into my lip, waiting for whatever he will say.

"Lexy…"

"Please don't make me give you some long, sappy speech." I laugh.

"Are you sure? I don't want you to feel like you're following me for my dream or what I want."

I nod. "This is what I want, T—you and Oregon. My mom made it seem like she never had a choice when she would abandon her life, and me, for a guy. Maybe she thought it was the only way to be loved. But you make me feel like this relationship is as much about me as it is about you and like I do get a say because you'll love me no matter what I choose."

The receipt paper crinkles between his hand and the side of my head as he pulls me to him and crushes his mouth to mine. He breaks our connection just enough to say, "You just want easy access to my motorcycle, don't you?" with a smirk.

"You think you know me, don't you?" I remember the first time I said those words to him, annoyed by every time he could read me, and I didn't understand how. Now, I know why.

"I'm just good at my job." He winks then looks behind him through the windows at the bar glowing under soft orange lights. "Babe, I'm about to own this..." He's so excited, and I'm confident this is the right choice.

"Oh yeah, about that." I feign hesitation.

"What about it...?" Worry flashes across his face.

"I'd like to interview for a job, as long as fucking the boss is allowed."

He responds by burying his hand in my hair, using his grip to tug my mouth to his. I feel him smile into it, and he shakes his head slightly before pulling out of our kiss. "God, I love you."

I smile back. "I would love it if I could actually try these dumplings now."

"Deal. Then we are going back inside to celebrate."

"Or we could go *home* and celebrate." I grin right before taking a giant bite of my dumpling.

EPILOGUE

One year later

TROY

"Thanks for letting me help. I'm so excited!" Maci smiles brightly at me as she rips off a piece of tape for me to stick the receipt covered in my handwriting to the front door.

"Thank *you*." I respond, but I'm not talking about her help with this.

"You're welcome!" She bounces inside when I open the door to let us back into the bar.

My eyes scan the room, making sure everything is exactly how I want it. Maci must sense I'm not following her anymore because she turns around.

"It's perfect. She's going to love it."

"It's not too sentimental? She's not going to freak out, right?"

"Oh, she's totally going to be shocked and thrown off. This isn't on her radar at all. But she's not going to freak out. You make everything better for her, Troy."

"Thanks. I feel the same about her."

"I know you do. It's so great. And crazy, huh? How life worked out this way."

"Who would have thought the one time I felt like the biggest asshole would ultimately lead to the best thing that ever happened to me." I laugh. I can't even feel bad about the time I ghosted my girlfriend's best friend a year before I even met her. If I hadn't done that, my life would be totally different now–all of ours would be.

She grins. "I guess it goes to show that everything happens for a reason. We are all exactly where we should be and with who we should be. It's like somehow we knew life had something bigger in store for us. I never could have imagined then what that was."

I take a step forward until I'm close enough to pull her into a hug. "Seriously, Maci. Thank you. Lexy is everything to me, and I wouldn't have her if it wasn't for you," I whisper into her hair before I release her.

She smiles at me before pulling out her phone. "Okay, you ready?"

"Everyone else is coming in an hour right?"

"I texted everyone this morning to make sure. Except I gave you two hours."

I look at her confused. That wasn't the original plan.

"In case you want to celebrate on your own first." She attempts a wink, but it doesn't quite land.

I laugh. "Perfect. Thank you."

"You already said that. Are you nervous?"

"I've never been less nervous about anything." I mean it. I know my girl.

She smiles at me again as she pulls her phone to her ear.

"Hey, Lex, I had to come to the bar to give something to Jess. Can you just meet me here instead?"

Maci chews on her lip waiting for her best friend to respond to her lie.

"Okay, cool. Just come in when you get here."

Another pause.
"See you soon."

LEXY

I check my makeup in the visor mirror of Troy's car. Since we work together, between this and his bike, we haven't found a need for another vehicle. I feel like over the past year I've been in Oregon, I've changed, but in a way that's more me than I've ever been. I'm never anxious. I'm never worried about impressing anyone. Even bartending doesn't feel like the show it was in Hollywood. That being said, I'm excited about my night planned with Maci. We are going to a winery on a girls date like I used to force Maci to do when we went to bars in California. Yesterday, we got our nails and hair done and decided to dress up more than normal tonight. Usually I'm the one talking her into making a statement, so I'm taking full advantage of her being in the mood this week. I've got on my favorite red dress that I haven't worn since Troy and I went wedding crashing, and I'm having the best hair day. My blonde curls fall perfectly down my back and across my skin where my dress dips low. I swipe my light pink gloss over my lips and rub them together as I fold the visor up and get out of the car.

As I walk up to the bar I see a "Closed for private party" sign on the door. Weird, Troy didn't tell me they had an event tonight. Maybe because he knew I'd be busy anyway. I wonder what it is. As I reach for the handle, I see a smaller note stuck right above it with tape. It's a torn off piece of receipt paper.

Lexy, while you're here, check out the new beer on tap.

It's Troy's handwriting. It's strange he didn't text me. I walk in, hesitantly, not knowing what to expect inside. I don't see Maci, or anyone else for that matter. I'm still not used to the new hardwood floor Troy and Marcus got installed last month to replace the ugly brown and green carpet that had probably been here since the 70s. The new flooring is still retro style to stay in line with the vibe of everything else they kept. I love how worn and warm it feels here. This entire town feels that way compared to LA.

My eyes roam the room, but I don't see anyone. There are twinkle lights strung from the ceiling and smaller cocktail tables set up with candles flickering in the middle of them. It must be for the event. Soft music comes through the speakers, and by the time I make it behind the bar to the beer taps, I realize it's "Kiss Me Slowly," except an acoustic cover of the Parachute version. I've considered this mine and Troy's song since we danced to it at the wedding we crashed–not that I've told him or anyone else that.

I reach for the receipt paper note taped over a tap on the end. We've been out of the beer that was hooked up here all week. I pull it off, noticing the beer tap handle before reading the note. It's Golden Road Mango Cart–my favorite beer. We haven't found a place that sells it here. I look at the note in my hand.

Just the start of me making sure you always have everything you need and anything you want.

This is the best surprise. I wonder if Troy is here. He must be getting ready for the event. Why didn't he show me himself? As I look in the direction of the door to the back room, he walks through it. Holy fuck he looks handsome. He's wearing his dark gray suit with a black button up shirt underneath. His styled blond hair is perfect, as always. His smile is so big when he sees me, but as he walks closer it transforms into that look he gets when I'm naked. He stops a step away from me and runs his eyes up and down my body as he runs his thumb over his lip.

"Hey, T." I smile at him, giddy about my gift, seeing him dressed up like this and the way he always wants me. "Thank you for my gift." He grins as he listens.

"You're welcome." He takes a step closer, his hands falling to the nape of my neck. He leans forward to kiss me slowly before pulling back. "You look beautiful. You're perfect."

"I kind of wish I didn't have a date with Maci anymore. I'd rather be wherever you're wearing this." I run my hands over the lapels of his jacket.

He smirks in a way that confuses me. His hands drag down my body, from my neck to my waist, and I drape mine over his shoulders, the receipt note still in my hand.

"I love you, Lexy."

"I love you too."

"I can't thank you enough for giving me a chance, for giving Oregon a chance, and I'm so thankful you love both so much."

"What can I say? You're hard to say no to." Making him part of my life has been hard to resist since I met him.

"Is that so?" He questions with a raised eyebrow.

"Mhmm. Well, except that one thing you keep asking me to try. That's easy to say no to," I joke.

He laughs, but then gets serious. "Okay, I'll ask you something else then."

"What?"

"It's on the other side of your note."

Huh? Oh, my receipt. It's still in my hand. I pull away from where I'm wrapped around his neck to examine the note. I flip it over.

Will you marry me?

I glance up at him, meeting his gray-blue eyes, but then look immediately back to the paper in my hand, my mouth falling open. What. I can't process it.

When I look back up at him, he's not there. He's down on his knee in front of me. He reaches out for the note, pulling it from my fingers and setting it on the bar next to us before he takes my hands in his.

"Baby, since the moment you kissed me on New Year's Eve, you've taken over my world. I want to keep you there for the rest of my life. I love you so fucking much." One of his hands drops mine as he reaches into his pocket and pulls out a black velvet box. He pulls his other hand away to open the box and hold it in front of me. "Will you marry me?"

My brain can't keep up with what's happening. I want to respond and look at the box, and I'm overwhelmed in the best possible way. The box wins, my fingers running along the edge of it as I look inside.

Instantly, tears flood my eyes. It's *the* ring. "This is my ring," I whisper.

"I mean, yeah." He laughs as he stands. "Is that a yes?"

"Troy, you got me my ring." He grins, understanding what I'm saying now. "How did you find this?" It's exactly the ring I described, the one I made up at the wedding we crashed. It's a diamond band, with a teardrop halo, except the gem in the middle is a ruby. It's red, and beautiful, and perfect.

"I had it made for you, for the girl who was made for me." Those are the sweetest words I've ever heard. This man is everything I've ever needed to feel like love can be everything in a good way. He pulls it out of the box, my eyes following his movements. "So, what do you say?"

I go to speak but my voice cracks, and I realize for the first time I'm crying. I tip my head back slightly, running my thumbs under my eyes to wipe the tears. When my cleared eyes meet his, I nod. The word *yes* is barely out of my mouth before he's sliding the ring on my finger, where it fits perfectly. I hardly have time to admire it again before Troy is standing, his hands buried in my hair and his lips on mine. He smells sweet and spicy and kisses me hard and soft, and I feel it all the way to my toes.

And Then There's You Epilogue

The following epilogue contains a major spoiler for book one of the **Finding Home** series. If you have not read *And Then There's You*, proceed at your own discretion.

MACK

Sliding into the booth at Brail's, I adjust my backward hat before taking a sip of the water the guys ordered for me. The rest of my band still lives in California, but having all grown up in Oregon, this final week with shows in Eugene also serves as a trip down memory lane.

"All the guys we are interviewing next week are from Cali," Seth, our drummer, says as he pushes the non-prescription black framed glasses up his nose. The guys weren't thrilled when I initially talked to them about retiring from the band, but eventually they kicked into action and are on the search for a new lead singer. "It'll be weird having a local in the band." He runs his fingers through his dark hair with frosted tips. He's going through a phase, and nothing screams *California* more than that.

"I think we *are* locals at this point. I feel like a tourist here," Mason, our lead guitarist, chimes in. His dirty blonde hair pulled back into a man bun and the leather bracelet collection on his wrists make him look more like a California native than a lot of the locals.

I disagree. It feels so damn good to be home. LA was always meant to be temporary.

"Either way, it's going to feel weird without you." Seth directs his comment at me.

Weird, maybe, but not in a bad way. I've known these guys since high school, but I wouldn't consider them good friends—at least not anymore. We may have traveled and toured together, but outside of that, I don't have much in common with them now. They don't even know what is going on in my life, especially when it comes to Maci. Ever since Seth offered me drugs in front of her, I've been a little resentful. It created a lot of tension during our east coast tour.

"Yeah, weird because you'll have to find someone new to drive your drunk asses to get tacos at 2 a.m." I joke even though it's a valid statement.

"Hey! Don't act like you didn't suggest the tacos. You can't even get good tacos here." Mason isn't wrong, but even if I'm always down for midnight snacks, it's the neverending partying I can't get behind. They aren't ready to settle down yet–which is fine–but they can't even seem to comprehend why I would want to.

They don't know Maci.

Even before Maci and I got together, I knew I'd want a family someday and to be near Avery while we raise our kids since we didn't have a lot of fond family moments during our childhood. Being with Maci, though, has me wanting to fast-track it. I love the vision we have for our life. It's something I held onto every night on tour when I was away from her. My excitement to get on stage faded each time I stepped onto it, and not knowing how long it would be until I got to go home to her was rough. Although, knowing when she is coming home next isn't exactly easing my unsettledness either. I've been kicking myself for months for not communicating these thoughts or feelings well enough to Maci. Maybe everything would be different if I had.

"I will definitely miss the tacos." I attempt to stay present in the conversation. "New food is the best part of touring. I will, however, not miss babysitting you two every night." I chuckle. I love food, but a lot of our late-night adventures were to prevent me from spiraling. I was depressed as hell missing Maci and trying not to resent music for taking me away from her. Instead of leaning into her, I gave all my energy to each show, hoping our success could help build a life for us. That and all the babysitting.

"Mack?" Seth asks, snapping his fingers in front of his face to get my attention. I have no idea what he's talking about–something about food.

"What?" I can't focus on my future vision right now. I can hardly focus on the present. All I play over and over in my head is visions of all the ways tomorrow will go. I have so much more I want to say to Maci, and I'm worried I'll never get the chance.

Seth laughs. "What the hell are you going to eat?"

"Order me the breakfast burrito, please. I'll be back," I announce to neither one of them in particular before slipping out of the booth. I walk out the side door–only slightly chilly in the fresh spring air–and pull out my phone. My thumb hesitates over her contact info before I hit *call* and bring my phone to my ear. Part of me hopes she answers so I can hear her voice and maybe get an inclination toward her decision. The other part of me worries I'll know the moment she speaks what her answer is. I'm so unsure of what it is, it's fucking terrifying.

It rings three times then goes to voicemail. Her sweet voice talks to my ear. *You've reached Maci... well, my voicemail. I'm either exploring whatever country I'm in or sleeping because time zones are weird and you probably forgot to take that into account. Anyway, leave a message, and I'll get back to you.*

I can't help but chuckle at her outgoing message. Before the beep, I take a breath, having no plan for what is about to come out of my mouth.

Hey, Mace. I heard from Avery you'll be out here for the wedding. Look, I don't know what or if you've decided anything. I've been trying to give you your space, but I know it's going to be hard when we are stuck in the same place. I thought I'd at least remind you where I stand so there aren't any surprises. Despite giving you space and focusing on my other dreams, I love you. I never stopped. Every day I hate you're not here with me. My words are coming out rough and desperate, so I take another breath to refocus. *I have been sober every day since you left, and I hope when you see me, you see how hard I've been trying for us, in case there is still a chance when you're ready. I know this weekend needs to be all about Avery and Miller, and I don't want to take away from that, so I wanted to get it out now. Avery said you land tomorrow before the rehearsal dinner, so I'll see you then.* I debate saying it again, but I do anyway. *I love you.*

Hanging up, I shove my phone into my pocket, push up the sleeves of my baseball shirt and adjust my hat before rejoining the guys. One more day. Then I can say all that again to her face and so much more.

DEAN

My palms dig into the edge of my bathroom counter as I stare into the mirror. I drank in Costa Rica, but nothing more than a few beers here or there. Last night after Marcus picked me up from the airport we went to Jameson's. I was hoping for an early night, but agreeing to go out with my best friend to celebrate my return and his new business venture turned into an attempt to drink away my anxiety about knowing Maci will be in the same place as me soon–although I don't know how soon. Not knowing when she'll be back or what she's thinking is killing me.

I run my fingers through my hair realizing I need to get it cut soon. Between how much it's grown and lightened, and my skin being at least five shades darker, I hardly recognize myself. Mentally, I'm in a completely different place too. I have so much more direction than I did before I ran away, and I'm thankful as fuck I figured out my priorities. I hope it's not too late.

Grabbing my basketball shorts off the counter, I slide them over my briefs before walking to the kitchen. Marcus glances up from where he sits at the table looking at paperwork. "Morning. It's strange having you back," he says with a grin.

"Thanks for letting me crash until I figure out what I'm doing next," I say, taking a seat next to him and scanning the page in front of him–it is something for the bar. Jameson's has been our go-to bar since we turned 21, and Marcus is about to own it. Everything he touches turns to gold, and I know this won't be any different—except I can see this is finally a work endeavor he's excited and passionate about.

"Your room is always yours." Marcus has owned this house since we moved in junior year of college. I pay rent whenever I'm here, but he doesn't have to keep space for me. I'm thankful he does, though.

"Thanks." The word comes out less powerful than I intend.

Pushing the papers aside, he gives me his full atten-tion. "Are you hungover or is it something else? You're emanating unease, man."

"Do you believe in soulmates?" It's the only thing I can focus on.

"Just reviewing some light airplane thoughts I see." He chuckles.

"Yeah." I slouch in my chair, waiting for more Marcus insight. He might not be an expert on relationships, but he's still the smartest person I know.

"I don't know, man. If they do, I haven't met mine yet," he says with a sigh. As far as I know he's not actively looking for a girlfriend. He has a lot of reservations about sharing everything about himself–especially the type of things you should share with a significant other. Can't say I blame him. It's a tough line to walk. "But *if* they do," he adds, "Maci is without a doubt yours." A knot twists in my stomach at her name. God, I desperately need that to be true.

Tipping my phone in circles on the table, I think about how she is halfway across the world on the other side of a text. "The question is if I'm hers."

"I don't think the world would be cruel enough to not make soulmates align."

Tossing his thought around in my head, I open my message app and scroll until I get to Maci's name. I tried to leave her alone while she was on her trip, but fuck, it was hard. The last text in our thread was from a few weeks ago when I was pathetically begging her to give me a chance–to give us a chance.

"She texted me about a similar thought when she left Costa Rica." This new information pulls my attention from my phone back to him.

"She did? I mean, you are her favorite." I chuckle thinking about how many times Maci has told me how much she likes Marcus.

"Yeah." He smirks as he takes a sip of coffee. "What are you going to do?"

"Buy a brand new Land Rover like you did, and pretend I don't have problems." I laugh.

"Says the guy who's been making three dollars an hour for the past year and a half," he quips.

"Yeah, yeah. I'll get a job soon. I just can't focus on anything until I know where I stand with Maci. She's all I think about."

"When is she coming home?"

"Is it desperate to ask her?"

Marcus stares back at me like I'm an idiot. Before I can respond, he stands, collects his papers and walks out of the kitchen, leaving me with only my phone and my thoughts. Maybe I can manage to not sound so desperate this time.

Me: *I just got back to Oregon. I need to see you. Please tell me I can see you when you get home–that we can talk?*

Or not. There's no denying I'm obsessed with her. I put my phone face down on the table in an attempt not to fixate, but to my surprise it dings almost immediately. I flip it over so quickly it nearly slips from my hand.

Maci: *Of course we can. I'm actually about to board my flight home for Avery's wedding.*

My stomach drops and my heart races. She'll be here. Tomorrow.

MACK

The day Maci comes home

"Perfect. Thank you," Avery says, approaching me as I dump the bag of ice into the cooler on her back porch. As I stand, I scan the backyard, taking inventory of everything else we need to get ready before the rehearsal in a few hours. "Everything else is all set. You're released from your brotherly duties for now." My sister grins at me, but I can't manage to return the gesture. My anxiety about this entire day is consuming me.

"Everything will be okay," she says cautiously, reading my mind with a dissolving smile.

My eyes meet her equally green ones. "Okay." I don't know what else to say.

"Here's the plan." Avery's hands forcefully land on each of my shoulders.

I chuckle. "Aren't we going over the plan in rehearsal?"

"Well, yeah. But we need a plan for that." Her enthusiasm fades slightly, and I immediately know what she means.

"We do? Have you talked to her?" I ask hesitantly, my heart sinking.

She shakes her head slowly as her hands fall from my shoulders. "No. I mean, I have. But I don't know the answer to your real question. She won't tell me. She said she wants to talk to both of you first."

"That's what Lexy said too," I say with a sigh. I have no clue what the hell is going to happen when I see her. I don't even know how much hope I have–it changes by the second it seems. I watch Avery's eyes fill with concern as they scan my face. I rip my hat off my head, running my fingers through my hair in a nervous habit before adjusting it backward on my head again. "Okay, what's the plan?" Whatever happens, I don't want it to take away from Avery's big day if I can help it.

"The plan is... whatever happens, all emotions about it get out of our systems today or at least put on pause tomorrow."

"I'm not going to ruin your wedding day over this." I hope the declaration comes across more certain than it feels.

A sad laugh escapes her before she says, "Tomorrow will be perfect. I have no doubt. I hope it's perfect for more reasons than just me getting married, but if for some reason things don't play out how we hope, I want you to know I'll be there for you, okay? You're my brother, and I love you."

"Thanks. Whatever happens can be ignored until after. It's not like we haven't been doing that for months." My eyes shift to the floor, not wanting her to comment on how difficult that's been for me.

Thankfully, she doesn't want to go down that rabbit hole either. "True. So, you're good?"

"For now." I fake the best smile I can. "Are *you* good?"

"More than good. I'm great! I can't wait to be married."

I harness all my focus to put solely on my sister. "Then let's get you married," I say with a much more genuine smile this time.

"Okay. Everyone should be here by five. I'll meet you in my room at like quarter after? I'll start my walk to the altar from there."

"Got it," I confirm. "I'll be back in a bit." Digging my keys out of the pocket of my jeans, I head to my Jeep.

DEAN

Why the fuck am I so nervous? I rub my sweaty palms against my well-worn jeans before pushing the sleeves of my flannel above my forearms. I swear it's not usually this hot inside airports.

I scan the arrival screen again. It didn't take more than a quick search to find her flight—there was only one that left Thailand around the time she texted me and connected to Eugene in time to get her here for the wedding.

The word *Arrived* appears in white text next to American Airlines Flight 882 on the monitor above my head. She should be here any minute. I doubt she bought a suitcase since I saw her last, but she still has to walk through the baggage carousels to get to the Uber pickup area... or regular pickup even—perks of living in a town with a tiny airport. I doubt Avery has time to get her considering her rehearsal dinner is tonight. Plus, I would have seen her by now if she was waiting here too.

I haven't seen Mack either.

My stomach flips at the thought of him, and my eyes scan the room for the hundredth time. What the fuck am I doing here? Is there any way she's going to choose me over him? They have so much history and so many ties. How can I ignore that level of connection when family is more important to me than anything?

Anything besides *her*.

She said we could talk, but I'm not sure she meant she wanted to be ambushed at the airport. She's never been upset with me for showing up on a whim in the past, but this is different. I might not be the only one with this idea. Fuck, I'm worried. I take a deep breath.

I'm confident that I absofuckinglutely love this girl as much as she deserves. Maci said that Mack gave her a sense of security she never felt with me, but I can give her that. I can give her the love and safety that comes with years of knowing someone because I'll never leave and we'll have the rest of our lives together. We're meant to be together. We found our way back to each other when we least expected it. There's no way we aren't soulmates, and I'm praying that today the other half of my soul comes home with me forever instead of leaving me behind for good.

Maci says she doesn't believe in being fated for one person, but our connection can't be explained any other way—how else would she find me on a small, local beach in a different country?

A new flood of people exit the hallway into baggage claim. Some of them hurriedly make their way to one of the three conveyor belts, anxious to be on their way. Others are slow moving, looking exhausted after traveling.

And then there's Maci.

The moment I spot her it's like I've been punched in the gut. My breath catches, and anxiety unlike anything I've ever experienced knots my stomach painfully.

She's frozen in place as families weave around her. Her phone is in one hand. Her other hand is pulled inside the sleeve of her green school hoodie, pinching the string between her fabric wrapped fingers as she chews on the plastic tip. Her eyes are locked on mine.

She blinks hard as if she thinks I'm an illusion, and I can't tell if she hopes I'm real. There's no way of knowing until she decides to walk toward me or walk away.

Except fuck that.

I didn't come this far to only come this far. I catch half a step and a half a smile, but by then I'm already winding between other travelers to get to her. I come to a stop a foot away.

God, she's cute. Her chocolate brown hair is knotted on top of her head. Her skin still holds a perfect tan from her month on the beach with me. Her black leggings hug her thighs perfectly, reminding me of how much I love being tangled in the sheets between them. Seeing her reinforces my need for her to always be tangled up with me, in my life. I need her more than I've ever needed anything, and this is the moment where I find out if she needs me too. She's close enough her breath warms my skin, and I see the small gold specks in her brown eyes as she looks up at me. "Maci." Her name comes out with relief, as if I thought I'd never get to say it again.

I hear a small thud as her backpack slips off her shoulder and hits the carpeted floor, but every other chaotic airport sound around us fades.

Her body collides with mine before I even have a chance to wrap my arms around her and pull her to me, and any residual doubt I had about being here disappears like the space between us. We stay that way for at least a minute, clinging desperately to each other in the middle of the airport as people detour around us to get to their carousels.

Pulling back slightly, I grip the side of her face and run a thumb across either cheek. Tears threaten to spill out of her eyes.

"I love you, Maci. I love you so fucking much. I always have, and I always will."

The unexpected sob that breaks out of her startles me. Her cry racks through her as she shakes against me, pulling us together by her grip on the back of my shirt. Her hands twist into the fabric like she never wants to let go of me again, and it's the best fucking feeling.

"God, I love you," I confidently repeat the words I've only said once before today, intending for her to hear me this time. "I'll keep my promise and remind you every damn day," I add in a whisper against her hair.

She leans her head back without loosening her hold on me, her eyes red and her skin streaked with tears.

"I love you too," she whispers in an attempt to find her voice after crying. Before the last word is out, my mouth is on hers as if I could capture the declaration that hit me even harder than I expected. My hands run through her fallen messy bun, cradling the back of her head as if I could possibly get closer to her this way.

The second our lips touch, I feel the familiar zing I always do with her. I don't have to live without it. Thank fuck. I pour every ounce of gratitude for that realization into our kiss, tasting her salty tears, like I did before she left Costa Rica.

Except they aren't the same because these tears are filled with all the hope that disappeared with the last ones. Reluctantly, I pull back. As my thumbs wipe away her tears, she chuckles.

"You're just always showing up when I least expect it, aren't you?"

"Start expecting it." I pause then wink as I add, "Girlfriend." She bites into her bottom lip in an unsuccessful attempt to fight the biggest smile I've ever seen.

Picking up her backpack from the floor, I swing it over my shoulder. I wrap my free arm around her, kissing her temple in the process. "Are you ready to get out of here?" I ask. Her eyes are wide with disbelief as she nods, like she can't believe I'm actually here.

She's quiet the entire walk to my truck. I don't push her. I get the feeling she's overwhelmed. Hell, so am I. Of course I wanted it to play out exactly as it is, but now that it has, it's like wrapping your head around a dream when you first wake up and wanting to drift back asleep to stay stuck in it.

Before I pull out of the parking space, I turn to her, threading my fingers with hers as our hands rest on her lap. Damn, I never thought I'd get to do that again. I need to get it together and stop getting all hung up on every single thing I no longer have to live without.

"What's the plan?" I ask. "What time do you need to be at the rehearsal dinner?"

"Well, my plan was to go to Troy's first."

I freeze. "What?" She laughs, and I immediately relax. "Yeah, not funny, Maci."

She shrugs and squeezes my hand, a smile still lighting her face. "It's a little funny. But for real, I need to go to Troy's. Well, Cooper's, I guess? I need my car to pick up my parents late tonight and all my things are there with Lexy."

"Oh yeah. I met her a couple days ago."

"You did?" Her excitement transforms into confusion then horror at what else that must mean.

"Yeah, him too," I answer the question I see in her eyes.

"Oh, God. I'm sorry, Dean."

Hearing her say my name again temporarily makes me forget the topic of conversation, but I recover. "It's fine. Troy was there as a buffer. It was a party." I laugh, recalling the memory that doesn't sting anymore. I steady my elated emotions before slipping into the supportive boyfriend role I want to assume for her. She still looks stressed, but I know it's not about me meeting her ex. "Maci?"

"Hmm?" Her eyes fall to where my thumb is rubbing against hers.

"Are you going to be okay tonight?" I know it's going to be rough. I wish I could be there to comfort her. "I'd offer to go with you, but I don't think I should."

"Yeah," she says softly, meeting my gaze. "I'm... I don't know." She looks away like she feels guilty about what-ever she's thinking.

"Babe." She doesn't look at me. "Hey, come here," I say gently and tug on her hand.

She reluctantly climbs onto my lap, and I wrap my arms around her as her head falls to my shoulder.

"Are you overwhelmed?" I ask.

She nods against my chest.

"I can only imagine how hard this is for you. It's okay that you still care about him, Maci."

Her head lifts slightly as she looks at me. "It is?"

"Of course it is." I sigh, looking into her worry-filled eyes. "He's been a big part of your life, even before you two were together. And it's not like you'll just never see him again. I know that. Do you know what you're going to say?"

She shakes her head slowly, and I catch a single tear slip down her cheek before she leans against me again. "No. I've been trying to think of something, but nothing feels right. I don't want to hurt him, but I know it's inevitable." Her voice sounds so small.

Even though I'm getting what I want, I hate that she has to do this. I want to reassure her that he'll be okay, but that feels like a lie. If the roles were reversed, I would be anything *but* okay realizing I lost the girl curled up against me again. "I wish I knew what to say right now."

"It's okay. What you said helps. Thank you." She pulls back and kisses me before sliding back to her seat.

"Where are we going?" Maci questions as we pull onto my parents' street. We have four more hours until she has to be at the rehearsal dinner, and I don't want to wait any longer. I park my truck in the driveway of the midnight blue house that mirrors the sage green one next to it.

She leans toward the dash, peering at the house through the windshield.

"There's someone I want you to meet." The memory of Maci telling me how much she wanted to meet my mom when we were together the first time floods my mind. Mom all but begged me back then. It seems like that was both last week and a lifetime ago. I'm not messing anything up this time around.

Maci immediately knows where we are and hops out of my truck before I can even open the door for her. She takes off, doing some cute half-walk, half-skip to the front door and knocking. I can't help but laugh at her impatience. By the time I reach her, she's rocking back and forth on her heels, waiting for my mom to answer the door.

"You can just go in," I say, reaching for the handle.

Maci slaps my hand. "Don't you ruin this moment for me. I've been waiting for this forever." Right as her head turns to look at me with a grin, the front door opens, Mom's eyes bounce between the two of us.

Maci's eyes snap forward in time to see my mom's hands fly to her mouth in surprise. I stopped by to see my parents yesterday, but I didn't warn them I'd potentially be back today. I didn't want to get Mom's hopes up.

"Hi, I'm–" Maci's peppy greeting is cut off by Mom.

"Maci! I know who you are, sweetie." She barely gets the words out before she's wrapping my girlfriend in a hug under the door frame. I lean against the wood paneled wall of our front entrance watching the scene when my mom's tear-filled eyes meet mine. Her happiness radiates off her as she takes in this moment. Only she and Marcus know its significance.

When they finally part, Maci looks back at me, her eyes watery again. I push off the wall and pull her into a side hug, her head falling to my shoulder, and she wraps her arm around my waist.

Sensing we need a moment alone, my mom says, "I'll go get lunch started. If you two can stay?"

I nod, and she heads to the kitchen, leaving the door open for us to follow her when we're ready.

"You've never introduced anyone to your mom before," Maci states.

"Oh, that was me introducing you?" I laugh. She hits my chest playfully before shifting into my arms. "Okay, okay. In all seriousness, I'm sorry it took me so long. I know you've been worried our relationship won't be as strong in the real world, or whatever you want to call it. I'm going to prove to you it can be even better. No holding back this time. Wherever we are in the world, you are my world, Maci. I love you." I tuck a stray strand of fallen hair from her messy bun behind her ear, the three words flowing out of me in a way that makes it hard to believe I was ever hesitant to say them.

She smiles as she leans into a hug, and I kiss the top of her head before pulling her inside.

MACK

"I can't tell you how much it means to me that you're here," Avery says as she floats into her room where I'm waiting to trial run her walk down the makeshift aisle in the backyard. As far as I know, the rest of the wedding party is already outside in their places—which means Maci will be waiting for us by the altar. When I returned to the house, I made a beeline for Avery's room. I want so badly to run to her right now. Knowing she's so close makes me unsure if I can wait another minute not knowing. But even though it's *the* day, it's also Avery's day, and I refuse to take away from that–if I can help it.

I wrap my arms around my sister in a hug. "I'm sorry Mom and Dad aren't here for this." I pull away as I finish my thought, focusing on keeping my anger contained. We don't have any sort of contact info for Mom, but Avery sent an invitation to Dad. He never acknowledged it.

"I have everyone I need." Her smile is bright and believable. "Okay, glad that's out of the way too. You better not cry when you give me away tomorrow. I'll kick your ass if you're the reason my makeup is ruined."

"No promises, Sis."

"Uhhh, we just agreed to all the emotions going on hold tomorrow, so figure it out, dude."

I shake my head with a grin. "Fine," I lie, knowing I'll probably be a wreck from how happy I am that my sister found the husband she deserves. "Are you ready?" I ask, as she loops her arm through mine.

"Yes!"

We make our way down the hall, veering into the kitchen at the end. The sliding back door is open, but I pause when we reach it. The sudden stop jerks Avery back slightly. She turns toward me, her hand reaching to squeeze my arm. "Maybe we should have had a better plan," she whispers. "We can have dinner first, if you want. Then finish rehearsal?"

I wonder if all siblings have each other's backs the way we do, or if it's special to us since we never had parents in our corner. Whatever happens, I'll get through it. "Nope. Whether I talk to her now or later, her decision will be the same." I take a breath. "I'm good."

The look on her face tells me she doesn't believe me. I don't believe me either. I told Maci I wanted us to make sure we don't take moments away from Avery and Miller. That's what's keeping my hope up despite her not coming to find me as soon as she got here.

I tell myself I'll stay focused for the next five minutes, but my eyes betray me, wandering to Maci the second we are in the backyard. She's standing near the fence wearing a sundress I've never seen before that's fluttering in the light breeze.

Avery and I take slow steps toward Miller and their friends, and the closer we get, the more clearly Maci comes into view. She looks like the same Maci I've always known, besides the golden glow of her skin that's darker than it's ever been.

That, and the fact that she's not mine anymore.

The eyes that once held so much love for me and no longer do is all the confirmation I need.

The realization hits me in a way I've only ever felt once–when I realized my mom left. My heart pounds against my chest, but then I swear it all but stops beating. I somehow manage not to misstep with Avery despite the sliver of hope abandoning me and begging me to crumble right here.

Halfway down the imaginary aisle that will be marked by chairs tomorrow, I run my free hand through my hair in an attempt to keep my emotions at bay, but I can't take my eyes off her. From a few feet away, I can see her clearly enough to watch a few tears silently escape before she looks away, shifting her gaze to my sister.

It's the only option I have right now, so I do the same. Thankfully, Avery has blurred out anything but her future husband, her face glowing as her eyes lock on his.

When we reach the end of the aisle, my sister leans in to hug me. The extra tight squeeze she gives tells me she wasn't oblivious to what was happening around her. I let her go and step back, but instead of sitting in the non-existent chair in the front row, like I will tomorrow, I retreat back inside the house.

I can't be out here anymore, and my only duty in the ceremony has been fulfilled.

Only a few minutes pass before there's a soft knock on my bedroom door. I don't respond, but it creaks open slowly anyway. I look up from where I'm sitting on the edge of my bed, my elbows resting on my knees, my head held up by my palms. My gaze falls back to the floor as Maci makes her way into the room. Even though she leaves space between us, the mattress next to me sinks a little with her weight.

"Mack," she whispers, and I can tell she's trying to hold back more tears. She patiently waits for me, and I don't know how much time goes by before I look at her. Her face is red, her eyes are puffy as silent tears stream down her cheeks. I know this isn't easy for her, but it doesn't make it hurt any less.

"I'm sorry," she says, her voice still quiet as it breaks on the apology. She looks like she's struggling to find her next words, and I'm not even sure what I want to hear. Nothing she says will make a difference. I know she doesn't want to hurt me. I believe she still loves me even though it's not in the way I want. I wish things could have been different, but they aren't, and nothing will change that. "Are you okay?" she asks so softly I hardly hear her.

"No." Tears burn at my eyes as if I gave them permission with that admittance.

She starts to reach for me but must think better of it because she pulls back. Her voice cracks, her tear filled eyes locking on mine. "You know that I love you, right?"

"I know," I admit, believing her, before a rush of spite floods me at the thought of how demeaning those words feel. "Just not enough." The truth fills the space between us.

"Mack." Hearing my name from her lips in a hushed voice used to be everything I wanted from the girl in front of me, but now it rattles me to my core. "Love is only one piece of the puzzle. It's not enough."

My eyes shoot to hers, locking on them, waiting for her to elaborate. She reaches for my hand, and I haven't touched her in so long I let her lock her fingers with mine. God, I miss her, and she's right next to me.

My gaze falls to our hands tangled together. "Why?" I don't know exactly what I'm asking, but I hope she gives me the answer I'm looking for.

"You love me so much you'd do anything to make me happy." Her thumb rubs across my hand, sending both comfort and rage through me.

"You say it like it's a bad thing," I mutter.

"I love you so much for it. You've always been there for me, and I know I've taken it for granted more often than not, but I think you lost yourself a little in loving me. It's time for you to find yourself and be with some-one who can help you do that." Her words are soft, but they hurt as if they're rocks.

"I want that person to be you."

She's silent, as if she either doesn't know what to say or doesn't want to say it.

"But you want to be that person for Dean," I add, feeling like there's a vice grip tightening around my heart as I say his name.

Sighing, she says, "I want us to both be happy."

"And I don't make you happy." I say it somewhere between a question and a statement.

"Of course you do, but I think we both care enough about each other that we would be willing to sacrifice our own happiness to give the other person what they need. We don't need the same things, Mack. It wouldn't be a healthy relationship. We'd be holding each other back."

"Seeing you happy *is* what I need. It's what makes me happy." I can hear the desperation in my voice as I silently pray she'll see a new light.

"Then maybe I'm just selfish." She pulls her hand back from mine, and I immediately feel empty without her touch. "There's things I want in life I know you'd give me even though you don't want them yourself. I'd let you give them to me, and you deserve more than that. You deserve someone who will give you as much as you're willing to give them, and for it to be what you want rather than a sacrifice." She looks to where she's wringing her hands in her lap.

I fall back onto my bed, my hands running down my face. As much as I knew this was a possibility, I sure as hell am not prepared for it. I'm torn between denial and understanding, between wanting to keep fighting and knowing it's time to quit, between telling her to leave and not wanting her to go.

"Will you lie down with me for a minute?" I stare at the ceiling, waiting for her response. She hesitates, but then I feel her next to me.

I lift my arm and she rolls into me, her head settling on my chest. Her arm shifts uncomfortably at her side, but then it lands softly across my stomach. I wrap my arm around her shoulder, rubbing my thumb across her bare skin. I feel her pinch the fabric of my shirt at my side between her fingers like she's picking at a thread.

We have to make it through this weekend. Hell, this isn't going to be the last time we have to pretend we were never more than friends. A dozen future instances where we will have to be together without being to-gether flash through my mind, and I watch them fade from visions of us being happily together, taking in a scene, into awkward interactions between strangers. I don't want that for us. I want us to be okay someday even though I'm not okay today.

I squeeze her tightly and her grip around my waist tightens. A cry catches in her throat before her tears run silent as she lets us lie together one last time. When I realize it'll never last long enough, I break the silence. "After this weekend, I can't see you for a while." Thinking about going another five months without her sounds terrible, but it's the only option. It's the only way to move past this.

"Okay," she breathes against my chest.

I let her go, and she sits, looking down at where I remain lying on the bed.

"Whatever you need from me, just let me know."

I nod as I sit, picking my hat up from the bed next to me and smoothing it backward over my hair in an attempt to start collecting myself. By the time I glance back up, the door on this chapter of my life closes behind her.

Managing to pull myself together quicker than I expected, I rejoin the party. I reach into the cooler for a water bottle, catching Miller's eye across the yard as I stand. He motions for me to bring him a beer. Pulling an IPA from the ice, I take a step toward Miller and his groomsmen. Maci crosses the yard a few feet in front of me causing me to freeze. I can't do this.

I turn on my heel, abandoning my task for the groom and walk straight through the kitchen and living room until I'm out the front door. Not wanting to actually leave or having anywhere to go, I sink to the concrete and lean against the porch wall.

The sun is setting by the time someone notices me. "Are you planning on drinking that?"

I look from the unopened beer can I'm tipping in circles in my hands to the stranger in front of me. "No, I don't drink anymore," I mutter.

Confusion flashes across her features as she stands there, staring down at where I'm sitting on the concrete front porch, leaning against the light blue wooden panels.

"I've been sober for six months. I was getting this for Miller." I hold the beer in the air, leaving out the part about how I was too acutely aware of every move Maci made—every smile that lit her face—to be in the backyard anymore.

"Wow, good for you," she says, and her genuine pride causes me to give her more attention than I did a moment ago. Her hair is shoulder length and light brown with faded lavender streaks running through soft curls. Her leather leggings, plain t-shirt and jean jacket tied around her waist complete her artist vibe. Somehow, I just know. The camera in her hand is a pretty big clue as well.

"Thanks," I manage, not particularly capable of feeling good about myself.

"I just hit my year mark," she adds, surprising me. Not a lot of people our age don't drink.

"Congrats." I make a conscious effort to look at her eyes so she knows I mean it.

"Are you okay? Do you need a meeting?"

I've been to a few NA meetings, and I'm sure they are similar to AA, but I don't need one now. "No. I'm fine. Thanks, though."

Compassion seems to calm the stormy gray swirling in her irises, but I look back to the beer can in my hands. "Well, you're missing the party. Who are you to Avery anyway?" she asks, taking a seat on the ground next to me even though I turned down a meeting.

A sad chuckle escapes me. "I'm Mack. Her brother."

"Duh. I should have guessed. You two look just alike. She's beautiful."

The sideways compliment vaguely registers, and I wonder if she's flirting. I don't have the energy to figure it out or care. "Yeah, she is. Sorry, I'm not good company right now. The girl I thought I was going to marry is here."

"Oh." Her understanding is evident in the way she says the word.

"Yeah. I'm just the epitome of love in this love-filled weekend," I say, sarcasm lacing my voice.

"I can see it." She's not joking at all.

I glance over at her again. "Ever had your heart ripped out?"

She nods. "And stomped on. A year ago." I assume the connection between that and her no longer drinking. "I'm Ella, by the way. Short for Stella."

"Like McCartney?" I joke.

"Exactly." She laughs, and I raise my eyebrow in question. "Dad loves the Beatles. Mom does too."

"Do you?"

"I don't mind them. I love all music really." She holds up the fancy camera that's sitting in her lap. "I'm actually a music photographer. I do cover art, marketing and concerts, of course."

"That's cool. My band's last show is actually in a couple days."

"You're in a band?" I can't tell her opinion by her tone.

"Yeah."

"Where are you playing?" She seems genuinely interested.

I hesitate, flashing to a vision of the small stage we first played on years ago. The image of Maci in the crowd fades away when I remember she won't be there anymore. My hands run through my hair. The next second they are slamming into the concrete at my sides, my eyes filling with unwanted tears. Fuck. I press my palms into my eyes in an attempt to keep from completely breaking down in front of this random girl. I take a deep breath and pull my hands away from my face. "Sorry." I glance in her direction and see concern written in her body language. "You can go back to the party. I'm fine."

"No, it's okay. I can stay."

"Don't you need to take pictures or something?" I question, assuming that's why she's here, although the leap from music to weddings seems big.

"Nah. I took some. Mostly I came to the rehearsal to get a feel for the set up since I don't usually shoot weddings. Miller is a good family friend."

"Oh. Okay."

"Let's go for a walk. Come on." She stands, staring down at me expectantly.

I stare back, unmoving.

She reaches for my hand, and even though I don't acknowledge it, she bends to latch onto my wrist and pulls anyway. "Come on. You'll feel better."

"Will I?"

"You won't feel worse."

DEAN

"I'm so excited to see our new home!" Maci bounces excitedly on the toes of her pretty gold sandals as I slide the key into the lock of our residence for the next six months. True to her word, Maria, the woman who runs the human trafficking victim sanctuary in Costa Rica, opened a second location in Spain. Only a month into us being home in Oregon, Maria called to offer Maci a paid volunteer position to help get the new place up and running. When our plane landed this morning, it was 78° and sunny. The timing could not have been better with the October weather in Oregon starting to feel a little too chilly and wet for my liking. Maria helped us find a studio condo in Alicante, a smaller town down the coast from Valencia.

Maci pushes the door open before I even have time to pull the key out of the lock. I laugh at her impatience as she bounds into the room, her eyes quickly taking it all in before she conducts a more in depth investigation. The white exterior is typical Spanish coast architecture with a flat, rust-red roof. The inside is as small as my place in Costa Rica which is plenty big enough for us. I stand just inside the door, our luggage haphazardly dropped by my feet, unable to take my eyes off her. She opens every door–the bathroom, the closet, the fridge and every single dresser drawer. My chuckle goes unacknowledged as if she doesn't remember there's someone else with her. The longer we're together, the more free she seems, as if the weight of anything that's ever held her back continues to float away. I had gotten glimpses of her free spirit, here and there, the rare times she let the most genuine parts of her shine. But Maci has found her herself, and I'm so grateful I've gotten to watch her overpower her insecurities and lean into her happiness in the process.

When she makes it to the floor to ceiling sliding glass door, she stops in front of the sheer white curtain hanging in front of it. Pulling them back slowly, her excitement is replaced by awe. "Dean, come look at this view," she says, pulling her eyes away to glance at me over her shoulder for only a split second. Without waiting for my response, she slides the door open and steps onto the balcony.

"Be right there, babe," I respond anyway, realizing I'm still stuck in the place my feet first landed. I pick up our bags and toss them on the bed before digging through mine for a moment. I make my way to join her on the balcony, but freeze in the doorway, leaning against it, with my hands in the pockets of my black joggers.

As I take her in, she scans the unobstructed ocean view, not even realizing I've joined her. She's leaning into the corner of the black bars that make up the balcony railing, her fingers wrapped around the metal. Her jean shorts border the edge of *too short*, but only because I don't want anyone else looking at what's meant just for me. She's wearing my friends' band tee–the shirt she stole from me the first night we had sex–tied in a knot in the front. Somewhere along her new home tour she kicked her sandals off, so she's barefoot against the cement. God, she's perfect.

I take a few silent steps toward her before caging her in between me and the perpendicular bars at the corner of the balcony. I brush her wind blown hair off her shoulder, letting my fingers feather down her arm before gripping the bar next to her hand. When my lips land on her soft skin at the collar of her t-shirt, she relaxes into me, still focused on the view, giving me the perfect moment I need.

"Hey," I whisper into her ear.

"Hmmm?" she breathes with a happy sigh.

"Do you have a husband?"

She laughs as she twists into my arms and says, "No." Her eyes find mine, and the glimmer in them tells me she thinks I'm playing. I've never been more serious about anything.

"Do you want one?" I ask, and watch her expression shift to confusion, like I started a role play without warning. "Maci."

"Yes..." the word trails off slowly as it comes out of the lips I desperately need to kiss. So, I do, smiling at the electricity of our touch that still hasn't faded as I pull back.

"I've been yours since the moment I saw you on Halloween two years ago–before you even knew I existed." Her eyes flick across mine, like she still doesn't know where I'm going with this. "If you'll let me, I'll make sure you know there's no one else for me, every day. I don't want to be your boyfriend anymore. Be mine, forever." I reach back into the pocket of my joggers and pull out the deep purple velvet box. Her eyes shift down to it then back up at me, a small gasp escaping her lips.

"Dean..."

"Maci, I love you more than I can ever put into words, but I want to spend the rest of my life trying. Will you marry me?"

I flip open the box to reveal the gold band, the sun reflecting off the round solitaire diamond–as if on cue–filling the space between us with a rainbow glare. She glances down again before her eyes are back on me. Her mouth opens like she wants to say something, but no words come out. I chuckle at her speechless-ness. "Babe?" I bring one hand to her face, my fingers weaving into her hair as my thumb strokes the skin below her ear.

She nods, one of the tears welling in her eyes finally escaping.

"Is that a yes... ooooor," I joke.

"Of course," she spits out, her voice shaky. "Yes," she adds in a bold, assured tone. "With you, everything is always a yes."

I grin as I kiss her, realizing the ring box is still in my hand when I move to pull her closer. Confusion splashes across Maci's face when I break our kiss. She follows my gaze to the ring. "Oh, yeah." She chuckles.

Pulling the ring from the white satin, I hold it out, waiting for her finger. Her hand comes between us, but right as the gold touches the tip of her finger, she reaches to pinch it from me instead.

"What's this?" She tips the ring to examine the inscrip-tion on the inside.

"The coordinates of our beach," I tell her.

"The day we found our way back to each other," she whispers with a smile as she slides the ring on her finger herself.

"I already knew we were meant to be together, but this was the place the Universe helped me prove it to you."

"It's perfect," she says.

"You're perfect," I whisper against her lips before resuming our kiss. I lift her by her thighs, her legs wrapping around my waist, her arms around my neck at the same moment her lips meet mine. I pull back just enough to not trip over the door track, and then our mouths are joined again. Freezing at the edge of the bed, I break our kiss, my forehead pressed against hers.

Her breath is heavy from our few seconds of heated kissing. "What is it?" she asks at my hesitation.

"Nothing," I say in place of sharing my jumbled memories flashing through my mind–the first time we had sex, the time I thought would be the last time, when I finally got to feel her again in Costa Rica, the first time she was officially mine.

Laying her gently on the white comforter first, I toss our bags onto the floor. When I turn back, she's watching me, her hair draped across the pillow, one hand playing with the knot of her shirt, her other thumb rolling against the band of her ring, twisting it slightly.

Her smile brings every part of my body to life as I crawl toward her. I straddle her legs, reaching for the button of her shorts without breaking our eye contact. I tug down the zipper and loop my fingers on the band, tugging them down slowly as she watches my movements. With her shorts on the floor, I run my hands up her calves, her thighs, placing soft kisses up her leg and reveling in the chills left in their wake.

Sometimes she's impatient, but not today. She's letting me soak up every inch of her. I kiss her skin at the edge of her silky underwear before sliding my hands under her shirt, dragging it with them as they slowly rake up her stomach. She lifts her arms for me to tug it over her head, and before I can get back to undressing her, her hands find my hair, tugging my head to hers, some of my blond strands brushing her forehead. Her lips connect with mine and still, both a jolt of electricity and a rush of calm wash through me simultaneously. I pull back slightly, letting her keep me close with her fingers lazily twisting into the hair at the base of my neck as I hover over her.

Her hands smooth along my neck, down my chest and slip under the hem of my t-shirt where she tugs. Obeying her unspoken command, I shift my weight enough to pull my shirt off then kick the rest of my clothes off too. I remove her underwear as I kiss torturously slow up her stomach, stopping only when I reach the wire of her plain black bra. God, I'm so in love with this girl. She's simple in all the right ways, never needing anything extravagant to be happy. Hell, how she's watching me love her makes me feel like the only thing she needs is me.

I slide my hands between her and the mattress, unhooking her bra, before slowly starting to slip the straps down her arms. She sighs as my fingers trail against her skin, and I glance up, the adoration she has for me evident in every glimmering speck of gold in her brown eyes. I know she sees the same look reflected back in mine.

Her eyes shift to the side when a breeze causes the sheer white curtain to flutter, but they lock back on mine in the next instant. As I lean in to kiss her, she whispers, "I love you so much, Dean," right before our lips touch.

The words and connection leave me needing all of her. I adjust myself until we align, and I push inside her slowly, giving her time to adjust. She was more than ready for me, but I still inside her anyway, savoring the level of intimacy a moment before slowly pulling out and pressing back in. We stay that way for a while, moving only enough to feel every place we connect as our tongues tangle in soft kisses. Her hand has found its way back to my hair, her fingers massaging through the strands. I'm propped up on one arm hovering over her. My other hand caresses the side of her breast. My thumb rubs over her nipple and elicits a moan from my fiancée. I swallow it in our kiss and pick up the pace, unable to contain my restraint.

She rolls her hips to perfectly meet my gentle thrusts into her. I break our kiss when my head falls to the pillow next to her, a groan escaping my lips. "You feel... indescribable," I mutter against the skin on her neck, unable to find the right word. Her breathing picks up as her hand migrates to my hip, her fingers digging into the skin on my back.

"Dean," she begs, searching for her release.

"I've got you, babe," I whisper against her lips before I kiss her as hard as I thrust into her. I rock my hips, creating a new, faster rhythm. My fingers thread into her hair, keeping my kiss steady against her as the rest of our bodies move in sync. She bites into my lip, and I feel her breath catch as she tightens around me, waves of her orgasm pulling me to my own.

MACI

"Babe, how black is my tongue right now?" I stick my tongue out with a giggle at Dean. We are almost finished eating our squid ink paella.

"Stop laughing so I can see," he teases then sticks his tongue out at me, the pink almost completely black. The rest of his skin has continued to darken after long adventurous days in the sun, and his hair is at least a full shade of blond lighter, swooshed across his forehead in a way that looks both styled and messy. I know I'll be happy as long as I have the man in front of me.

We drove to El Palmar, which is about an hour from where we are staying in Alicante, to try this paella restaurant one of Dean's coworkers recommended. In Costa Rica, while we were daydreaming about perfect career paths, Dean envisioned a job we weren't sure existed until we arrived here. Now, a few days a week he partners with a local guy at the Santa Bárbara Castle that's within walking distance of our place to lead tours. Two days a week he makes the two hour drive to Valencia to work with a tourist company. He tag teams the tours, Dean helping to translate when necessary–which is often with all the American tourists. It only took him a week or two to master the differences between Central American Spanish and the European dialect.

I try to hold my giggles in as he examines my tongue. "It looks pretty black, but I think I need a closer look." He leans across the armrests of the wicker chairs dividing us, his hand wedging between my thighs before his lips touch mine. His other hand grips the nape of my neck, pulling our mouths together with more intensity. My lips part immediately, allowing him to deepen our kiss, the taste of authentic Spanish food on his tongue. God, I love being here with him. I love being anywhere with him. Remembering we are the only ones in the outside seating area, I melt into the kiss, the tingles I love so much traveling across my skin as Dean readjusts his fingers to thread through my hair.

He pulls back just enough to break our kiss. His fingers run along the side of my face before cupping my cheek. His mouth twinges with a smirk as he says, "Tastes like your tongue is pretty black to me." He kisses me on the nose before readjusting himself back in his own chair and takes his last bite of paella.

As I pick up my fork to take one more bite too, my phone vibrates on the table. Being eight hours ahead of the West Coast, I wonder who could be texting me. My eyes widen as they scan the picture from Avery of a white stick with two pink lines. "Oh my God!" I scream as I happy dance in my seat before responding to the text with a string of the most exciting gifs I can find.

"Are you going to tell me what that ridiculously adorable dance was about or do I need to guess?"

I set my phone back on the table and turn toward Dean, my leg bending up on the chair. "Avery is pregnant!" I squeal. The way his smile brightens his face makes me think he's happier about my happiness than he is about the news.

"That is exciting," he says. He pauses then adds, "Do you want to go home for a bit, once we're finished here?"

"Oh, umm." I hadn't considered what we'd do next. We still have four months here, and we've been winging life since we got back together–making decisions in the moment. "Maybe when the baby comes? Would that be okay?"

"Yes, of course. She's family. I miss mine too. We can stay as long as you want."

I let my gaze drift to the rice fields behind us as I think back to a vision that's consistently appeared over the past decade of Avery and me raising our kids together. I'm not sure when it shifted, but that's not what I want anymore. I shake my head. "Maybe we can just spend the holidays at home?"

His eyes glimmer with the smile void from his face as he asks, "You don't want to stay and raise your kids near her?"

"I'd rather show our kids the world." The words come out before the realization that we've never had this conversation hits me, and it occurs to me I've made a huge assumption. "I mean..." I try to backtrack. "Do you want kids?" I ask, nervously picking at the wicker at the edge of the table.

"I want *you*," he says softly, running his hand sensually up my arm, and he waits for my eyes to lock on his. "You're enough for me, Maci. But any other adventure you want, I want too."

"Really?" I search his eyes for the truth in his answer.

"Really. I think we'd be great parents."

"Me too. But..." He rubs his thumb across my skin where it's settled at the nape of my neck, encouraging me to finish my thought. "I think I want you all to myself for a little longer first, though." I grin thinking about how many adventures we'll get to have together, just the two of us, and how many more we'll have with a family.

As he leans in to kiss me, the side door to the restaurant opens, our server walking through with two shot glasses of what look like milk. Dean pulls back to address the server. I watch in adoration as my fiancée converses with him in Spanish.

I smile as he walks away, not having picked up on much of the conversation. You'd think I'd be more fluent by now, but the speed the locals speak makes it hard for me to understand. Luckily, the volunteers and women we're helping at the sanctuary slow down for me. "I understood 'shot' and 'rice.' I think." I laugh.

"Close enough," he says, handing me one of the shot glasses. "He said it looked like we were celebrating something and thought these could help. This is rice cream liqueur made from rice grown in Valencia."

"Oooh. That's so cool." I clink my tiny glass to his and we both tip our heads back to try the celebratory drink. I expect the burn of alcohol but am surprised when it's sweet, like liquid rice pudding with a hint of cinnamon or a light version of eggnog. Setting the empty shot on the table I say, "Thanks for being my personal translator and for not making fun of me for not picking up on languages like you do."

"You're welcome." He stands, pulling euros from the wallet in his back pocket to leave on the table.

I stand too. "Hopefully you don't get tired of doing it everywhere we go."

"I never get tired of anything we do together," he says, taking my hand and leading me away from the table.

"Well, remember you love me when we are in country number 87, and I'm making you learn *another* new language."

He stops on the sidewalk, pulling me to him, bringing our conjoined hands to his lips so he can kiss my fingers. He firmly presses his other hand to my lower back before kissing my lips. "Maci, I will love you in every language, in every country, every single day."

MACI

"Hey, babe," echoes through the entryway as the door shuts. I look up from where I'm sitting on the couch to Dean and Marcus walking in from their game of basketball in the driveway.

"Yeah, hey, babe," Marcus adds, a grin on his face.

We came home from Spain a month ago and have been living with Marcus, in Dean's old room. He's always been my favorite friend of Dean's, and living together has been smooth. We get more than enough alone time. Marcus and Troy spend a lot of time at their bar. We don't mind having him around, he doesn't seem to mind having us around either, and we really appreciate having a place to stay until we decide on our next adventure. The only real plans we have are to spend time with Avery and the new baby, and Brooke is coming to visit from Thailand in a few weeks.

"You look incredible," my fiancé says as I stand from the couch and he pulls me into an embrace. I'm wearing a simple black fit and flare dress, but the way Dean's face lights up makes me feel like it's so much more. He kisses my lips as he smooths his hands over my lower back, pressing me closer.

I pull back scrunching my face. "Gross you're so sweaty."

"You like me sweaty." Mischief glimmers in his eyes as he attempts to kiss me again.

I push against his chest playfully, not able to stop my smile. "No. We have to go. You two," I wave my finger between the boys, "need to shower and change." A simultaneous sigh leaves both of them, as well as mutual grumbles of acceptance. I chuckle as Dean reluctantly releases me before they head to their respective rooms.

Fifteen minutes later the boys return to the living room. "How did everything go, by the way?" Dean asks. His messy-styled blond hair starkly contrasts Marcus' neatly tied back brown locks, but they both look extremely handsome in black slacks and button ups.

"I left before Lexy got there, but I'm sure it went perfectly." I smile, thinking about my best friend's proposal.

Marcus chuckles. "I'm just happy I don't have to hear about the anticipation anymore." I'm not fooled by his comment at all. Marcus is secretly a hopeless romantic at heart, and he thoroughly enjoyed helping Troy plan tonight, especially since the two of them have become so close now that they own a business together.

"Okay, let's go!" I usher the men out the door, anxious to see Lexy.

When we walk through the front door of Jameson's, everything is exactly how I helped arrange it with Troy earlier. Only now it's full of our favorite people.

I spot Lexy immediately, and Dean leans down to kiss my temple. "I'll get you a drink," he says, knowing I'm about to make a beeline for her.

Lexy meets me in the middle of the room, her blonde curls falling perfectly over her shoulders and her silky red dress hugging her body in a way that makes her look like a movie star. "I hate you," she says through a bright smile.

I shrug. "It's not my fault you didn't catch on to me wanting to get all dolled up for once." Grinning, I reach my hand out and wait for hers to land in it. I've already seen her ring, but I'm just so excited. I love Troy and Lexy together so much. I've loved the idea since it first crossed my mind during our weekend in Vegas. Both the diamond of my ring and the ruby of Lexy's catch in the twinkle lights strung above us.

"It's perfect." She sighs dreamily. Watching my best friend's transformation when it comes to love and relationships has been so much fun. I love where she is now, where all of us are. As if on cue, Mack fills the space next to us, a grin covering his face as he pulls Lexy's hand out of mine to examine her ring for himself, holding it in front of his face and twisting her finger.

"Damn, Lex."

"I know, right? This is so weird," she says, once again her words not aligning with the smile on her face. Her gaze shifts to somewhere behind me. "Oh, Melissa just got here. I'll be right back." She takes off toward her future mother-in-law, leaving Mack and me alone to-gether–for the first time in a year.

Technically, I saw him last week for the first time, but we didn't have any moments to ourselves. We were both at the hospital, meeting Canaan, Avery's baby. It was probably the best way for it to happen–in a room full of love and attention solely focused elsewhere. It was inevitable for us to be together at some point though, so now will be the test of where we stand. The last time we talked was Avery's wedding weekend, but I'm confident he's doing well based on reports from Avery and Lexy. I'm hoping with the baby, maybe this can be our turning point, and we can get back to some sort of friendship. I'm one hundred percent happy with my choice, but I still miss him.

"I hear another congratulations is in order?" Mack's words break through my thoughts, leaving me con-fused, until his gaze shifts to the ring on my left hand.

"Oh, yeah," I say shyly.

"I'm happy for you, Maci." He looks and sounds gen-uine. He always does.

"Thank you." I stare into emerald green eyes I haven't locked onto in a while. "How are you?" I ask, nervously twisting my ring around my finger. I don't know why I'm anxious. I think I just want him to be as happy as I am.

A smile lights his face, and immediately my body relaxes. "I'm great." His eyes drift to behind me, and I turn, following his gaze to a girl leaning against the bar talking to Cooper. She's wearing a navy blue body-con dress with capped lace sleeves and has lavender streaks twisted through her light brown hair. She's gorgeous, and Mack's eyes hesitate on her before coming back to mine. "It's new," he adds, "but it's going well."

I can't help my smile of relief. "Tell me about her."

He pauses as if he's contemplating if this is a weird conversation but speaks anyway. "Ella. I met her at Avery's wedding. She's a friend of Miller's." Apology fills his eyes, as if it wasn't okay he met her the weekend we officially called it quits. I try to reassure him with a look of my own. "A few months ago, I wanted to plan something cool for my kids at work, to make them feel like rockstars for their first show. She's a music photographer. I reached out about having her do a photoshoot with them. I guess it just kind of went from there."

"She sounds great, Mack. I'm so happy for you. So, work is going well? Do you miss the band?"

"I love it. It's exactly what I should be doing, and I'm glad to be back here. Especially with the baby." His eyes sparkle even more at the mention of his nephew.

A wave of peace floods me as I focus on Mack, and the feeling distracts me enough I don't see Dean approaching. I become aware of him as he's reaching out with a whiskey sour. "I snuck you extra cherries," he wiggles his eyebrows at me, like he's proud of himself, but his face falls when he moves to lean into me and realizes I'm talking to Mack. "Oh, hey, man," he says, refraining from getting closer to me. God, I love this man. He could easily be putting off a different vibe right now. Regardless, I still feel a little weird.

"You're best friends with the owner." I roll my eyes as I take the glass from him and pinch one of the stems between my fingers. "We can have as many cherries as we want." I bite the cherry off–my attempt at avoiding any awkwardness that could potentially ensue.

I glance up from my drink to assess the situation, stopping mid-chew as I watch Mack reach his hand out. "Hey, it's good to see you. Under better circumstances this time."

The men chuckle as if their shared mutual understanding and time have bonded them. I stand there as if I'm in a twilight zone.

"Yeah, you too. Congrats on the new family member," Dean says, returning Mack's handshake.

"Thanks." He beams. "Well, I'm gonna go find Ella. I'll see you two around." His eyes find mine one more time before he turns away, and the way he looks at me makes me feel like he's thankful for how everything worked out.

"You alright?" Dean asks, pulling me to him by the hand that's now caressing my lower back.

I hold my drink between us and let my other hand fall to his chest. "Yeah, I was just thinking."

"Oh yeah? About what?" His fingers smooth along my cheek before threading through my hair and resting at my neck.

"I'm just happy for everyone." He smiles at my words but stays silent for me to continue. "It's crazy how everything really worked out, isn't it?" I ask Dean for confirmation, with my earlier conversation with Troy on my mind, but he knows my question is rhetorical. It's hard to find the right words to describe it. I scan the room, my eyes briefly landing on where Mack is leaning into Ella as she looks at him like he's everything she's been waiting for. I continue on, finding Troy and Lexy, his arm wrapped around her waist, her head on his shoulder as they talk to Cooper's mom. I can't help but grin as Cooper tugs on Sophie's hand, pulling her into the corner of the billiards room with a mischievous look on his face, as if no one will notice them. I look back to Dean where he's silently watching me with adoration. "Who would have thought choosing the right seat in math class would lead to all of this?" I laugh, standing on my toes enough to brush my lips against Dean's, knowing so many decisions led us all exactly where we are meant to be. Home.

Acknowledgments

Life is crazy, time is weird and I'm so thankful to every person who has spent any of theirs helping me make my dreams come true. Specifically:

Brooke for always hyping me up.

Alexa for helping me perfect my playlists.

Heather for highlighting every line she loved.

Katherine for making sure I didn't leave sentences unfinished.

Amber for turning another cover vision into reality.

Steph for tossing a million ideas around with me.

My ARC readers for putting off the TBR lists for this book.

And the 87 other things that can't be wrapped up in one line but I won't repeat because I got way too mushy in book one! Just know ILYSW is a lot more loveable because of them.

More by Tisa Matthews

If you loved this story, check out the **Finding Home** series on Kindle Unlimited.

And Then There's You is book one, following Maci's love triangle with Mack and Dean.

I Love You, So What? is book two, following Lexy and Troy's story.

Can We Just Be Happy Now? is book three, following the story of Dean's sister Sophie, and Troy's best friend Cooper.

Tied Up In Riches is book four, following the story of Brooke and Marcus.

While books three and four can be read as stand-alones, books one and two of the series should be read in order for the best experience.

Home is an extended epilogue featuring a POV chapter from each main character in the series! It's meant to be read after you've finished the series!

Unhitched is a standalone, modern day romance jam packed with 2000s nostalgia and swirled around with the turning 30 identity crisis. It's written by a millennial for millennials.

PLAYLIST

Dress — Taylor Swift
Islands In The Stream — Karaoke
CWJBHN — Jake Scott
Mistakes We Knew We Were Making — Straylight Run
In Betweenin' — AUSTN
Die in LA — Hunter Daily
She's Why — Russell Dickerson
Scared of Falling — Abigail Osborn
Obsession — Mitchell Tenpenny
Walls — Trevor Holmes
Wreckage — Nate Smith
Feels Like Love — Noah Schnacky
Love You a Little Bit — Tanner Adell
ILYSoWhat — Hannah Ellis
I Hate Love Songs — Kelsea Ballerini
J.O.Y. — Canaan Cox
If It Weren't For You — FINMAR
Kiss Me Slowly (Acoustic Version) — Jonah Baker

About the Author

Tisa (like Lisa with a T) Matthews is an indie author currently living in Florida with her husband. She's a firm believer in taking chances even when it's scary—everything from moving to new places completely alone to quitting her job to dive into author life. She loves reading and writing relatable romance and roller blades her in free time.

<u>CONNECT ONLINE:</u>
@tisa.matthews.books